Her Curse and Lullaby

Book 1 of The Chimera's Requiem

M. A. Morales

All rights are held by the author

Cover art by Miblart

Title page images by Canva

Written by M.A. Morales

Copyright © 2022 by Michelle Morales

First Edition: March 2023

ISBNs:

979-8-9871958-2-6 (paperback)

979-8-9871958-3-3 (ebook)

For more content by this author, go to:

elleoaks.com

Send inquiries to author at

Gmail: mamoraleswrites@gmail.com

Or contact via form on elleoaks.com

Other Books by this Author:

Light from a Broken Lamp

FOR MY AMAZING PARENTS AND
BEAUTIFUL FAMILY. YOU'VE INSPIRED
ME TO ALWAYS PERSEVERE AND BE THE
BEST I CAN BE.
THANK YOU.

Chapter One

The Ulton Residence
"Humana vera solum theoriis"
(Human truths are only theories)

BOTALIA WIPES THE DEW and pollen from the bronze plaque outside the door to her family's villa. With a softened expression of nostalgia, her hand rests there a moment more than it needs to. She turns her gaze to the tropical plants on the veranda and the dense forest of trees and shrubberies surrounding the house. Petrichor and the scent of the first opening blooms of the morning float on the breeze, brushing against her cheeks. The many creatures' calls and whistles reach her ears. Tranquility.

A honeybee settles on the flower of a potted hibiscus. Goldenrod against a fresh coral petal, the flower perfectly hydrated and ready to share its pollen with the scavenger. Botalia steps slowly toward the natural phenomenon. A smile spreads across her face, the beauty of nature never tiring her.

A pulse reverberates through her. Her hand rises to her chest, and she squeezes at the collar of her shirt. Botalia's eyes shut with urgency, as if she had foretold the blinding light to appear in front of her. A disturbance. Birds squawk and fly from the trees, disrupted in their morning calls.

Botalia leaps from the porch to the front lawn. Her eyes scan the tree line, searching for any unidentifiable movement. With an extra measure of precaution, Botalia kneels to the ground. She places her hands on the moist blades of grass, pushing them into the wet soil of dawn. A deep inhale precedes a flow of her life force to her hands. The power travels through her fingertips and into the earth, scouting the surrounding area. It passes by the worms and beetles burrowed into the soil, twists around the roots of the tall aleoak trees and those shallower roots of her genetically engineered bushes. On top a pile of dried grasses and large leaves, lay a distressed animal near a pool of its own blood.

Her hands lift from the ground in an instant and Botalia propels herself in the direction of the creature. Like a bolt of lightning, she passes through the forest, focused on arriving as soon as possible. The cry of the creature finds her ears. Botalia slightly changes direction to find the line of least distance to travel.

Botalia passes a bush with the leaves curled up to the sky. A smile cracks through her struggle to find breath in her hurried sprint. The cries of the creature grow louder as she approaches. The beast lay on the ground, blood matting the hair near its back end. Horns curl about its face with a long snout protruding from the center. Four cleft toes on each of the four feet of the creature dig into the nest it had created. It faces Botalia and panics as its condition hinders its desire to protect. Botalia empathizes.

Inching forward, Botalia places a palm on the forehead of the creature, a ranadune.

"Shhhhh," she whispers in a calming tone.

The creature's panic settles, trusting in Botalia, the island's caretaker. Cries transform to mutters. The creature closes its eyes, exhausted.

Botalia crawls to the pool of blood, the dried grass crinkling under her hands and knees. The smell of the iron in the blood causes dizziness, the image of the pool of crimson causing her heart to race. Botalia takes a deep breath. She gently lifts the fluffy on top, dripping blood underneath tail of the creature. Under its tail lay a tiny, breathing ball of matted hair, no larger than the size of a domesticated house cat. Botalia smiles in joy of the new inhabitant of the island.

Her hand hovers over the newborn. A pulse of life force emits from her palm, ensuring the small one to be in good health. After examination, Botalia directs her palm to the mother. The creature will live and quickly recover. Botalia nods and walks to the outer rim of the nest. Her eyes scan the trees, wondering if any of the other creatures witnessed the miracle. She giggles and takes off at a jog toward the beach.

The long, undisturbed sand displaces under her feet. The salty ocean air kisses her cheeks. Botalia looks out to the crashing waves. She doesn't bother to focus her eyes as she knows nothing lingers over the horizon. None would dare steer near the island. Rumors of disappearances and monsters of the deep, all false with records considered 'hidden,' are told to any licensed merchants, captains, or navigators as a warning not to stray near to the island. Threat of penalty and prison time is often directed to those more daring.

Botalia sighs. She turns her back to the mainland on the other side of the sapphire sea. The invisible chains pull at her to return to the villa. Her mind wanders to her musings of civilization, her daydreams of helping Professionals and Scholars alike at the Magistrate Association. Unlimited resources to perform her experiments. Infinite occasions to administer her help. Ability to demonstrate her skills. To learn from others with more experience. The ultimate wish.

"Unfortunate for me, to wish and to dream are no more than weapons to destroy an individual..."

Botalia shakes her head and searches for a distraction. A release. Her arm flies up at her side to form a perpendicular line to her body. She aims her palm at the ocean. With a focused stare and concentration of life force, the waters swirl, contained and controlled. An orb of water rises and circles about the invisible walls maintaining it. Botalia, in a burst of despair, raises her other hand and shoots an energetic dart at the orb. With an explosive force, the orb breaks the bounds. Botalia's hands meet in front of her chest, forming a circle with her fingers, shielding herself from any water spraying in her direction. Once the water settles into the sand and tide, Botalia sprints toward the villa.

A pulse emanating from her chest, Botalia clutches at her heart and hums to calm the beast within. She pauses on the porch, recovering her breath and easing the hum to a steadier tune. A haunting lullaby. Botalia understands the predictions of the beast's afflictions before it hits her. As an animal before an earthquake or tropical storm, it warns her.

A pain surges throughout her chest, causing her heart to stop then race in a matter of milliseconds. Botalia stretches for the door and falls through the doorway, her trembling legs losing balance. The air grows thick and her aura surrounds her in a torrential current. The hard, wooden floorboards sustain her weight, though she feels heavy and pressed. As if gravity has increased, the pressure chokes her breath and her ability to rise. Within a minute, the pain disperses throughout her body. A jolt of energy strikes her, life force falling away in wisps from her fingertips. Losing too much at one time could result in something dangerous. Botalia, knowing this, controls the increments in which the extra energy seeps away. She curses the monster she is.

The grandfather clock in the study tolls. Eight o' clock in the morning.

Botalia rises from the floor, not wishing to stray from her daily schedule, and walks to the study.

She draws the curtains of the study to allow the sunlight to filter in. It hits the hideous scarlet patterned wallpaper, that which her parents insisted on having as it appeared like the walls of the study at a palace in Divesregio. Botalia rolls her eyes at the memory. A set of two, pine tables sit near the bookshelves, dented and scratched to prove their history of utilization. Botalia opens a drawer of a desk and retrieves loose sheets of paper and a pen (permanent and proof she is human when evidence arises for an inaccurate hypothesis). She grabs the binder of interest from the bookshelves, this particular one labeled 'Life Force Theory.' Sitting in a cushioned chair at a pine table, Botalia thumbs past the pages of her parents' writings. She smiles with the ease of distinguishing her mother's quick scribbles and her father's tiny yet elaborate cursive. Each style tells a story of its own.

She arrives at a page of her own writing, the theory which she wishes to elaborate upon. Botalia pushes the binder away and positions the blank papers in front of her at a slight angle, her preferred writing position. With a deep breath, Botalia leans back, cracking her spine, before hunching over the desk. The expectations of society no longer restrict her, nor the need to labor to earn a living or maintain her magistrate status (which was never recalled after her exile).

Botalia writes her hypothesis.

Emotions are a quantifiable unit decided by laws of the universe, therefore life force is a quantified unit dependent on specific factors including emotion. Stronger emotions, a larger unit of energy(?) result in stronger bonding of life force.

Botalia considers her hypothesis and what evidence she can collect to prove her hypothesis true. Though she feels past experience may be enough to strengthen the claim's validity, physical evidence is crucial in any scientific field. When it comes to emotions, physical evidence proves a difficult task. Perhaps through electrical circuits she can determine brain activity and link the currents to the basic human emotions. Or she could test the potency of her aura given the state of emotion she needs to be set in... But how would she quantify how strong the emotion would need to be? Are there some emotions stronger than others? Botalia read the research of many acclaimed Life Force Scholars, the number able to be counted on one hand as the field had yet to be heavily studied. They state that when in a mind of panic or anger, life force can expand beyond the storehouse of said user, as if the life force equivalent of an adrenaline rush. Beyond the storehouse... Panic... Anger...

"Could a person force themselves into an elevated stage of panic or anger and manipulate their life force and storehouse to expand over time?" Botalia mumbles.

She clicks her pen on the desk as she leans back into her chair to stare at the ceiling, consumed in her thoughts. She squints and manipulates her facial muscles as a river of thoughts pour over her.

"Fear.. fear... fear..."

Botalia repeats this word as she hustles to the bookshelves. Her pointer finger slides along the pristine spines. She grabs *Life Force Fundamentals* by Alidina Vazgard, a Scholar who often visited her parents. Botalia fails to remember what they discussed, as they often moved to the lab in their basement in Dominia where they once lived. Understandable how a child would not be invited to such important meetings.

She sets the book on the table and hovers her hand over it. It opens with the force of a gust of wind and the pages ripple back. Her eyes focus to find the chapter she searches. The bold text **Repository and Battery** appears and the pages freeze. Botalia skims the text.

"Areas facing constant states of panic and distress, such as in war zones and areas most at risk of natural disasters, have been proven to increase the repository of said population's life force. While the repository expands, life force will not. Only in intense moments of panic and distress would a life force user be able to achieve an execution of life force of a greater caliber than normally capable, thus filling the repository. Excess life force will escape and may take many forms. *Flip to Page 348 for information on external manifestation."*

Botalia bites her lip in deep thought, staring at the blank piece of paper before her. She grabs her pen and squeezes it in her grip, thinking through the words with care.

"Panic, distress, fear... expand the storehouse but don't fill the battery."

Botalia writes her thoughts and blinks at the sentence she's composed. Her right hand raises to her chest. Her heart races, pounding, her hand feeling the pulses. She closes her eyes and all she sees is the crimson red of her eyelids, as if a strong light shines in front of her. Botalia knows no such source exists. Memories stained in blood present themselves. Images not her own but seen in dreams and flashes of thought throughout the day. Pictures conjured in moments of pain. Others' moments of panic and distress. Their emotions expand her storehouse. Her genetics charge the battery.

Botalia slams the pen down and leans on the table, the palms of her hands shoved into her eyes to act as a blockade to emotion. But the images appear once more.

"Go away," she whispers, hoping her verbal wish to will it so. But her curse refuses to be controlled. A parasite with no cure. Her heart accelerates, a twinge inside her chest. Expand the storehouse. Charge the battery.

The creature within her rattles the bars of the subconscious cage, forcing her to jump. It awakens her. Allows her to separate the curse from the afflicted. Allows her to feel human, even if only a little.

Botalia rises from her chair and exits the study, leaving her notes on the table and the book flipped open to that page should she return. As her mind constantly churns with thoughts and theories, multitasking increases her flexibility in switching from task to task. It also increases the odds to keep the intrusive thoughts at bay.

The glass door slides open as she exits into the backyard of the villa. The sun heats the air with quickened pace, beads of sweat forming on her chest with the rising humidity of the island. Botalia strips of her sweater, an emerald, stretched ribbed tank faded by the sun presents itself. It hugs her body, skin showing where its length fails to cover. After ten years of wear, Botalia understands her luck of having a wardrobe that still somewhat fits. With a breath of fresh air, Botalia skips to the greenhouse.

She opens the glass paneled door and a gust of mixed hot, humid air and cool, dry air hit her. The fans spin to create a favorable current. Plastic trays and pots of many sizes sit on the crudely constructed wooden shelves and tables. Several plastic bags of fertilizer sit against the back wall, a barrel of compost at their side.

Botalia examines her many trials in botany and horticulture. She checks the cuttings, taken from shrubberies and flowers from the island, to see if the roots have taken to the different types of soil. Using her life force, Botalia analyzes the aura of the plants, telling her which nutrients may be lacking in their development and which growth hormones may need to be applied.

Botalia walks over to a table with several test plants upon it. The shrubs, no taller than thirty centimeters, stagger the table, each with a label signifying its test number. The notebook lays to the side, many colorful tabs sticking out of the pages. Caressing the leaves of the plants, judging whether they may need more water or not based on touch before aura analysis, Botalia decides they are well hydrated and picks up her notebook.

Reading over her notes, Botalia finds her pencil and writes her daily entry on the test subjects. Each test subject exists within the same environment and receives equal parts water, this based on previous experiments to determine optimal results as far as climate and hydration is concerned. Her current tests analyze soil composition, the nutrients necessary in contributing to fast growth and a strong root system.

Botalia squints her eyes as she observes the aura of the plants. She notices one plant with an incredible amount of life force, its aura beginning to affect the plants next to it. Botalia decides to space the plants, giving them the room necessary to expand but also so she can better see the individual auras. Though she desires to take notes on all of the plants, this one holds her attention. Opening up to the page in the notebook labeled '005B20N10P20K5pH,' Botalia checks her past examinations of this particular test subject. She nears the plant and removes the ruler from the drawer to her side. Bringing the ruler up to the leaves, Botalia focuses her eyes. She gasps. The last time she measured the auras, they were incredible in comparison to other adult plants with well-grounded roots. However, in less than a month, this plant's aura has doubled.

"Impossible," she whispers, a smile spreading across her face. "A person could be no more than a novice and perform high-level life force transmutation or manipulation with life force suctioned from this plant... perhaps even an atomic shift..."

She dances around the room, in her excitement kicking a metal stake across the floor. With explosive laughter, she kneels down to pick up the fallen equipment which has slid beneath the table. Stretching her arm as far as possible, her shoulder digging into the metal rack hastily installed to the wooden legs of the table, she finds the cold metal stake. Her fingertips brush against it but her length proves just short. Moving her life force to her fingers, she uses it to pull the stake close enough for her to grab it.

In her victory, she rises with a high jump and touches the base of a hanging basket suspended by a lasso. A dizzy spell hits her like a flash of vertigo as she lands on her feet. Her knees jiggle out from under her and she falls to the ground. Botalia uses her life force to cushion the fall, but an excess escapes from her in her panic. Her eyes widen.

Botalia drops her notebook and runs to the villa. She stares out the long, slim window by the front door and carefully examines the tree line. She places a palm on the pane and waits. Closing her eyes to increase her other senses, Botalia listens to the change in the animals' calls.

Squawks of the birds fade into the beating of their wings. Shouts of the mammals and rodents grow quiet as they hide themselves. A subtle tide crashes against the sides of a metal object. A strong aura presents itself, as if the wind carries flames and ash to her island. A burning heat, like fiery rage, finds her fingertips. She moves her fingers from the glass. The life force swells in her chest as her heartbeat matches that of the beast within her.

Someone is coming.

Chapter Two

The motorboat pulls up to the abandoned dock. An air of caution present in his aura, he ties the boat to the rusted cleat. With the presence of another within her area of detection, he knows he must be careful. Botalia knows him to be experienced in the art of life force, the control of his aura and his attempt to mask it worthy of praise. However, intuition tells her he does not mean to hide his presence, only test her.

His aura fluctuates with the soft ripples of air above heated coals. His immense pride allows him to maintain a cool and calm composure. The visitor struts to meet her, a feigned confidence accompanied by hostility in every heavy footfall. Not a hostility for the one he seeks to meet with but an inward hostility. A hostility that derives from shame; shame for asking another for help after so many years. A hostility stemming from his own self-conceit and arrogance.

He walks the stone path, every second closing the distance between the two of them. The creatures of the island stare, their curiosity of his unknown scent, his unknown power, cause the creatures' hesitation in their movements. Though unaware of his intentions, they express an awe in the aura emanating from his person. The same awe resonates from Botalia, fear an unwelcome accompaniment.

The man continues forward, never showing indecision in his steps. She senses his strength. He grew stronger, his aura larger and more refined. Wondering why he may be here, she formulates the many responses she may need to any number of actions on his part.

She trusts her instincts, however, in her anxiety and the presence of another human after a decade of solitude, she understands the need to be prepared. No surprises. Not this time.

The trees part as a lawn spreads before him and the silhouette of the villa reveals itself to the visitor. He takes a large, anxious breath, his steps getting smaller as he nears the house. The team is well aware of his social anxiety, or what may be more apparent as asocial behavior, and yet sends him to handle the communication with her. They say he was best to go because he not only operates the team for the time being, but he and Botalia are familiar with one another. The first reason provides a legitimate excuse in his eyes, however, the latter is all the more reason for him to stay away.

The visitor lets out a sigh and raises his leg to continue up the steps of the porch when she opens the front door.

"Why have you come here?" Botalia asks, standing in the middle of the doorway as if daring his entry.

"I, uhh... I didn't really have much say," he raises his left arm to scratch his head. He dislikes confronting others with words and his anxious speech reflects that. "Although, I was the one who recommended someone come to see you."

Silence falls between them. He looks at her, shocked to see the resemblance to her parents despite her, as the community deems, unnatural creation. She is average sized in height and build yet he can tell she's well-toned. She has her father's eyes, sharp and bright, never missing a movement. Focusing his eyes, he can see the immense life force she possesses, though simply standing in her presence was enough to assure him of her power. Her concentrated aura emanating from her pores sends a chill down his spine as he wonders how one can gain so much power and strength with so little physical repercussions. However, he wonders why most of her life force concentrates itself in her chest.

She looks at him, seeing the same man she encountered ten years ago. Not much seems to have changed. His unkempt, black hair, his vagabond style of clothing, and his lack of care about what others think of him still resonates. The deep terracotta coloring of his skin proving he spends many hours in the Dominian sun, where she presumes he resides, most likely practicing combat with his life force. He's more confident of himself, and the flow of his life force shows it. His aura flares to the same effect of a flame and extends about six centimeters from his body. "He is strong, much stronger than the last time we met," is the first thought to cross her mind.

"We all kind of felt this would happen when we sent you off. The President of the Association warned us and yet we kept denying it." The man releases a sigh. He looks up to the sky and smiles. His gaze returns to her. "The situation was far beyond the comprehension of any of us on the Council it seems."

She walks onto the porch toward the visitor. An anxious and weary expression covers her face and exudes from her body language as she approaches. Her shakiness is in part due to the power she can sense within him, but mainly derives from her solitude on the island and not having been able to mature her social skills.

"Mr. Flynn," she begins.

"You can address me by my first name," he smirks, tipping his head toward his shoulder.

"Uhh... Tanten." Botalia pauses. Her eyes close and she brings her hands to her chest, placing one hand atop a clenched fist. She looks to Tanten, closing the distance between the two of them. His initial reaction to step back is countered by his inability to appear frightened, no matter the situation. She extends her right hand out to him.

"It's nice to have a visitor after all these years. Even if it's you." Her hazel eyes peer into the dark, cocoa irises of his, the pupils hiding themselves so as to mask the window to his soul. The sounds of the environment around them fade. Tanten, shocked by her gesture, not knowing whether it be a trap or a friendly hand shake, hesitates to make any moves. He can't sense any hostility, but her superior strength causes him to question everything that has or will transpire.

She realizes his internal conflict and drops her hands to her side. Biting her lip, she looks to the ground, trying to silence the thoughts echoing in her head.

"I'm sorry, I-" she begins.

"No, I'm-" Tanten interrupts, believing his refusal to shake her hand far more impolite than cutting off her sentences. "...sorry. I sincerely apologize for my coarse behavior, Botalia."

"I know I'm a monster. But I'm really trying. Really." Botalia looks to the ground, unable to face Tanten. Her tone remains grounded but the voices in her head scream out to her, clouding her thought process. "It's as I feared, I can't go back to the mainland. I can't ever go back. They'll never revoke the terms of my exile. Not even a marauder like Tanten is willing to accept me as human. Strange how I thought isolation was for the better... how I deserved it. Yet I thought if I proved my worth, showed them all what I could do... No. It doesn't even matter. With no more than a focused glance Tanten has raised his guard." Her hand rests on her chest to resist the pounding calls of the monster. In Botalia's curiosity and naivety, she defends Tanten's visitation despite not wholly understanding the motive.

"Err...," Tanten scratches his head as he peers at Botalia. Not being good with social commentary, he does not know what to say, discomfort pricks at the hairs on his arms as if a chilled aura meets him, though that may be his own aura extinguishing. He tosses away his concerns and guilt as he extends his hand. "Uhh," he clears his throat, "Ms. Botalia Ulton, please accept my apology for my actions. But, if you please, I have some rather important news I wish to discuss with you."

"Of course."

She grabs his hand and time freezes. Botalia grits her teeth and squeezes her eyes shut, a slideshow of images and sounds play in her head. Moments of absolute suffering, of Tanten's suffering, dissolve into her interior. She absorbs the cries and pain of those moments, with flashes of light blinding her every time she tries to open her eyes to escape. The current transports to her a phantasmagoria of audio and visual; the initial potential difference enough to cause her body into a state of shock. To Botalia, the incident seemed to last minutes though to Tanten, the shock left as soon as it came. At first, Tanten didn't feel anything but a short zap. However, feeling Botalia squeeze his hand and analyzing the look of anguish on her face, he understands there is much more that transpired in that instant.

Botalia loosens her grip and quickly reaches for her heart. Her heart rate almost tripled from the shock, and she realizes it's as though gravity increases around her, pulling her down with a greater force. Her eyes carry the look of disbelief yet intuitive understanding of the situation. Her breaths grow short and deep to try to calm her heart. After a few seconds, Tanten reaches for his heart, too. To him, his heart feels lighter. He looks to her, his confusion and concern covering his face.

"Bo-"

"Please, come inside." Botalia opens the door for him, trying her hardest to avoid eye contact. Tanten glimpses at his right hand, continuing to wonder the type of trap that may be set.

"Who would set a trap that causes them pain as opposed to their target?" Tanten asks himself. He senses the nerves emanating from the girl, that is, if he can still picture her as a girl. Tanten reacts the only way he knows how: abandoning rational thought and listening to his intuition. For the time being, he must trust her, or his plans will go nowhere.

As he enters through the doorway, Botalia directs him towards the sitting area. Two sofas and cushioned armchairs surround a square, glass topped coffee table. Pictures, paintings, and certificates clutter the walls. Hutches and cabinets full of trophies and impressive artifacts fill the corners of the room.

"The remarkable appearance of this space alone would lead one to never doubt the high regard with which the Ulton family was held," Tanten thinks, his jaw dropping. Once he arrives at the chair and sits, he regains his cool and collected composure.

"Sorry, I wasn't expecting any visitors so there's no meal prepared. Would you like a drink?" Botalia, being unaccustomed to having visitors, attempts to be, if only a little, hospitable. From the time she began calling this villa home, Botalia never had guests. For ten years, she was deprived of direct contact with all humans, the only contact being the mysterious shape to leave food and other supplies she may need and annual letters from the Association to guarantee she had not left. Or to check she was alive.

Botalia's question catches Tanten off-guard.

"Uhh, whatever you have is fine," Tanten answers. She does not stand but rather places her hands on the clear, glass surface of the table and closes her eyes. When she opens them again, she leans back in her seat with tilted head, observing Tanten with a straight look.

Tanten clears his throat and addresses her with a serious expression. "Botalia, do you stay updated on the news?"

"Yeah. I watch the world news everyday as well as read it on the internet. Not to mention, I frequent the forums of the Magistrate Association's website. Despite not being a part of the world, I like to know what's going on in it."

Tanten looks at her in shock, an elitist glare forming on his face. At that moment, a wispy, humanoid figure enters carrying a silver tray with their drinks atop it. Tanten's attention never shifts from Botalia. She turns to her conjured servant, smiling and bowing her head in thanks. It sets the tray on the table, bows, and vanishes in a whirl of smoke. Botalia leans forward to pick up a glass, gesturing Tanten to take his. Seeing that he remains unmoved, she leans back and locks eyes with him.

"How are you able to access the website?" Tanten asks in a deep, serious tone. His look reads anger, causing Botalia to raise her guard. She furrows her brow, takes a sip of her drink, and sets the glass on the table, all without breaking eye contact. Botalia takes a breath, attempting to calm her constantly heating temper. The longer she sits in his presence, the more she remembers the writings of his critics, one of them the world renowned Professional, Merwyn Giacobbe. Narcissism. Immaturity. Botalia senses it in the carelessness of his aura, the flames licking at the air as if testing his limits.

"What? You thought the Association cared enough to revoke my license when they exiled me? I was too insignificant for that little detail to even cross your minds. None of you cared what became of me, as long as I never showed my face again." Botalia turns her head from Tanten, who remained unmoving throughout her explanation. He stares at her, examining how her aura transforms.

"You are well aware of why we sent you away." Tanten rolls his eyes and takes up a mocking tone, whether accidental or not. "You had committed a serious crime. You were dangerous-"

"I was fourteen! I had just lost my parents! And what do I get?!? No sympathy but a summons which resulted in my exile! I had barely recovered, and I was thrown into the wilderness. Naked. Devoid of anything... and everything. I was an empty vessel. No wonder this monster found a suitable nesting ground in me." Botalia feels the tears begin to swell in her eyes and controls her breathing in an attempt to regain control of her emotions and aura. Though Botalia had often thought about the situation, she never said it aloud. The weight of her thoughts transforming into reality in front of her creates a host of strange connections in her mind, ones she'd have preferred remain in her nightmares. When her emotions escalate and her energy surges, she sees the day it all began. The fluctuation of her aura and release of life force urges Tanten to lean back and take a more defensive stance. He feels her raw life force surround him. He knows her sheer power far outweighs his, however, he trusts that Botalia will not attack him. He intuitively knows Botalia wishes him no physical harm.

Botalia retracts her life force, absorbing it back into her pores, and turns her head to face Tanten.

"We're getting distracted. I assume you're running on a strict schedule. So let's get to it. What do you want? Why are you here?" Botalia takes on a belligerent tone, expecting a straightforward answer. She knows how brief Tanten can be, while fully being aware of how stubborn he will be if she doesn't respond to his liking.

Tanten picks up his drink and swirls the liquid inside. He takes in its sweet scent, concentrating on the path on which he will lead the conversation.

"Have you heard or read anything about the Schism?" Tanten asks, following with a sip of his drink. He raises his eyebrows as the drink was sweeter, but also more satisfying, than he anticipated.

"So my assumptions were correct." Botalia stands and walks toward the window to peer outside, relaxing her nerves and tension in this movement, for staying seated made her anxious. She stalls for a minute, taking in the forest surrounding her lonely home, wondering if he will further expand his question or let on to his own knowledge. After no response, she speaks. "I didn't know if I was reading too much into it or if it was subtly being hinted at while trying to avoid the general public from fully grasping what was actually going on. But if you're bringing it up, it must be true. The Council must be horrified." She crosses her arms, knowing full well what Tanten will, or in the least should, say next.

"I resigned from the Council," Tanten responds, shifting his eyes to the contents of his glass. Botalia closes her eyes and grins. She continues to face the window, her back to Tanten. Her grin quickly turns to a scowl as she pieces this information and her prior knowledge together. Botalia waits to catch Tanten in lie, though she knows thus far he has been honest with her. However, she realizes that honesty and the whole truth are far from being the same.

"But you weren't the only one to resign, right? Others left after the explosion of the "Schism" issue within the Association," Botalia states, trying to pry more information from Tanten or simply tempt him into making a wrong move, as if looking for a legitimate excuse to vent her anger towards him, if not the Magistrate Association as a whole. Tanten sets his glass on the table.

"You're correct. Three others and I left the Council, leaving them with thirteen members, how unfortunate." Tanten rests his head on his hand, wondering how much information he'll have to give up before being able to ask the question. He knows he has to wait for the perfect moment or she will reject him. And once she does, there's no changing her mind. Although, his instincts inform him that his current attempt to form an alliance with her are falling short of succeeding.

"The Council is meant to remain unbiased with such ordeals, so those who chose sides were forced to leave. However, you predicted this, so you left earlier. Am I correct?" Botalia asks. Her fists clench at her sides. Normally she is extremely patient, but her ever-growing restlessness around Tanten pushes her to her limits. She wishes for him to come out and ask the question. She knows her answer, but he seems to be delaying it. The suspense tortures her.

"Aye. I sensed the tensions in the community well before the explosions. Granted, the tension has always existed, but lately it was becoming a bit too much for anyone to ignore, though the Council tried their best to. The weight of the Schism and the President's death caused a lot of problems within the Council. The death of the President seemed inevitable to me, though I'd hoped my intuition was wrong," Tanten scratches his head, a nervous habit of his. He lets out a sigh. "All would be well but the Vice President resigning shortly after the President's death led the Council into a pit of chaos. Those posers try to act level-headed but they're an absolute mess. So I left before the situation got any worse." Tanten takes a drink, emptying his glass. He sits up straight and glimpses at Botalia who remains unmoved, staring out the window. Tanten feels an odd sensation, so he focuses his eyes on Botalia, revealing her frigid aura.

"You didn't just leave. You ran away," Botalia remarks in a matter-of-fact, cold tone. "No... but that's not quite it." Her life force tries to manifest, but she works to prevent it from doing so. Ten years of wishing for visitors turns to wishing for eternal solitude. Her rage builds as she questions how some people can possess such disgusting character traits. She finds relief in that she hadn't had to deal with such people for ten years. Botalia thinks that being lonely was the exchange for not being violated by such corrupt persons. Her exile wasn't prison but freedom.

"You had run away from the Council long before you informed them of your resignation. You betrayed their ideals long ago, betraying the entire Magistrate Association along with it. But you've never devoted yourself to the Association's ideals. Everyone knew that, but they still voted for you."

Botalia's rage builds the longer their conversation lasts. Tanten analyzes her aura, sensing her anger and seeing her control over its strength. Her aura forms a helix around her, the waves moving at such high velocities they appear to create a solid entity surrounding her. Tanten cannot help but be in awe over her aura because never before has he seen an aura take such shapes or move at such speeds. He smirks. "Her parents would be proud."

As he observes her, Tanten notices Botalia utilizes her own aura to contain her life force. Often people manipulate their aura to take the form of a viscous medium to slow down another person's life force, rendering an attack ineffective. In this way their aura acts like a one-way window: they prevent another's life force from entering while allowing their own to freely enter and exit. However, Botalia alters her aura to act like a wall. Not only will it prevent life force from entering, but her aura prevents her life force from exiting as well.

"So much control. Precision. Is it only my presence that forces her to act as so or does the monster always wish to come out to play?" he thinks.

Simply by being in the presence of Botalia, Tanten realizes she's on a much higher level, not even comparable to those magistrates considered the best. The separation is as vast as the difference between a puddle and an ocean. Tanten wonders what she had to sacrifice to gain such power.

A whirl of smoke circles a singular point by the table. As the smoke rises vertically, the form of the wispy, humanoid servant becomes visible. It gathers the glasses onto the tray and walks toward the kitchen. Her aura calms down. Tanten deduces she manifested a fraction of her life force into the conjured servant in order to regain control over her aura.

Several minutes pass in silence. Botalia remains facing the window and Tanten leans forward in his chair, both of them with their eyes closed. Tanten's cellphone vibrates, breaking the silence. He looks at it, presses a button, and returns the phone to his pocket.

"Maybe we can wrap this up tomorrow," Tanten suggests in a tired, inattentive tone. He stands. Botalia turns to face him as he readjusts his clothing.

"Why don't I give you my answer now? Then you won't have to worry about making room for me in your schedule." Listening to her tone he can easily guess her answer.

"How can you give your answer when I haven't asked you the question?" Tanten snaps. Whether it's his innate stubbornness or merely clinging to hope, Tanten must know why, above all else, Botalia denies him before having properly laid out his proposition.

"You were going to ask me to join your side, or your team, rather. Were you not?" Botalia glares at him and he returns it.

"Yes, but-"

"So, my answer is no. End of discussion." She maintains her calm composure, but she can sense Tanten is on the verge of exploding. She understands how he could be frustrated, attempting to set up the perfect moment to ask, even divulging some information to gain her trust. He's not a patient person, and while the length of their meeting seemed to deteriorate her wits, she can't help but feel entertained by it all. However, if he persists, she knows her amusement will quickly turn to anger.

"You can't simply say no and expect me, of all people, to just walk away!" Tanten fires back, eyes widened. His aura often acts like a gentle flame, but at the moment it appears more like a wildfire.

"This was never going to be easy, was it?" Botalia whispers to herself more so than to Tanten. A grin slips for a split second, knowing she is in full control. "Listen, Tanten, you came here on official business, not to visit with me. So accept my answer for what it is. No." Tanten raises his clenched fists and throws them down like a child throwing a tantrum. Botalia rolls her eyes and crosses her arms.

"How can you expect me to accept your answer and be done with it?!? I can't expect someone like you to comprehend the scope of the situation after being isolated for ten years; I don't expect you to understand given the brief discussion of the topic but-"

"Stop talking to me like I'm still a child! I understand. Maybe not as much as you, but I know enough to piece it together." Botalia knows she cannot concede in failing to complete the puzzle. She simply lacks the data and the pieces necessary. She marches to the front door and opens it. Tanten stomps toward her.

"Give me one reason, one reason why you reject me, and I'll walk out now and never look back." Tanten cools himself and stands, head held high, awaiting a response.

"One reason..." Botalia repeats. She has many reasons to deny him, but she wonders which will give her the most satisfaction as a response. Before she can process it, the answer she truly knows she most wants to give slips out. "To a child, having parents that can serve as role models means everything. My parents may have messed me up, but they never abandoned me." Botalia locks eyes with Tanten. "That is my reason. I could never work with someone like you. So I don't intend to."

Tanten breaks eye contact and struts out the door. It's his own fault. He asked for a reason and she gave one. He can't be angry at Botalia. He was mentally unprepared for the response he received. Apathy, such a common trait to those with which he aligns himself, works against him in his time of most need.

As he steps down the path, Botalia calls out to him, "If you're not satisfied, I'll tell you another reason." Tanten stops in his tracks, curiosity getting the better of him. "I've thought about it quite a bit, and I disagree with you. Ten years ago, when the Council was deciding what to do with me, the decision wasn't unanimous. I know the Vice President and you voted against exiling me. For years I wondered why, whether it be sick tests and experiments or training me to work and operate as one of your dogs. I don't need to know your reasons, moreover, I don't want to know. But I do know one thing. You were wrong. I was a danger to myself and more importantly to others. My feelings toward Atlas are independent of my feelings toward you. I know you and Atlas had different reasons for rejecting my exile. But your choice, putting your desires over other's safety was selfish. That vote signified your betrayal of the community that supported you." Botalia stops for a few seconds, wondering if Tanten will respond. He offers up no comment, so she continues. "That's why I refuse to join you. I could never help someone who pledges loyalty only to themself."

Tanten drops his head and continues walking away, never looking back. Botalia watches him until he escapes from her vision. Tanten follows the path that had led him to the villa. He observes nothing, listens to nothing, feels nothing. He blocks out his reality and ends all thought processes. Tanten escapes into his imaginary realm, where he often goes when faced with an unsatisfactory reality; where he goes to escape self-reflection, whether it be out of stubbornness or fear.

When he reaches the dock, he boards the boat and leaves immediately. He sails away never once returning even the slightest gaze to the island. Tanten sets the course for his motorboat and decides to rest. Binding his thoughts exhausts him. He closes his eyes. The only thought he allows to escape is an inward command, "Just forget this ever happened." The boat sails toward their destination, the distance between the island and the boat only increasing over time.

Once his presence disappears, she enters her home, closing and locking the door behind her. She sits in a chair, head in hands, knowing all that was said cannot be taken back. She will not break the terms of her exile, for the time being. But the temptation to leave the island grows as she thinks of the possibilities for herself and all she could accomplish. She looks to the ceiling.

"I have no regrets."

Chapter Three

The sound of a horn blares. The screams of irritated, rambunctious sailors and calls of the gulls reach his ears. He feels a slight disorientation with his center of gravity. Tanten sits up in the boat and observes the sun's position.

"It's about six in the evening."

His eyes widen as he locates the source of the horn and screams coming from a giant trade ship heading directly towards his motorboat. He quickly maneuvers the motorboat out of the path of the ship, handling the boat elegantly, even at quick speeds. Tanten pulls into the docking area and jumps out, fixing his unkempt hair from the gust created in his panic to avoid crashing. He places his hands behind his head, lets out a deep sigh, and smirks.

As Tanten walks the crowded sidewalk, he smells the food from the vendors around him. He realizes he hasn't eaten since early morning. He looks up and down the street, seeing what food appeals to his empty stomach, allowing the savory smells to lead him. He spots a sub sandwich vendor ahead and decides it's better than nothing.

While sitting on a bench, eating his sandwich, Tanten observes the passersby. Normal people going about their normal business: shopping, laughing, enjoying their luxurious and carefree lives.

"How do they live like this?" he wonders. "No adventures, no risks, cycling through their life day after day, never falling behind but never moving ahead. If one wants to move ahead, one has to make sacrifices. Sacrifices like-"

Tanten's phone vibrates. He blinks his eyes a few times as he returns to reality from his thoughts. He hopes it's someone who has called the wrong number and not- He checks his phone. Of course it's him, he thinks. His face turns grim and irritated.

"Atlas, what do you want?" Tanten asks, snarling at the phone as he brings it to his ear.

"Ahh, still alive, huh? When I called earlier, you didn't answer, so I assumed the worst. Oh well, got my hopes up for nothing, I guess," Atlas replies. Tanten rolls his eyes, having expected nothing less.

"What do you want?" Tanten questions, more assertively than the first time.

"Whoa, someone seems a bit hostile," Atlas chuckles. Tanten prepares to hang up, but Atlas continues. "What's the news?"

"I'll tell you when I get there."

"Well, listening to your tone, I can only assume... oh, by the way, Bysciw's here." Tanten's eyes open wide at the sound of that name. His heart rate quickens pace, and his left-hand squishes part of his sandwich, the condiments forcing their way through the sides of the foil. Atlas chuckles again, "So get here quick. Or don't."

"When did he arrive?" Tanten tries not to sound alarmed, but his voice gives him away.

"I'll tell you when you get here," Atlas answers and hangs up.

Tanten clenches his right fist, on the verge of breaking his cellphone. His frustration increases the more he repeats that name in his head, but he can't stop. Should he leave and return another day? Hoping that, when he returns, Bysciw will be gone? The questions keep echoing in Tanten's head, "Why is he here? Did someone tell him? Does he know? What's the best choice: seeing him or waiting? Maybe I can learn information from him. But what if he's angry I've been leading in his absence?" Tanten stands and disposes of the remainder of his sandwich, the finishing of which would only add to the uneasiness of his stomach. "No, I can't run. Despite the nausea his presence provides, I must face him." Tanten marches on, heading toward their base of operations.

As he stops in front of the building, he uses his life force to sense any unwelcome visitors and suspicious characters. The watchful eyes of his team members find him, from stories up in the building, out of the third and fifth window to the east side. Tanten smiles. His own skills never cease to amaze him.

Tanten enters the building and heads straight for the stairs. He looks around the empty room and wonders why no one is patrolling the ground level. He opens the door to the stairwell and heads down. Nausea hits him due to his unsettled stomach. His heart accelerates, more so than it had done prior, for now the confrontation seems all too real. He wonders what sin he committed in his past to deserve such torment in one day. He punches the code into the security lock, the likes of which Tanten knows will not keep out any enemy they should really be concerned about, and opens the solid steel door.

All the banter dies down. He peeks around the edge of the door and sees the team, including Atlas and Bysciw. They gather in a circle and watch as he enters the space. Tanten examines all their faces. Whatever they were discussing before he entered could not have been bad news because they all appear rather enthusiastic and excited. Tanten looks at Atlas, who returns a wide, deceitful grin. Next to Atlas sits the one haughty and arrogant as can be. Bysciw.

Bysciw peers at Tanten, his eyes spelling out his excitement. A shiver runs up Tanten's spine as Bysciw reads him. Tanten feels exposed, knowing he's hidden a lot of information from the team members. If Bysciw can read him so easily, and the greater risk accurately, there is no chance Tanten can lie and get away with it. Bysciw continues to observe Tanten and gestures to the open seat across from him. Tanten trudges to the chair, his recalcitrant attitude to superiors a trait he has never cared to hide. The surrounding team watch his every step. He feels trapped, like an animal led to the slaughter. No option, continuing on or running away, is satisfactory.

Tanten sits in the chair. He takes a deep breath and accepts the situation, showing no trace of fear on his face. He examines his 'boss'. Bysciw wears his fur-trimmed cape and accessorizes with gaudy jewels about his fingers and his ears, trying to appear as a king. He seems to be in good spirits, but Tanten knows Bysciw's emotions change as quickly as Juhm's tides. Tanten must remain cautious, and tread lightly throughout the conversation that will ensue. "Atlas is bad enough, but adding Bysciw to the mix makes for an even more uncomfortable situation," Tanten thinks.

"Well, boy, you look exhausted," Bysciw directs at Tanten, breaking the silence. "Gather round everyone, take a seat. Atlas, shall we get this meeting started?"

The group organizes itself. There are four chairs seated in a circle. Bysciw sits in front of Tanten, Atlas sits to his left, and the others stand in a circle surrounding them. Tanten notices that the fourth chair in the inner circle remains empty. Bysciw senses Tanten's interest of the empty chair. "Ah yes, I've hired another Professional to assist us. I will not tell you anything else about their identity until they turn up. At the moment, they are rather busy, so we will begin the meeting without them." Tanten exhales in relief. "Who wishes to start?" Atlas raises his hand and lets off one of his cheeky grins.

"I'll start with my report if there are no objections." Bysciw nods. "The Schism growingly becomes an inevitable situation which many believe will lead to a civil war within the Association. Many from the separatist groups fear for their lives, but are willing to fight for what they believe to be a just and noble cause. They wish to end the disrespect and unequal treatment by the funding committees and international labor and education bureaus which they believe to be instituted by the Magistrate Association itself. However, both sides believing they are the ones being wronged have now come up in arms with one another. Professionals, though more so disciples, versus Scholars, more often than not informants.

"The vice chieftain of the Sorcerics, being of the Professional and disciple classes, and I discussed the possibility of delaying the first attack on an opposing group, but he stated that the chieftain is growing impatient. Their opponents, being those of the Scholar and informant classes, have left threats on multiple occasions, calling for the surrender of the Sorceric Separatists. They continue to train and grow their troops, even admitting those who are not official magistrates. Their training techniques are sub-par, but among their soldiers, there are plenty of potential. However, none of extraordinary potential, and therefore their soldiers are insignificant." Atlas holds out his hand and a glass of wine is placed in it. He takes a sip, holds out the glass, and one of the members takes it away. Atlas resumes.

"A few days back I met with the lead advisor of the Scholastic Loyalists. I asked how long he can delay the start of the war. He stated he can indefinitely delay it if he pleases, but to do so would betray the interests of his supporters. He's prepared to fight whenever, simply holding back to please what he believes is the Association's wishes, as if they are manifesting some plea deal to prevent what could escalate to the involuntary manslaughter of hundreds of innocents. Though more so than this, one noticeable factor did concern me. Their armies are growing at a rapid pace, much faster than that of the Sorcerics. I fear if we wait too long, the Sorcerics will crumble under the sheer numbers of the Scholastics. This devastation would create an immense imbalance within the Magistrate Association's Professional to Scholar ratio and thus lead to a decrease in funding by nations. Not devastating in the slightest for us. Perhaps our jobs, but as a group, this may be a tricky outcome to deal with leading up to our expedition, not giving us the time necessary to prepare."

Bysciw scratches his head. He squints his eyes, looking at nothing in particular, but concentrating in deep thought. He questions Atlas, "What are your projections?"

"Assuming the current rate of growth within both groups remains constant, I project that we have at least two weeks, no more than four weeks. Though both sides are ready to fight at any moment, they both desire more time to strategize. Neither group has a satisfactory plan and, if battle commences too soon, absolute chaos will ensue. Chaos meaning civilians will certainly get pulled into the mix. The Council will be at a much greater disadvantage, as will our main rivals. If we don't desire the chaos, but simply want a distraction, we must wait until both groups have at least a blueprint of a plan. My projections for this matter range from one week to three weeks. However, their strategies can easily be manipulated if I pull some strings. If I were to inject them with doubt, I'm sure the projections I gave can increase by at least a year. So don't worry about their strategies. The real problem here is the growth. Also of note, many more individualist groups are sprouting up. Their power and influence over the two major groups are minimal, however, I fear they may start causing problems for us if they act independently."

"Interesting. This gives us something to think about. Thank you for the report. Be sure to keep us updated," Bysciw remarks. Atlas nods and leans back in his chair, shifting his eyes to Tanten. Tanten knows Atlas is challenging him, but he has no desire to impress Bysciw, and Tanten knows his news won't impress anyone present.

"Tanten," Bysciw looks to him, excited for the news he'll never hear. "Tell us about your trip."

Tanten glances at Bysciw, with a straight expression on his face. He throws away the possibility of even trying to feign good news. Atlas grins as he feels he is victorious. Bysciw's smile turns to a frown. Everyone surrounding begins to murmur words of discontent and impatience. They all stare at Tanten. Tanten closes his eyes, his heart speeding. "Is this how it feels to be interrogated in front of so many? Having to reveal the grim truth to those who look up to you? Having to admit failure?" he wonders. Bysciw raises his hand and the crowd silences.

"Boy, give us the news," Bysciw commands.

"When I arrived at the island, I immediately felt her presence," Tanten begins. "I approached the villa, and she stood in the doorway. I can confirm she is alive... and powerful. As we talked, it became obvious what her answer would be, however, she kept talking, trying to extract more information out of me. When I felt her mind was made up, when there was nothing I could say to convince her otherwise, I stopped and demanded her answer," Tanten stops. The surrounding team members look at him with wide eyes, the suspense of waiting for Tanten to finish apparent on their faces. Atlas places his hands behind his head and closes his eyes. Bysciw continues to focus solely on Tanten.

"So?" asks one of the members from the crowd.

"She said no. She outright refused," Tanten states. The group looks displeased with this answer. Tanten locks eyes with Bysciw. He feels as though Bysciw searches into his mind, trying to pry out the entirety of his and Botalia's meeting. Tanten maintains his calm and cool composure, leaning back and observing the faces of those around him.

"Tanten, be honest with me. If that girl were to have accepted and joined our team, how much of an advantage would that have given us? Was her rejection a great loss to our team?" Bysciw questions. Tanten feels surprised, and somewhat relieved, for this type of follow up to his news. He sighs.

"There is no denying it, having her on our side would put us leagues ahead of everyone. Her aura is comparable to none. Her life force and control over it is incredible. She truly is a monster." Tanten leans forward and attempts to read what Bysciw is thinking.

He appears disappointed from the news, but his curiosity of this girl appears to be far greater. Tanten looks at Atlas, who still seems pleased with himself. Tanten thinks that he himself may see victory yet.

"I see," Bysciw responds.

"But we don't have to worry," Tanten continues. "Her rejection is no great loss. It would be advantageous to have her, but it's not to our disadvantage to not. After our conversation, I can assure one thing. She doesn't want to get involved but rather sit back and watch. She has no interest."

"She refused because our mission doesn't sound adventurous enough for her?" Atlas asks in a cold tone. "How do you expect us to believe that? A girl, no less the child of world-renowned Scholars, who's been isolated for ten years, has no desire to accompany us on our mission. You're not telling us the full truth."

Tanten and Atlas glare at one another. The murmuring from the crowd signifying their agreement with Atlas. Tanten tries to think of how to dig himself out of this hole.

"When she refused, I asked for her reasoning, but she constantly dodged the question. Eventually, I got irritated and left. There is nothing I could have done to persuade her," Tanten answers. Atlas opens his mouth to make another comment, but Bysciw raises his hand. Tanten looks to him.

"Tanten, how certain are you she will not join our enemies?" questions Bysciw. Tanten thinks for a moment.

"Our rivals, the Crusaders, don't know of her existence nor the power she possesses, just as none of you had. To be honest, I'd bet no one, excluding myself, remembers her." Tanten answers with semi-complete honesty, however, his response does not completely reassure Bysciw.

"You mentioned, when we were discussing this option, that the Council knew before exiling her the possibility of her becoming a threat. Is there a chance they would ask for her assistance, given the chaos that might ensue?" Bysciw doesn't know much about Botalia. All he knows is what Tanten and Atlas have told him. However, Bysciw has developed an interest in Botalia. If he could control her and her power, the possibilities for what he and his team could accomplish would be endless. Being power hungry isn't an exclusive trait to him, so he knows if others discover her and her power, they will do whatever it takes to claim her.

Tanten thinks about Bysciw's question. His eyes widen, remembering the discussion he and Botalia had. Tanten closes his eyes and exhales. "Well, this could definitely be a problem," Tanten sighs.

Everyone's eyes widen and they listen intensely to what Tanten has to say. "If the Council does as we expect and begin scanning their files of all registered magistrates looking for the strongest to enlist into their forces, they may stumble upon her name. During a conversation between Botalia and myself, she mentioned she still had access to the magistrate's official website, which we know is only accessible if you are a licensed magistrate. When asked about it, Botalia said when she was exiled, they never revoked her license." Tanten drops his head to look at the ground. He lets out a barely audible laugh. He wonders, "Why didn't I see it before? How could I be so stupid? I know I lied to them about why she refused, but I thought she had no desire to involve herself. In truth, being asked to join probably excited her. She refused simply because I was the one who asked her. Granted, she would have refused if Atlas asked her as well. If anyone else from the team, especially one as seemingly respectable and intelligent as Bysciw asked her, she would probably jump at the chance, the chance of being useful and escaping after so many years..."

Atlas frowns in disappointment. Atlas hoped Tanten would be humiliated for failing in his mission. Atlas thought he was victorious, that Bysciw would be impressed with his report and promote him to second-in-command. However, the poor news Tanten delayed seems to captivate Bysciw. Bysciw has not moved his eyes from Tanten since they got onto the topic of Botalia. Atlas knows his own report had nothing but satisfactory news, and yet Tanten, the smug-faced con, delivers less than acceptable news and still holds Bysciw's attention. He glares at Tanten, disgusted that he continues to work alongside this man.

Bysciw places his head in his hands. His shoulders move up and down as he begins to laugh. His laugh grows more boisterous as he thinks about the situation. Some of the other group members join in with the laughter, looking at each other, confused about what's happening. Atlas continues to frown, now glaring at Bysciw. Tanten looks up, also confused by Bysciw's actions. Bysciw continues to bellow, everyone wondering if the noise will alarm those meant to keep watch.

"Excuse me," Bysciw says, trying to regain his composure. Everyone stares at Bysciw. "I apologize for my outburst. Oh, boy, you never cease to entertain me," he addresses Tanten. Tanten's eyes widen and his eyebrows raise. Tanten wonders how he got on good terms with a man he wants dead. Bysciw continues, "The situation amuses me is all. If the Council finds out, we'll have quite a race on our hands. Atlas, you worked within the Association for several years, do you think they'll ask her for help?" Bysciw looks to Atlas, who immediately changes the expression on his face to one of surprise. Tanten glares at Atlas, who, feeling the heated look, answers with a smile.

"I can't answer with certainty, but if the Association crumbles as we hope, they may feel they have no choice but to call anyone they can to their aid. Whether they remember her or not is a great question. I'm aware the Association never disposed of her information. I was assigned with that job and, well," Atlas chuckles,

"I never followed through. I thought it would be fun to stumble across her files, years later, when everyone else had forgotten her. I never expected to be in a situation such as this." He smiles. Bysciw, however, is not smiling, nor is anyone else in the room.

"Well," Bysciw responds. He puts his hands on his knees, sighs, and stands. "If we can't have her, no one can." Those surrounding drop their jaws. Atlas frowns and leans back. Tanten looks at the ground in horror, his heart playing what seems to be the melody of the day. "Atlas, how quickly can you contract a small group of assassins for her extermination?"

"Tell me when, and they're there," Atlas answers, his eyes closed.

"Very good," Bysciw smiles. "Eliminate her by the end of the week. Try to keep assassin forces to a minimum, and only hire from the professionals. They know not to let information about any of their victims leak."

"As you wish," Atlas replies, standing up and walking away from the group. Tanten continues to stare at the ground, wondering what he should have done differently.

"Nice work, boy," Bysciw says. As he walks past Tanten, he pats him on the shoulder. "Be sure to keep everything under control while I'm away. Failure is not an option." Bysciw glances at the untouched fourth chair. "I guess our newest lead was busier than expected. I'll contact them and retrieve the information they gathered. I'll send a messenger to pass on any vital information. However, the first order of business is to get rid of that girl."

Bysciw walks away. The other team members disperse, most returning to their tasks from before the meeting. Tanten remains motionless. He blames himself. He is the one who recommended they contact her.

Tanten looks up and sees Atlas return to his chair with a drink. They look at one another, expressionless.

"Back so soon?" Tanten asks Atlas.

"Business is brief when dealing with professionals," Atlas answers in a monotone voice. They share a moment of silence. "Don't look so glum." Atlas stands, deciding his desire to be in Tanten's presence any longer is nonexistent. "You seem to forget who we're talking about." Atlas walks away. He calls back, "I have some business to attend to. Ciao." He lifts his hand and waves back.

Atlas's words ring in Tanten's ears. As much as Tanten hates to admit it, Atlas is right. Tanten softly laughs. He thinks, "Bysciw has no idea what he's gotten himself into. A group of assassins, even professionals, won't be able to kill Botalia, let alone touch her. She's too powerful. Bysciw underestimates her abilities. But I know better." He leans back and relaxes a bit. "Your ignorance will be your demise, Bysciw. I won't have to wait long, especially after this move. It's checkmate." Tanten closes his eyes and smiles.

Chapter Four

Two days have passed since the visitor appeared. The first visitor in ten years. Botalia waters the plants in her garden, still thinking about their conversation. She examines the blooms and feels the leaves of each plant, making sure they are well fed and strong. She focuses her eyes and analyzes each plant's aura and life force.

"Stupid brain and thoughts and... Why can't they all just forget? Why can't I forget?"

Botalia mumbles to herself as she attends to her chores. The wish to distract herself is met by her desire to understand. Her aura flares in a wave of rage, wisps of life force seeping into the ground.

She starts to water the last row of plants when her life force returns to her in a panic. Whether it be the instinct of the beast within or her own senses, an unknown presence enters the vicinity of the island.

Dropping the watering pot where she stands, Botalia rushes to the villa, jogs into the sitting room and pulls a crudely drawn map of the island out of a side table drawer. Botalia hovers her hand over it, index finger extended, and closes her eyes. Her hand moves without hesitation. When she opens her eyes, her finger is by the dock.

"They're entering on the dock... they must not be hostile. Right?... Well, they may be, but often enemies don't use the front entrance." Botalia, shocked at the thought of having another visitor, tidies the room a bit, for she knows she has plenty of time before the guest reaches her front doorstep.

With the help of her life force, she can sense how far away a person is if she focuses. When they get close, she'll know. It's strange, though. Botalia knows it's not Tanten because the plant by her front door responded to the newcomer. The plant's name is "herba aduolant" (plant of sensing) and Botalia created it through her experiments. She has planted many other of this specie of plant on the island. They are all interconnected, so when one senses a change in the environment around it, the others follow suit. The plants respond by having the leaves curve upward in alert. This is how Botalia monitors the island. The plants help her gauge when a creature has delivered a newborn or if a foreign insect somehow migrated to the island. The plant adapts to the newcomers within an hour, so after that time period expires, the leaves return to a downward position. Because of their interlocking network, if one plant adapts to a newcomer, all plants adapt to the newcomer.

As she paces back and forth, Botalia wonders who the visitor could be. When she learned of a visitor the other day, she almost had an anxiety attack, forcing herself to employ the deep breathing exercises from her days as a child with the fury of a monster. When she learned it was Tanten, her panic deepened. She places her hand on a wall and closes her eyes. After a few seconds pass, she finds the visitor's footsteps. They feel light and springy, often how those excited and optimistic walk. She doesn't recognize the person's aura, however, she feels she has a connection to the person. Intuitively, she knows they have never met, but it's as though she knew they would meet one day.

They stop in front of the villa, whether it be of fear or preparing for an attack. Botalia removes her hand from the wall and heads to meet her visitor. As she opens the door, her eyes widen and her mouth grows agape. Standing in front of her is a copper-skinned, young boy in a white tank top and black cargo pants carrying a worn and dirtied backpack. He looks at her, smiles, and waves. Jogging up to her, the young boy holds out his hand.

"Hello. My guardians sent me here to ask for an *apprentaship*. My name is Koepp Flynn," the boy says, smiling all the while. Botalia nervously laughs and smiles in return. She looks at his hand and hesitates to shake it. The incident with Tanten is still fresh in her memory, though she feels this boy's past is probably not as tragic as Tanten's. But still, she fears the inevitable pain.

Despite her fear, she grabs his hand. A slight jolt shocks her, like being hit in the stomach with a baseball, but the pain soon passes. When she closes her eyes, she could see the sufferings of the boy's past, the darkest moments of his life. Though more colorful than Tanten's sufferings, she can still see that this boy has experienced much pain and heartache. She clenches her fists and wonders if the pain would be less had Tanten acted like a real father.

"Oww," Koepp says, pulling his hand away from Botalia and shaking it. He appears confused by her tight grip, but quickly brushes it off.

"I'm so sorry," Botalia says, putting her hands up to her chest. "Please forgive me."

"It's fine, really." The boy looks up at her, his dark cocoa eyes equal to that of his father's. "You look a bit young to be a master. Is there anyone else here?" Koepp asks, looking around.

"Nope, just me," Botalia grins. She doesn't understand the purpose of Tanten's son being here, but it doesn't change the fact that he stands in front of her. The only person she can think responsible for him coming to her island is Tanten, but she assumed he didn't involve himself with his son.

"So, what's this about you wanting to be my apprentice? Are you lost or did someone send you here?" Botalia scans the area, but she knows he's alone. "Who would send a young boy off on his own?" she wonders.

"Well, my caretakers gave me a piece of paper saying that I'm to find Ms. Botalia Ulton on this island and ask to be her student. They told me I had to leave, so I left right away," he shrugs. "And now I'm here." He looks around, taking in all the surroundings. The clear skies, the dense forests, and the colorful array of tropical flora on the veranda. His smile widens as he watches the birds and insects fly about. He breathes in deeply, inhaling every aroma nature offers him. Botalia senses Koepp truly loves nature and possesses a kind spirit. She focuses her eyes and observes his aura. Koepp's aura imitates a gentle flame and, though his knowledge of utilizing life force is nonexistent, his aura appears just like his father's. Every aspect of his aura is a facsimile of his father's.

"Koepp Flynn. I, Botalia Ulton, would feel honored to have you as my student," Botalia declares. His smile radiates his excitement and joy. She can't help but feel happy just from looking at Koepp's expression, as if his overflowing emotion is contagious. Botalia knows he's never had a proper role model in his life, so she wishes to prove her worth as someone he can look up to. Botalia questions whether she's made the right choice, after all, she's meant to be isolated from people. However, she believes the experience will benefit both her and Koepp, a mutual relationship. She knows she can teach him a wide variety of subjects, from math to science to geography to language. She will teach him combat as well as techniques in using life force. By looking at him, she knows he doesn't have any control over his life force, but if anyone were to teach him, it should be her. Koepp has incredible potential, she can feel it, and with her as his master, he may grow stronger than his father someday.

"Follow me," says Botalia, leading Koepp into the villa.

His jaw drops as he sees the extravagance of the interior.

"This will be your new home. I hope you can find some entertainment while you stay here." She looks at his face. The smile of the innocent, young boy is a memory Botalia will come to cherish. Koepp runs around, investigating every nook and cranny of the villa. His hands press against the glass of the cabinets housing dozens of awards and specimen. A rush of curiosity steals him away to squeeze the faux ranadune hair pillows and test the cushions of the sofas. Things she had taken for granted growing up with a semblance of wealth.

"Come. This way," she beckons him. Arms thrown behind his back, Koepp darts toward her.

Botalia leads him to a guest room on the second floor. No one had entered the room for years, a layer of dust and dangling cobwebs covering the walls and furniture.

"This will be your room, however, we'll have to do some dusting first." Koepp laughs.

They spend the rest of the day cleaning out the guest bedroom and exploring the villa. She decides it is best not to show him some of the rooms for the time being. When night arrives, they sit on the back patio by the fire pit, gazing up at the night sky.

"All the lights in the sky are beautiful," says Koepp in awe. Botalia smiles.

"Haven't you seen stars before?"

"I'm from the city. There are too many bright lights on the ground that prevent the people there from seeing the stars. I bet if people there could see how pretty they are, they would be a lot happier." Koepp continues to look up in amazement. Botalia drops her head and closes her eyes. She smiles. "Ahh!" Koepp gasps. Botalia opens her eyes and looks around. "Look!" yells Koepp excitedly, tugging on Botalia's arm. He points to the sky. "It looked like a star was falling out of the sky! Is it gonna hit someone?" He turns to Botalia. She giggles.

"It'll be fine. What you saw was probably just a meteor entering the planet's atmosphere and blazing due to its velocity and resistance of our atmosphere. The meteoroid will probably crumble before getting anywhere near the ground," Botalia states. Koepp appears enlightened, but slightly disappointed by Botalia's words. "Do you want to know a secret?" she asks Koepp. He turns to her, excitement covering his face, nodding vigorously. Botalia smiles. "Alright, I'll tell you, but you have to promise not to tell anyone. Only tell those you would trust with your life." Botalia holds out her pinky finger, and Koepp quickly wraps his pinky finger around hers. He nods in agreement, his face now serious. "There is an old tale that if a person sees a falling meteor, they are granted one wish. It can be any wish in the universe, and if the falling meteor was a lucky one sent as a message by the gods, that person's wish will come true."

"How will I know if that was a lucky meteor?" Koepp asks, concerned.

"Make a wish, and if it comes true, you'll know," Botalia responds. "But you can't say it out loud. Just think of your wish really hard in your head, and the gods might hear it." Koepp nods and closes his eyes tightly, his fists and jaw clenched in pure concentration. She smiles at the innocence of the boy. His unkempt brunette hair, his slim, but well-built, figure, his bold brown eyes; there was never any denying this was Tanten's son. Botalia gazes at him until he opens his eyes. His smile appears indestructible. Koepp puts his hands behind his head and lays down on the patio, staring at the stars once again.

"If there's another meteor, I'll let you make the next wish," Koepp tells Botalia. She finds she doesn't even need to change her expression to show her gratitude. She never stopped smiling.

"Thank you very much," Botalia says. They both gaze up at the sky for a few minutes, silently. Koepp yawns and Botalia sees him struggling to keep his eyes open. "It's been a long day. Why don't we call it a night? Because your room isn't ready yet, you can sleep in my room." Koepp sits up with an astonished look.

"But where will you sleep?" he asks.

"I can sleep on the couch tonight. I don't mind," Botalia replies. "And no playing around because tomorrow we start your schooling."

Botalia stands and extends her hand. Koepp grabs hold and pulls himself up. They enter the villa, their home, and ready themselves for sleep.

As Koepp slips into Botalia's bed, she turns the lights off and closes the door. She retires to the sitting room, retrieves her book, and begins reading. After twenty minutes, she closes the book and allows her thoughts to flood her.

She smiles as she thinks about her day with Koepp. While he looks like Tanten's son, he differs from Tanten, the term antithesis not far from the truth. Koepp is innocent and kind-hearted, his smile contagious. Tanten is corrupt and heavy-hearted, he trusts no one. She wonders if Tanten is responsible for Koepp coming to the island. She can't think of anyone else who would be willing to send their ten-year old son to apprentice her. He said his guardians were given a letter calling for Koepp to learn from her. Perhaps instructions from Tanten? While pondering this thought, a disturbance stirs in the back of her head. She closes her eyes to focus on it. When she understands the source, she rises from her seat and heads to her bedroom.

She opens the door and sees Koepp turning from side to side, his face twisting and his body perspiring. Botalia rushes over to him, hoping he hasn't contracted some sort of illness. She wipes his forehead and senses that the pain is derived subconsciously, like he's trapped in a painful dream. She runs her hand through his hair and closes her eyes. She sings:

Close your eyes little warrior
Return to your dreams

Walk upon the red clouds
And sleep
Lu Li La Le
Feel the pain disappear
No need to fight on, fight on
The darkness draws near
Lu Li Lu La
Approach with gentle heart
Sense the monster's release
And sleep, and sleep
Sense the monster's release
And sleep
Lu Li Ly La Li Ly Le

AS SHE SINGS, KOEPP becomes calm, his breathing and heart beat relaxing. He lays still and reenters his REM cycle. Botalia hopes only good dreams will encapsulate him for the rest of the night. She grasps his hand and intuitively knows her hopes take shape. Koepp's mind swims in a sea of pleasant dreams. Curiosity grabs hold of Botalia and she follows her life force into the depths of his mind. As she travels down the hall of his memories, Botalia examines each door, a memory hidden beyond each one. There is a door a bit farther down that shines brilliantly, almost calling her to open it. Botalia approaches the red oak door, the light escaping from every crack. She reaches for the doorknob but stops herself. She closes her eyes and steps back. The guilt of almost giving into her temptation gets to her. Botalia decides not to violate Koepp's privacy. She'll allow him to tell her about his life as he feels appropriate.

With eyes still closed, she focuses her attention on controlling her muscles. Botalia releases Koepp's hand. Her eyes open as she reenters reality. Koepp lays in a deep sleep. Botalia lets out a sigh.

She exits the room and stretches out on the couch. She stares at the ceiling, thinking.

Botalia raises her right arm and observes it. Her fingers and hand sway as she thinks. She stops moving them and focuses her eyes. Nothing. If everyone else can see it, why can't she? She feels it, she senses it's there and yet she can't see it. It seems unfair, in her mind if in no one else's, that a person is unable to look upon their own aura. Why must something considered impressive, at least in Tanten's eyes, be hidden from her? Why can't she view her aura, just once?

She drops her arm and sighs. She begins thinking once again and laughs, wondering, "If I could wish for one thing, what would it be? I'll have to think of something good so I don't disappoint Koepp." She closes her eyes and takes a deep breath. "Don't fail me now, imagination. I don't want to disappoint Koepp... I never want to disappoint Koepp." Botalia yawns and falls asleep.

Chapter Five

"Today we'll start our math lessons," Botalia states, Koepp nodding his head in agreement, though his eyes reflect his nerves. Botalia grabs a jar of jellybeans and places it in front of Koepp. His eyes widen. She walks over to the desk and picks up some sheets of paper and a pencil. They sit in the study, where she has been teaching him for the past two days. The grandfather clock strikes to signify a new hour. Botalia hands the papers and pencil to Koepp, who readily accepts them.

"What you see in front of you are one hundred math problems. They only involve addition, so not too complex." She sits across from Koepp who appears confused. "If you get stuck, use the jellybeans to help. Simply count out the first number in jellybeans, then, count out the second number in jellybeans. Put the two groups of jellybeans together, and you have the answer. Any questions so far?"

Koepp shakes his head, but then changes his mind. "Actually, I do have one question. Am I allowed to eat these?" he asks, pointing at the jellybeans.

Botalia laughs and stands up. "Yes, but don't eat too many because then you may not have enough to solve the more difficult problems. Once you get the answer, write it down, and when you're all done, I'll grade it. We won't move to the next level until I feel your grade is satisfactory. Also, you have a time limit. After the time is up, I'll collect your paper whether you're done or not. Any questions now?"

"Yeah, uhh, how long do I get?"

"I'll give you fifteen minutes. There are one hundred problems, so I expect you'll do fine," Botalia responds, expressing a reassuring smile. "I'll just be sitting at the other table, so if you have any questions, feel free to speak up." She leans down to look at him, eye level. "I trust you'll do fine."

Koepp nods in agreement, eager to begin. Botalia takes her seat. Koepp moves the jar and his papers to the rug on the floor. After adjusting, he looks up at Botalia, ready to start. She looks at the grandfather clock across from her, waiting for it to hit a fresh minute. The seconds hand reaches the twelve.

"You may begin."

Koepp does not hesitate. Like a runner hearing the gun at the starting line, he takes off.

While Koepp works, Botalia conducts work of her own. She constructs her lab write up for the ongoing experiment with her plants. Granted, she has many ongoing experiments, but after viewing the aura of the plant in her greenhouse, this one piques her interest the most. If she succeeds in achieving her goal, she could change the world, that is, if the Association allows her to contact others in the scientific community to share her findings. But she knows the experiment would interest more than scientists. The world would be captivated by her success. A plant that offers a battery of life force for even the most novice of life force users to utilize... Yes, there may be dangers. But no scientific field could progress if one only thinks of the negative impact it may have when the information falls into the hands of those with bad intentions. Perhaps the Association would allow her to return to Dominia... perhaps... Her daydream breaks as she remembers she must keep her eye on the time.

Botalia glimpses over at Koepp. He bites his bottom lip and squints, counting jellybeans and scratching his head, wondering if he has time to double count or trust that he counted right the first time.

She smiles. He may not be the brightest, but he's got time to learn. He radiates potential, and Botalia decides she won't stop until he does.

Once the fifteen minutes expire, Botalia grades his paper. Koepp stands next to her, nervously sucking on a jellybean. To him, waiting for the results is more nerve-wracking than taking the test. Botalia puts down her pen and stands up. She walks over to the rug on the floor and sits, patting the ground next to her. Koepp joins her on the rug. He tries to peek at his score, but Botalia hides it from him.

"Not yet," she says. He looks dejected, but he doesn't see disappointment on her face so he feels a bit less worried. She looks him in the eyes and smiles, he returns it. "You finished fifty-three out of one hundred problems," she starts off, "so there is plenty of room for improvement. However, out of the fifty-three answered, you got forty-nine correct. It's not amazing, but not terrible. To be honest, I'm impressed you did so well given that you've never participated in any elementary level education." Koepp doesn't know whether he should be excited or disappointed by his results. He settles with disappointment.

"I'll do better next time, I swear," he says. Botalia giggles.

"I know you will. Just in case, we'll set goals for you to reach, and if you fail to reach those goals, there will be consequences." Botalia smiles and tilts her head to the side. Koepp attempts to force a smile, but he doesn't quite succeed. "Tomorrow, when you take the updated version of this test, I expect you to finish at least seventy problems, and get at least sixty of them correct."

"What will be my punishment if I don't?" asks Koepp.

"That will be a surprise," answers Botalia. She stands up and Koepp follows her lead. She continues, "I'm sure-"

Botalia's heart doubles a beat, and her life force shoots through her fingers and into the ground.

Impossible.

Koepp perks up and looks around, having never seen Botalia with a frightened expression. Botalia peers at the boy sitting in front of her. Before, she only had to worry about herself. Before. Things were different now.

She grabs Koepp's hand, and she pulls him behind her as she rushes up to his room. This was the safest place in her mind for two main reasons. One: It's on the second floor. Two: there is only one window and a door, limiting the number of entrances and exits. As they run up the stairs to the room, Koepp remains silent, too scared to say anything. Though he doesn't know anything about life force yet, the moment he met Botalia he sensed her power. If whatever is happening scares her, it should scare him, too.

Botalia closes the door and leans against it. Koepp sits on his bed, staring at Botalia. Botalia puts her right hand on the wall and closes her eyes. After a few seconds, she feels it. She knew she sensed multiple presences, but now she knows just how many they are dealing with.

Four.

Botalia senses four human presences heading for her house, all coming from different ways. And they are powerful. She knows she must exert some life force, and she focuses it into determining their exact location.

One of the visitors jumps from tree to tree, effortlessly making his way toward the villa. She can sense his hostility, ready to kill at any moment. With his light step and agile movements, she can only assume he's an assassin or an elite hunter. His aura is dark and whirls around him like a violent tornado. She guesses from his concentration of life force that he is strong, not as strong as her, but still strong.

She shifts her focus to the next visitor. Number two swiftly approaches from the back of her villa, on the ground. He also intends to kill, judging by his hostility and aura. Botalia can feel from his light step that he's not only dexterous but young. She senses his life force is not well harnessed. He's either very impulsive or barely a threat.

The third visitor she checks on travels from the opposite side of the villa from the first visitor. Botalia senses she's rather athletic by her speed and movements. She appears to be an assassin like the other two. She hides her hostility better, but her aura radiates. Botalia guesses this assassin enjoys the thrill, for her aura spells out her excitement.

As Botalia moves her attention to the fourth visitor, she notices something off. The fourth visitor, a man, is walking up the same path taken by Tanten and Koepp, in other words, walking casually up to her front door. Instinct tells her the four are working together, but why is the fourth member so nonchalant? An odd stirring occurs in the back of her head while attempting to interpret this fourth person. His aura is dark and misty like the others, however, while his aura seems most familiar with a hostile essence, it creates a shape she can't seem to recognize. It feels like a strange hybrid of emotions, but she can't determine the components from the solution.

In the time she was analyzing the fourth visitor's aura, she realizes the others have stopped moving.

Have they gotten into position?

"They have us surrounded on four sides. I know for certain three of the four are assassins. I assume the fourth is as well, but he must be better at hiding his murderous intent." She peers over at Koepp who looks at her nervously. She walks over to him. "Don't you worry. I won't try to act like these are nice people because they're not. But it seems they don't know whose island they've stumbled upon," she says with a reassuring smile. He slightly grins. She grabs him by the shoulders and they lock eyes. "I will never let anyone hurt you." She releases her right hand and holds up her pinky finger. "I promise." Koepp grabs her pinky finger with his and smiles.

Botalia looks out the window from his bedroom and notices nothing immediately suspicious. As she stands there, she is hit by the eyes of another. Botalia doesn't know who is watching her or from where, but they've seen her. She puts her hand on the wall and closes her eyes once more. The three visitors have not moved from their positions. The fourth continues his casual walk up the path. At this rate, she estimates he'll be at her front doorstep in two minutes. She wonders if she should leave Koepp here or take him with her. "What a stupid question," she thinks to herself. "I have no choice but to take him with me. I can't let him out of my sight. If he leaves my side, any number of events may occur. They may hold him hostage, hurt him, or even kill him. That settles it. Koepp stays with me. But what if I get hurt? One, three, and four feel like strong adversaries, while not more powerful than myself, they may have developed an infallible strategy. With their ability to conceal their auras and life force, no ordinary magistrate would have been able to sense their presences. It was only due to my heightened senses I was able to feel them approach." She thinks about it some more. "That may give me the advantage. They may think of me as no one other than an ordinary magistrate. However...assassins don't blindly kill. People hire them to do their dirty work. Who would want me dead?" Her eyes shift to Koepp.

She hears the knock at her front door. Lost in her worries, Botalia didn't pay attention to the time. She has a tendency to over-analyze, but now she has to rely on her instincts. The visitor knocks again. Botalia gestures for Koepp to follow her. They descend the stairs and walk toward the door. She signals for Koepp to stand back. He obeys her every command for he knows she wishes him no harm. Botalia closes her eyes and exhales before opening the door.

As the door swings open, their auras clash before she sees his face. The hybrid of emotions become known to her in that instant. A mix of nostalgia, curiosity, and hostility meet her. Botalia bites her lip as she turns her head to look upon the visitor. His aura constricts her, unable to move. But it's not by any power of his that she feels this way. Botalia's anxiety resumes where it left off after Tanten's visit, strangling her. Frozen by her own fears, Botalia stares at the frame of one she once knew.

"I see you've grown up," says the man at the door to Botalia. He grins, appearing almost deceitful. He leans to peek around her, looking at Koepp, smiling and raising his eyebrows. "And, you have a son?" The feelings constricting Botalia release her. Her petrification caused her to lose sight of all around her, even Koepp whose protection should be her top priority. Botalia regains her composure and returns to reality. She locks eyes with the visitor.

"Not quite. He's my student," Botalia responds.

She focuses her eyes to examine his aura. It still appears in the hybrid form, though, more sinister than before. He harnesses his life force to be accessible at a moment's notice, the control incredible. Botalia senses he is sizing her up as well. Though the visitor does not express his thoughts, he can't help but be impressed by her aura and life force. Simply thinking about her great power excites him. Koepp remains quiet and his eyes constantly shift from Botalia to the visitor. Immense power radiates from both people, keeping Koepp frozen to his position.

"Hmm... interesting," responds the visitor. He scans the space and then returns his gaze to Botalia. Her eyes fixate on him. He chuckles. "Well, if you're not going to invite me, I guess I'm forced to ask. May I come in?" As he asks, he scratches his arm, which she notices has the faintest markings upon it. Botalia squints, wondering what sort of trap this may be.

"Right this way," Botalia says, leading Koepp and the guest to the sitting room. He may be a hollow frame of who he once was, but he definitely appears to enjoy the mold he's set himself into. His spiked silver hair and slim, muscular build prove he's grown up from the greasy haired, lanky boy she once knew, or she thought she knew. The visitor looks at her transformation, thinking about how the once frightened and tragic girl grew into a powerful and confident woman. Though, he observes that her charitable heart and lack of trust remain unchanged.

Koepp sits next to Botalia on the couch, their visitor sitting in a chair across from them. Once they sit, Botalia and the visitor lock eyes. She bears a straight face with sympathetic eyes and the visitor grins, his eyes glowing with his curiosity and hostility. Botalia breaks the silence the only way she knows how.

"Would you like something to drink?" she asks, in a serious tone. The visitor chuckles and leans back.

"It would be rude to decline."

Botalia follows procedure by placing her hands on the table and closes her eyes. Koepp watches carefully, expecting to see something impressive, but nothing happens. The visitor's smile grows. Focusing his eyes, he could see a fraction of her life force flow from her hands, across the table, to the floor, and move in the direction of what he assumes to be the kitchen.

"Strange the extent people can evolve independently of the help of teachers," remarks the visitor.

"I find it strange an intruder would walk right up to my front doorstep and ask for entrance to my home," Botalia retorts. The visitor chuckles, despite Botalia's harsh tone.

"It's not too strange. The plan worked, did it not?" smiles the visitor. Botalia rolls her eyes and sighs.

The wispy, humanoid servant enters carrying a tray with three glasses and a pitcher. Koepp's jaw drops in awe of the figure. The visitor analyzes the conjured servant. "She effortlessly managed to conjure a fully functioning humanoid and enable it to keep shape and control without it being in reach of her vision," the visitor thinks. "Many life force sculptors never reach the level of constructing a completely controlled humanoid outside of their sights, and it takes an expert to do so with little effort. Her power excites me."

The servant places the tray on the table and fills the glasses. Botalia bows her head in acknowledgment, thanking the servant. The humanoid bows and disappears in a whirl of smoke. Koepp remains with mouth agape, impressed by the show of her abilities. He turns to Botalia with an inspired smile. Botalia does not smile but returns her eyes to the visitor, who joyfully watched the show. He leans forward and grabs a drink, sipping from the glass and licking his lips before returning it to the table.

"Shall we reminisce or get straight to business?" the visitor asks. Botalia grabs her glass, Koepp following suit. She takes a drink and places it back on the table, thinking of her response all the while. Botalia places her hands on the table once more and closes her eyes, recalling the servant. The visitor, aware of her conjuring her servant for the second time, wonders why but keeps the silence unbroken. Botalia leans back and sighs. After ten seconds pass, the wispy servant enters carrying three additional glasses. The visitor raises his eyebrows.

"Those aren't for us," Botalia states. The visitor puts his head in his hands as he chuckles. He lifts his head and smiles.

"Business it is," the visitor answers.

Unaware to him, Botalia called the servant the second time as a decoy, allowing her to execute her actual plan. She wanted to determine the location of the others, which did not take long because they moved closer to the villa from their previous positions. However, she decided it was no longer to her advantage to act as if they were not present.

The man in front of her continues, "Why the serious face? You know you've won. Why not lay out the terms of our defeat and call it a day? After all," the visitor stops and glimpses at Koepp, "teaching a Flynn must be exhausting." Koepp gasps and stares at the visitor. Botalia's expression remains serious.

"Tenebrant," she pauses for simply saying his name causes her heart to freeze and stomach to sink. "I believe I know why you all are here, but what I want to know is who. Who sent you?" She prays Tanten's name won't escape his lips, for Koepp's sake. However, there is only one other name she feels is even a possibility: Atlas. Strange how the two people who voted against her exile, probably the only people to remember her existence, would wish for her death.

"I don't know the details, a friend asked me if I wanted to tag along. When he stated you were the target, I couldn't resist," Tenebrant responds.

Botalia releases a laugh. Koepp looks at her in confusion. "Well, I suppose I shouldn't ruin all of their fun," she says, standing up. "After all, that one seems pretty young. This may be a great learning experience. For all of them." Botalia stretches her arms and legs. Tenebrant smiles. She glares at him. "If you as much as move from that seat, I will kill you."

"Don't challenge me, I might just be tempted," Tenebrant replies. He closes his eyes. "Ten minutes. I give you ten minutes to round them up. Dead or alive doesn't matter, as long as you bring them here."

"Challenge accepted," Botalia responds, smiling back at him. She peers at Koepp, who appears terrified. He wraps his arms around his legs and sets his head atop his knees. "I'll be back soon, Koepp, don't you worry." He nods. "Tenebrant." He opens his eyes. "If anything happens to Koepp, I won't hesitate."

"Again, don't tempt me," Tenebrant says. He raises his eyebrows. "Are you ready?"

"Tell me when."

"Go."

Botalia closes her eyes and places her hand on the floor. She'll take out the man first, then circle around to the young boy and woman. Botalia runs up the stairs and heads to an empty bedroom at the east end of the villa. She opens the door and cringes at the amount of dust. "Worry about that later," she thinks. She opens the window, grabs onto the tree branch hanging near, and climbs up into the tree. Botalia senses that her target doesn't realize she knows. She must be cautious and catch this one off guard. He's the strongest of the three, so she must take him down quickly and quietly.

She jumps from tree to tree, proving her agility to the nature around her. She moves near to where he stands. Botalia closes her eyes and places her hand on the tree branch. Her life force flows through the trees much faster than it does on the inside of her villa. In her home, the life force travels across lifeless objects, which create a source of friction. The life force provided by nature accelerates her life force by adding to its energy. He's not far from her current position, and it appears she is doing quite well hiding her aura because he doesn't notice her and does not appear to suspect anything outside of what is considered a procedural assassination.

To get closer to him, Botalia uses her life force to silence her movements. She sneaks up, positioning herself on a branch about twenty feet behind him. She knows she must continue to focus her eyes because a slight change in his aura will tell her to act immediately. She wonders how she can capture him without injuring him too badly. One minute expires.

She claps her hands together and concentrates a portion of her life force into them. As Botalia separates her palms, the life force spans between them like a spiderweb. She jumps at the assassin, holding her hands out in front of her, positioning them as if she were going to catch a ball. The man's aura flares as he senses her presence. Her eyes widen. She completely concealed her aura yet he reacts to her. She bites her lip, knowing she must focus on her mission.

The life force extended from her hands wraps around the man's face, acting as a medium which will muffle any sound he makes. She releases the life force from her palms. It sticks to the assassin's face, and Botalia simultaneously kicks his side. The kick forces Botalia to twist her body in order to control her landing on the tree branch. The man springs his legs and raises his arms to grab hold of another tree branch. He utilizes the force of her kick to swing to a lower branch. He takes a defensive stance, sensing her power.

Botalia lunges at the man, concentrating her life force into her right hand, ready to hit. He reacts to her movement by jumping to the ground. Her hand makes contact with the tree, just as planned. She predicted he would dodge. The moment her hand strikes the tree, her life force flows to the ground. It raises from the soil and constricts the assassin. Two minutes have passed.

She jumps to the ground and smiles, he returns it. Botalia delivers a sharp strike to the back of his neck, not hard enough to kill him but strong enough to knock him unconscious. His body falls to the ground as she releases the life force which binds him. She picks up his body and lays it at the side of the villa, out of sight of the other assassins.

Closing her eyes, Botalia places her hands on the ground, and locates the young boy. He has shifted slightly from his previous position, but he's clueless as to what has occurred. The third minutes ticks over.

The boy stands on the ground behind a tree, waiting for the signal from the others to strike. Botalia approaches him from his side. Unlike the other assassin, she knows it will be impossible for him to sense her. She approaches his back, moving like a gust of wind, silently treading on the ground. His eyes widen, but before he can react, a sting originates from the nape of his neck. His vision blurs and he falls into Botalia's arms.

Botalia lifts his motionless body over her shoulder, feeling sympathy for this young boy who must live only through his assassination training. As she carries his body to the location of the first target, she realizes this lifestyle is not unique to this young boy alone. "The other two assassins also had to endure rigorous training and various exercises. It's no wonder their aura moves so freely like a gust of wind, they are empty. They've been trained not to experience emotions because it may hinder their performance during the job. I thought I was a monster, but at least I have feeling. They, the assassins, are devoid of even raw emotion. Their excitement derives from their sole pleasure, killing others, a successful mission."

She places his body next to the other. Again, she closes her eyes and locates the woman assassin, she has moved closer to the villa. Botalia stands up and wonders how she will approach the final assassin. After developing a plan, she heads toward her final battle. Minute number four expires.

Botalia walks casually toward the woman, not out of arrogance or over-confidence, but because she wants a fair fight. No sneak attacks or dirty tactics. She wants to gauge her opponent's abilities. Also, the woman assassin seems very excited in her hiding, so Botalia would feel guilt to deprive her of a proper fight.

The assassin spots Botalia and conceals her presence. Botalia stops, facing the tree the woman hides herself in. Botalia holds her hands out in front of her, placing her right fist in her left hand. She concentrates her life force in her right hand and aims for the tree trunk.

The assassin jumps out of the tree, nanoseconds before Botalia makes contact. However, Botalia reacts almost instantaneously, moving her aura from her right hand to her left leg, manipulating the force to act like a springboard and project her in the direction of the assassin.

The assassin jumps up, dodging Botalia's dive, and kicks out her left leg, aiming for Botalia's spinal cord. Botalia stretches out her right hand and pushes off the ground, rotating her body one-hundred and eighty degrees. As she twists, she grabs hold of the assassin's extended leg with her left hand and pulls the assassin to the ground with her. The fifth minute passes.

Botalia emits her life force from her hands to quickly get on her feet. The woman assassin performs a kip-up and waves a dagger at Botalia. The assassin leaps into the air to achieve leverage, but Botalia roundhouse kicks the assassin's calf mid-leap, forcing a moment about the point of contact. The assassin pushes off the ground with her left arm, and Botalia swings her right leg, aiming for the assassin's elbow. However, Botalia rapidly withdraws her kick as the assassin cuts through the air with her dagger to create a shield between them. The assassin lands her flip and Botalia rises to meet her. Leading with her dagger, arm extended, the assassin lunges. Botalia catches her arm between her left arm and her ribcage. She feels an uppercut from under her chin delivered by the assassin and swiftly responds with her right elbow colliding with the side of the assassin's face. Another minute dies.

The force of her elbow pushes the assassin, twisting her locked arm in the process. Botalia raises her right leg and knees the assassin in the side. As Botalia commits to this attack, the assassin lifts her left leg and forces it between the two of them. She anchors it in Botalia's core, focuses her life force on her foot and leg, and pushes back with all her might. The force is tremendous and sends Botalia flying backward, her back slamming into a tree. Her instincts take over and she dodges out of the way of the thrown dagger. It hits the tree, exactly where her head had been one second before. However, the dagger removes itself from the tree and returns to the assassin. Botalia sees that she has attached her life force to the dagger and is able to recall it after throwing it. Botalia stands up, wipes her arm across her mouth, and giggles. Using life force seemed too easy an option for Botalia if she solely wanted to win, but she wanted entertainment. However, Botalia knows if the assassin begins using life force, she can't simply counter with purely physical defense. Minute seven ends.

The assassin endlessly throws her dagger, Botalia constantly dodging the attacks, decreasing the distance between herself and the assassin. When Botalia gets within arm's reach of her, the assassin drags two fingers along the blade and uses her life force to lengthen her dagger. Botalia's eyes widen as she leans backward to avoid the horizontal slice dealt by the assassin. Weaponless, Botalia stops the dagger from hitting her by using her palms to continually knock the assassin's arm upward or to the side, preventing her from making contact. Both Botalia and the assassin know they need to end the fight soon, not knowing the limit of the other's stamina. They go for the critical hit. Botalia focuses her life force into her right hand. The assassin sets up for a fatal attack. Both pull back to add to the forward momentum of their attacks. Botalia lunges forward, accelerating her fist toward the assassin's core. The assassin sees her opportunity and begins her slice. Botalia makes contact and unleashes her strength, sending the assassin flying backwards into a bush.

Botalia stands, breathing heavily, and feels a sudden sting on her left cheek. The dagger cut her, but that is not all. It was laced with poison. Botalia scoffs. Being a scientist who works with unknown and foreign plants as a hobby, she has built up her immunity to a variety of poisons. It has no effect on her. The assassin finds herself laying in a shrub. She sees she landed the attack but is shocked when she notices Botalia still stands. The assassin breathes deeply, and she struggles to keep her eyes open. As an assassin, she naturally went through plenty of training with poison immunity as well. However, the shrub is one of Botalia's experiments, so no one besides herself has been exposed to the hybrid plant's poison. The bush the assassin fell into is called "sopor virgultum," or sleep plant. It combines the pollen of plants that cause drowsiness and those that cause paralysis, creating its own unique scent which puts those unaccustomed to the smell into a dream state. The eighth minute lapses.

Tenebrant and Koepp sit quietly. Koepp remains in his curled position, unmoving since Botalia left. Tenebrant, hands behind head, looks up at the ceiling, smiling all the while. Koepp worries for Botalia, but he feels she'll win this challenge. He hasn't seen her strength yet, but he knows her intelligence far outweighs any he's ever met. She won't lose.

For the duration of the challenge, neither have heard any noises from outside. The only sound comes from the wall clock. Koepp looks at it, noticing time is running out. Less than two minutes remain. He closes his eyes and hopes for Botalia's victory. Tenebrant glimpses at Koepp and his smile widens.

Just as the ninth and final minute begins, the back door opens. Three large, wispy humanoid figures enter carrying the unconscious bodies of the three assassins. Botalia walks in behind them, still breathing heavily. Koepp leaps out of the chair in excitement, a joyous smile spread across his face. Tenebrant turns in his chair and slowly applauds. The conjured minions gently place the bodies on the ground before vanishing in a whirl of smoke. Botalia admires her work and looks up, smiling at Koepp's reaction. She turns her head to face Tenebrant. He flashes a smile in her direction and then turns to take a drink from his glass.

A wispy servant enters the room carrying a vial. It hands the glass container to Botalia who thanks the servant before it bows and disappears. She kneels by the bodies. After opening the vial, she pours some of the liquid from within it into her cupped left hand. She sets the vial on the floor and raises her right hand. Botalia closes her eyes, focusing a fraction of her life force into her fingers.

She waves a pattern with her right hand, moving it up, down, in a counterclockwise circle, in, and finally out. She touches her thumb to her middle finger and moves it towards her left hand as if she's grasping a delicate thread, preparing to insert it into the eye of the needle. Then, she opens her right hand over her left, as if releasing whatever was being held. Botalia takes the index and middle finger of her right hand and runs them across her left hand through the mixture she's created. She rubs the mixture on the unconscious assassins.

After applying the mixture under the noses of the three, she grabs the vial and stands. She walks to the kitchen and washes her hands before returning. Koepp and Tenebrant sit mesmerized by her actions, despite not understanding what they just witnessed.

However, one thing is certain.

Botalia was victorious.

Chapter Six

Botalia returns to her seat, pouring a drink in the empty glasses. They all remain silent, staring at the bodies on the ground. After a minute passes, the bodies begin to stir. The older of the two male assassins sits up first. He looks around, confused by his location. He stands up and walks toward the others, silently taking a seat. The other assassins wake up in much the same manner, though the young boy hesitates before approaching the party.

The group sits in a ring around the table. They each hold their drink glass and often sip from it rather than attempting to fill the silence. Botalia and Koepp wear straight faces, their attention focuses on the three assassins. The assassins show no expression. The man, in his early twenties, shifts his gaze between Botalia and Koepp, Botalia holding his attention for a longer period of time. The woman assassin, a lady in her upper teens, looks around the room, trying her hardest to avoid eye contact with Botalia. The young boy, no more than eleven or twelve years of age, stares at the floor, glancing at Koepp from time to time. Tenebrant leans back and observes the scene, smiling. He decides he should be the one to break the silence.

"Well," Tenebrant says, peering at the assassins in turn. "If you desire to finish the job, now's as good a time as any. Wouldn't you say?"

The fear returns to Koepp's eyes, but Botalia maintains her composure, though she knows Tenebrant speaks the truth. The three assassins turn to Tenebrant, the woman and the boy expressing their shock by the reflection of light in their eyes. The man expresses no feeling in his eyes. Botalia notices and feels sympathy for his eyes are empty.

"We can't kill her," he replies.

"You can't kill her... now? Ever? Or you don't want to kill her?" Tenebrant asks, a humorous tone in his voice.

"We are incapable of killing her."

"Your client will be quite displeased, won't they, Naht?" inquires Tenebrant. Naht sighs and takes a drink. He glances at Botalia then back to Tenebrant.

"He'll be displeased, but I assume he knew we would fail," Naht replies. The two other assassins look to the floor. Naht glimpses at Botalia and grins. "Her presence far exceeds any I've encountered. Boss probably knew the difficulty of the task, which explains why he assigned all three of us." Naht pauses, turning to the other assassins. They avoid eye contact due to the shame of their failure, though, Naht appears indifferent. "The mission was futile. The client either deceived us or hired us hoping for the best, for his own sake. Though a combination of the two is the highest possibility." Tenebrant chuckles.

Botalia speaks up, "Your client, who is he?" She locks eyes with Naht. He sighs.

"As a long-time client and myself being top-ranked assassin, I am forbidden from telling you, the target, any confidential information that may expose our client to harm. Seeing your life force with my own eyes, I don't imagine it would be impossible for anyone to see you as a threat, so the possibilities may as well be endless," Naht responds.

"Except for the fact that only a few people can recall my existence," Botalia glares and crosses her arms. Life force dances on her fingertips.

"Was it Tanten Flynn?" Koepp asks in a soft voice. Botalia turns to him in shock.

"Koepp..." Botalia says, shakily reaching for him, sympathy swelling in her eyes. Tenebrant chuckles and takes a drink.

"No," Naht answers, looking at Koepp. "Tanten Flynn has no desire to hire assassins. He-," Naht stops, feeling Botalia's aura collide with his. Naht drops his head and grins, "Never mind."

Botalia faces the woman, who feels her gaze. Botalia sips at her drink. "You put up a good fight," Botalia compliments. The woman assassin looks up and smiles. "I could sense your excitement, so I couldn't resist. It's been a long time since I've last dueled a human, and I felt it would be rude to deprive you of a proper fight."

"I appreciate it," the woman assassin thanks.

"If the challenge had no time limit," Botalia glares at Tenebrant who returns a smile, "I wouldn't have ended the fight so soon. Anyways, I had the upper hand because you were in a foreign environment unlike myself. If you ever want a rematch, just tell me when." The woman assassin regains the light in her eyes, nodding. Botalia continues, "Actually, I have an arena in the basement. If you're still running on adrenaline, we can duel now." Botalia shares a friendly smile. "That goes for you three as well," she directs at Tenebrant, Naht, and the young boy.

They all face her, each with a different expression. Tenebrant leans forward, excited by her words. He enjoys fighting others, especially those who may pose a challenge, and he doesn't often lose. Naht shows no expression, he thinks of her superior strength and the pointlessness of a fight against her when the winner is obvious. The young boy appears frightened, remembering how easily she knocked him out earlier. He decides there is no point in strengthening his technique if it may lead to his death. The woman assassin opens her mouth to speak but is cut off by Naht.

"Neja," Naht snaps. "If you continue to make impulsive choices, I'll be forced to report you. We have failed in our mission. We must return."

"Then report me. It's not like Father will fire me, or any of us, for wanting to improve our abilities," Neja responds. "I'm not leaving until I get in a good fight. The suspense of waiting for our rematch may kill me." Neja smiles at Botalia, who returns it before changing to a solemn expression.

"I apologize," Botalia says, turning to Naht. "I don't want to cause any trouble. I went ten years without any visitors and in this past week I've had six. I'm finding enjoyment in being able to communicate and entertain myself with anyone who shows up. Don't feel pressured to violate your principles for my enjoyment," she states, directing the last line to Neja.

"I kinda want to see your full strength," whispers the young boy assassin. Everyone looks at him, shocked, most of them forgetting he was present. He looks up at Botalia and slightly grins. Botalia gazes at him and then turns to Koepp. Koepp smiles at the young boy, a light present in his eyes. Naht appears irritated. Neja peers at the young boy, excited to hear him speak up and express a similar opinion. Tenebrant delivers his signature chuckle.

"It seems I'm outnumbered," Naht shrugs, smiling. He glances at Botalia. "Lead the way." Botalia grins at him.

"Well. The people have spoken, I must deliver." She stands up, the others following her lead.

Botalia leads them out the back door. The party appears confused, thinking she was leading them to the basement arena. She follows the veranda to the right, and they notice a wooden door at the end. Botalia opens the door to reveal a stairway. They descend the stairs, the staircase twisting as it goes further down. They approach a set of doors with lanterns hanging off to the side.

The moment the doors come into sight, the lanterns ignite with bright orange flames. The group walks through the doors. The arena is the size of two basketball courts placed one next to the other. They enter through a tunnel that cuts through the bleachers, which line the extent of the wall. As the party walks onto the court, they feel an odd sensation. Looking to the floor, they notice a strange inscription along the perimeter of the court. Tenebrant, Naht, and Neja quickly jump out of the ring. Koepp and the young boy look at them in confusion while Botalia giggles.

"Don't worry about those lines. You felt the sensation, right?" asks Botalia. The three nod. The young boy and Koepp felt it as well, but they both classified the sensation as excitement and tossed away any concerns. The older three knew better, and now they feel as though they've entered a trap.

Botalia leans down and drags her fingers along the inscription. "It's what I refer to as a 'force field.' Like a wall that surrounds the ring, the force field contains all forms of life force within it. Any display of life force used on the court cannot break beyond the barrier of the wall, kind of like a particle in an infinite potential well.

However, instead of reflecting or refracting the life force, the field absorbs any life force that comes into contact with it. The sensation occurs because, when crossing the line, no life force can be present at any position inside of the wall itself. It's almost as if your life force is forced to the back of your body and out as you cross the line and, once completely on the other side, your life force reenters your body."

The group stares at Botalia, impressed and confused by her explanation. She smiles and continues. "I wanted a way to train without damaging anything else on the island and the idea just came to me. It took some time to perfect, and it's still not perfect. But it can withstand an immense explosion of life force, without allowing any to escape beyond the ring. Well," Botalia sighs, "Are we ready?"

The others look at one another.

"This is a one versus one battle, correct?" Naht questions.

"Whatever pleases you," Botalia answers. "Though, if winning is your goal, you'd only stand a chance if you all teamed up to defeat me."

"Overconfidence is not a flattering look on you," Naht responds, stretching his neck. Botalia smiles.

Tenebrant walks to the bleachers. Neja imitates, disappointment on her face. Koepp and the young boy look at each other before following. Naht and Botalia remain on the court, the others watching from the stands. Botalia walks to the center of the court, Naht follows. Once in the center, they stand across from one another, not breaking eye contact.

"Are you ready?" Botalia asks. She takes a defensive stance.

"I've been ready. I'm waiting for you," Naht replies.

He thinks through multiple strategies in his mind. He knows the only way to victory is to outsmart Botalia, to employ a seamless strategy. However, he's aware if he thinks too much he'll be delayed in his reaction if Botalia attacks. Despite the possibilities, Naht can only think of one viable option that will assure his victory. The trouble will be getting close enough to her to commence his plan.

Botalia decides not to wait for him to attack after observing him for a while. He tries to contrive the perfect plan, however, he does not know the extent of her abilities. She charges him, ready to side snap kick him, but he leaps into the air before she begins her set up. She pushes off the ground to level with him. Naht attempts a jab at her ribs, but she blocks with her arm. They land on the ground and jump back, increasing the distance between themselves.

Naht has to focus his life force into his hand before he can follow through with his plan, but with Botalia attacking him head on, he knows he can't leave the rest of his body undefended by life force. He knows he must attack her from behind, sensing the set up will be the difficult part.

Naht lunges at Botalia, attempting a butterfly kick but she blocks with her arms, lifting her leg to kick his exposed side. He pushes off the ground with his right hand and exerts enough force to cause a rotation of his body, swinging his legs around like a propeller. Botalia leans back slightly and grabs his right ankle. She tries to throw him, but his centripetal force exceeds her own, throwing off her balance.

Naht uses this opportunity to his advantage, kicking off with his left foot, right hand extended, aiming for her arm. Botalia tries to regain control before jumping into action, so she puts up her hand in defense, intending to grip his fist which will cause injury to his elbow if not careful.

In the moment Naht's fist contacts her hand, time freezes. She feels an agonizing pain, her eyes tightly shut, and she grits her teeth as if biting a bullet. The images flashing before her, the sounds and voices echoing in her head, torture her from the inside out. The tragedies occurring simultaneously hit her with the feel of a natural disaster, a disaster claiming thousands of lives and causing the suffering of many more. She feels her living body fall to the ground, but with the environment she's trapped in within her mind, she knows she has no control over earthly matters. All she can see and hear are the pain and suffering of a boy who knows no happiness. Tortured and neglected to transform him into an obedient shell. An empty life, a hollow vessel. Always trying to impress, but never being noticed. At one point, he stopped trying, understanding he'd never receive the recognition he sought. Blood rains on her face in a drizzle, still warm, still fresh. A robotic voice repeats the word "Again" and another shadow falls through the cracks. "Again." A different shadow bursts into a million tiny pieces. She feels her heart wrench, as if being split in half by titanic horses running in opposite directions. The slideshow seems endless. "How do I make it stop?" she cries out in prayer. The subconscious representation of herself slowly cripples under the weight. "Please make it stop." All goes black.

Botalia opens her eyes and finds herself back in the arena. She realizes not even three seconds have passed for Naht is in the process of back flipping away from her after his failed attempt at his plan. Once he lands, he peers at her with wide eyes and raises his hand to his heart. Botalia bends over, her heart screaming, but she doesn't break eye contact. She pulls together her remaining strength, though she feels a newfound power surge through her body, and lunges for him. Naht, surprised by the charge, can't decide how to dodge. Milliseconds pass and he realizes dodging is no longer an option, so he carefully observes her movement to determine how he should block.

Botalia kicks out her left leg, rotates one hundred and eighty degrees and kicks out her right leg. Naht easily defends against the kick, but he senses something strange. She applied no strength to her kick, rather the strength went to accelerating her life force to her left hand, which functioned as a support while kicking, but also enabled her to emit her life force. Her life force traveled across the floor, and rose up behind Naht, swiftly striking him at a nerve between his shoulder and neck. Naht falls to the ground, not unconscious but immobilized by exhaustion and the shock of the strike.

The group in the stands don't know how to react. They sit with their jaws agape, wondering what they witnessed. Botalia grabs Naht's arm to help him stand. After walking him to the bleachers, Botalia notices everyone staring at her.

"What?" she asks, still breathing heavily.

"What was that?" Neja questions.

"What are you talking about?" Botalia responds. They all continue to stare at her.

"Something happened... when he hit you. You both seemed to freeze for a second, and it looked like you were in immense pain, but you appear uninjured," Neja replies.

"The little girl has grown up," Tenebrant chuckles. The party continues to stare at Botalia, confusion and a slight fear covering their faces.

Nerves begin to overwhelm Botalia. "Stop looking at me like that," she thinks, "Stop looking at me like I'm some monster." She shifts her eyes from person to person, though she knows they're all thinking it.

"What did you do to me?" Naht speaks up, his voice soft and nonaggressive. "What kind of trap is this? My head... and my heart. What ability is this?"

"I-" Botalia begins but is interrupted by Naht.

"And why did my plan fail? You're hiding something more than just an immense storehouse of power. There's a secret behind it. You weren't simply born with that power. No. You did something, something awful to acquire that amount of life force," Naht states. He looks at Botalia. For the first time, she thinks she sees emotion in his eyes. She can't determine if it's hostility or sympathy.

"I think we should all eat dinner and continue the fights afterwards," Koepp interjects, his innocent voice distracting from the mood. The young boy nods in agreement. Botalia turns to Koepp and smiles.

"Sounds good to me," declares Tenebrant, standing up and walking to the bottom of the bleachers. The others stand and follow him. The last to rise is Naht, who stares at the ground. Botalia holds out her hand, offering to help him stand. Naht looks up at her and shakes his head. He stands on his own and walks to meet the others. Botalia frowns as Naht walks past her, only turning as the party exits through the tunnel. She catches up with them as they ascend the stairs.

The only conversation occurs between Koepp and the young boy assassin as they talk about their "unique" combat techniques. Koepp talks about fighting like a superhero from some absurd comic book and the young boy brushes it off, while seemingly enjoying the thought. He talks about his practice of mixed martial arts, and Koepp opens his mouth and widens his eyes in admiration of the young boy. Botalia's heart relaxes a little to see Koepp and the young boy developing a friendship, noting that it's probably the first genuine friendship either have experienced.

The party enters the house and gather in the sitting room, waiting for Botalia's instructions. She leads them into the hallway, passing the front door and opens the glass double doors. They enter an extravagant dining area with marble floors and a large oak table. The raised ceiling is adorned with a crystal chandelier. A balcony from the second floor looks down upon the table and chairs. On the opposite end of the room is another set of double doors, leading into the kitchen.

Botalia displays the room in a showcase-like fashion. "Take a seat wherever. Or you can wander around a bit until dinner is ready. Do any of you have any dietary restrictions?" She examines the group who continue to gawk at the luxurious furnishings and textiles. "Right," she says frowning and walking into the kitchen.

Koepp and the young boy assassin gaze at the room in wonder. Their eyes connect with one another and a devious grin spreads across Koepp's face. He tags the young assassin and takes off running, screaming, "You're it!" They run around the large table, the young boy chasing after Koepp.

Neja yells after them, "No running! Be careful!" but the boys ignore her. She sighs.

Tenebrant chooses his seat and relaxes, closing his eyes, head placed on his hands.

Naht glimpses at the boys, a disapproving expression covering his face. He rolls his eyes at Neja, and finally addresses Tenebrant.

"Did you know?"

Tenebrant opens his eyes. "About what?"

"Did you know we would fail when you heard who our target was? You seemed eager enough to join us. Most people wouldn't agree to assisting assassins with the killing of an old friend."

Tenebrant scoffs, "That is where you're wrong. We were never friends." He pauses. "And to answer your question, no, I didn't know. Though I'm not surprised." Tenebrant closes his eyes again, signifying the end of his participation in the discussion. Naht sighs.

Naht's mind spins as he tries to explain what happened in his and Botalia's fight. She appeared to be in immense pain, but it was by no method of his own. The uplifting sensation he experienced seemed the antithesis of her reaction. However, after she regained control of herself, her aura and life force pulsated with a newfound strength. He can't recall the last time he was unable to rationally explain an event with his intellect. He sits in the seat adjacent to Tenebrant, lost in his thoughts.

In the kitchen, Botalia searches for food suitable for a dinner. She panics as she sees the vacant cabinets and barren refrigerator. Opening the pantry, she finds rice, noodles, a variety of sauces, and an assortment of homegrown vegetables. "This will have to do," she shrugs. Botalia places her hands on the quartz countertop and closes her eyes. Four wispy servants appear, standing before her, ready for instructions. The moment a plan for the meal enters her mind, the servants don't hesitate. They remove pans and pots from the cupboards, food from the pantry, and utensils from the drawers, creating the meal. Botalia smiles and exits the kitchen, knowing she'd simply get in the way of her servants.

Upon exiting, she observes Koepp and the young assassin running around, smiles upon both of their faces. Botalia smiles.

When they see her, both boys freeze to their positions. The sudden silence grabs the attention of the others, and they look up.

"Dinner will be ready soon. I apologize in advance if the meal doesn't compare to the extravagance of the hall," Botalia states. "But, it's the least I could do for my visitors."

After the meal, the servants collect the dishes and silverware, and the party retires to the sitting room.

"Today has been... interesting, however, we must return," Naht says. Both Neja and the young boy appear upset with the news.

"What about my fight with Botalia?" Neja asks Naht.

"Botalia and yourself can select a day for your match according to your schedules," Naht responds. Botalia laughs, knowing full well that her schedule is wide open. Neja sighs but doesn't respond, knowing that an argument with Naht is a fight she will never win. The young boy frowns but doesn't fight back.

"Well, I'm glad you stopped by, even if you were trying to kill me..." Botalia expresses a half grin before her face grows serious. "Will you get in trouble? You know, because I'm still alive?" Botalia questions.

"If, as commented earlier, no one expected us to succeed, I doubt we'll be demoted or punished. However, a failed assassination dirties our record, possibly causing business to decrease because of clients questioning our reliability," Naht sighs. "The damage won't be catastrophic. However, we will have to perform our next missions flawlessly, which shouldn't be a problem for any of us," he says, looking at Neja and the young boy. He senses their desire of staying on the island awhile longer.

Naht grows confused, not only by their expression of emotions, but also their pleasure of the experience despite their failure. He worries. For the short time Neja and the young boy have been on this island, they have transformed. Neja felt excitement without having killed her prey, and the young boy smiled and laughed with what appears to be his first friend. Naht believes he finally understands.

"That is the secret of this island," Naht determines, "It not only transforms people into monsters," he thinks while glimpsing at Botalia, "but it also turns monsters into people."

Chapter Seven

The three assassins walk to the front door. Botalia, Koepp, and Tenebrant follow close behind. As they exit onto the porch, they turn to face each other.

"I hope we get to fight one another soon," Neja directs at Botalia.

"Whenever you feel ready for a fight, stop by and I'll be here," Botalia replies. Neja nods in agreement. There is a silence that lasts a few seconds.

"Well, I suppose we're off," Naht states. As the party turns to walk, Naht faces Tenebrant. "Are you coming?"

Tenebrant smiles and responds, "I figured I would stay and reminisce awhile, if the hostess is alright with that." They turn to face Botalia who rolls her eyes and gives an approving shrug.

"If you insist," Naht replies.

They arrive at the halfway point between the villa and the forest when Naht rotates and locks eyes with Botalia. "Bysciw," he says. "Our client, his name is Bysciw."

The other two assassins showcase their disbelief at his betrayal of the assassin's code. Their accelerated hearts are met with an ease at the revelation of this information, for they cannot deny they've come to respect Botalia, as a person and as a monster.

Botalia wrinkles her brow in an attempt to unload the information. She nods her head as thanks for the information. The assassins give a final wave before they resume their walk down the path.

"Until next time," Botalia shouts after them, waving her hand high in the air, Koepp joining in. Neja and the young boy glance back and then at one another, their softened expressions tugging at their humanity. Everyone takes a simultaneous breath, experiencing a deeper connection with one another through the power of the nature that surrounds them. The birds and beasts of the island offer up their goodbyes to the departing visitors. Naht chuckles.

"Next time..." he thinks to himself, and slightly grins.

Koepp continues to vigorously wave his arm until the three assassins are out of sight. Botalia turns to Koepp, smiling.

"Looks like you made a new friend, and he's about your age," Botalia says, Koepp nodding. "By the way, I never caught his name."

"His name is Nix Kufuta, and he's a top ranked assassin. Naht and Neja are his older siblings. They work for their father as assassins," Koepp responds. Botalia laughs and plays with the unkempt black tuft of hair at the crown of his head. His laugh fades into a longing stare in the direction the assassins took off.

"Oh yeah!" Koepp gasps. "I forgot to tell you," he says, looking at Botalia, a light shining in his eyes, "It was a lucky one."

Botalia thinks for a moment and then remembers. The meteor. She smiles as she thinks of what he may have wished for. Koepp beams as he thinks about his wish coming true. He's never believed in wishing because no matter how often he wished as a child, it never came true. But Koepp begins to think his luck may be changing, seeing as his last two wishes have been heard and answered. The messengers of the meteor granted his second wish. He's received the one thing he desired above all else: a best friend. Though their time together was brief, Koepp and Nix bonded and shared much about their lives with one another. Koepp and Nix saved each other from their tragic futures; futures achieved had they never escaped the cycle they had been riding for so long.

SLAVED BY HIS GUARDIANS, Koepp was always told he had no time or need for friends or fun. They forced him into carpentry and construction at a very young age to earn a wage, as no squatter deserves the air they breathe. His guardians claimed his pay as their dues and in exchange gave him a place to stay and food to eat, though only the bare minimum. When in the city, Koepp acted and was treated like an adult. He had no choice. A child without pay often got sold by their guardians into the trafficking rings. A child with work was not touched, for fear of angering the Bosses of the Big City. The dark side of the rich nation Divesregio. Marble cities laden with gold cast a shadow on the slums from which Koepp was raised.

Though Koepp accepted his plateaued life of performing nothing but menial labor, he always wished for adventure and to accomplish something greater. His soul began to decay, cycling from day to day, becoming a robot molded to society's will. At ten years of age, he never comprehended how his life could already be planned out for him.

Two days before arriving at the island, Koepp fell into a deeper chasm of his depression. His day at work had been incredibly exhausting. People constantly ridiculed, abused, bullied, and took advantage of him. This particular day he had met his breaking point. He wasn't aware people treated him immorally, as this was the way it had always been. He never complained despite the pit to fall into his stomach and the shaking of the dams with the pressure building up. His guardians taught him from a young age to never complain and accept all criticism with grace, otherwise you'll be a burden to others. He listened to their advice. Koepp never wanted to be a burden on anyone. He's always felt that's why his real parents abandoned him.

On that dark day, when he arrived home, he didn't eat but rather crawled into bed, stared at the ceiling, and bawled. He couldn't prevent himself from shaking. For the first time in his ten short years of life, Koepp openly accepted death as an escape. He wished for something, anything, to take him away.

When slits of moonlight crawled in through his barred windows, Koepp heard his guardians screaming at each other in the living room. Loud clangs and crashes occurred. The woman entered the room, letter in hand. She wrapped her dingy, second-hand, designer robe about her, half of her hair with cream and styling ribbons, the other half dangling in burnt strands. Her baggy eyes expressed her rage. She threw the letter at him and yelled at him to leave. In a hasty confusion, Koepp grabbed the letter.

He wandered the city with his work satchel, which carried his only belongings, and tear streams dried to his cheeks. He knocked at the kitchen door of the restaurant, the one that often hid their leftovers in the back of the building each night for the street urchins in more urgent situations than himself. The metal door swung open, and the chef smiled at Koepp.

"Sorry to bother you."

"Anything for the one who tiled our kitchen after the devastation two months back. What can I do ya for?"

Koepp pulled the letter from his cargo pants and handed it to the chef.

"I don't know how to read," Koepp said with an embarrassed expression. The chef, and owner of the establishment, softened her expression.

"It says:

TO THE GUARDIANS OF *Koepp Flynn*,

Your years of care of the boy Koepp Flynn are no longer required. You've raised and cared for him and for that I am grateful. However, now is the time for him to leave. You are to send him to the island circled on the attached map. Once there, he will become the apprentice of Ms. Botalia Ulton. I don't expect he'll return, so ensure he packs all his possessions. Again, I am grateful for your assistance these past years.

-Tanten Flynn

P.S. If I find that the boy has not left in a week's time, I will shred our contract without hesitation.

Koepp? What does this mean? Are you off by yourself? Ya can't think you'll get far in this land on your own?"

"I have to try. I'm not going back."

The chef checks behind to see if any listen. She reaches into her apron and pulls out twenty emerald pieces.

"Take this and go straight to Petro's Wharf. Tell him Dancho Wing Yui sent you. And take this." She stalks to the kitchen and grabs a prepared takeout meal, handing it to Koepp. The chef places a hand on his forehead and whispers a prayer of protection.

"Thank you, Dancho."

"Anything for a Flynn. Now go before midnight hits and the Wolves take to the streets."

He wiped the tears from his eyes as he ran down the street. The tears that were once shed out of suffering were now shed out of happiness. He felt a release within himself, his heart weighed much less than a few minutes before. His smile made a statement in the cold-hearted streets of this city. Others watched after him, confused and angry at his happiness. None of that mattered now. Map in hand, Koepp began his journey to the island.

Now on the island, Koepp's inner child escaped after being chained away for so many years. He was finally able to experience the simple joys of life. The opportunity to learn from Botalia of all he missed out on as a child excited him. He can say he has made friends, a thought he never believed would pass through his head. He felt so grateful to the sender of the letter.

His thoughts return to the present. Koepp sees Botalia and Tenebrant entering the villa in front of him. He smiles and can't help but turn around and inhale the fresh scent of nature, listen to the creatures, and fall in love with the beauty of the environment. The three of them head to the sitting area and take their personal positions of rest. After relaxing for a few minutes, Koepp decides he can no longer hold in his question.

"Botalia?" he starts, Botalia turning to him in wonder. "Who is Tanten Flynn?"

Botalia freezes for a moment before closing her eyes and sighing. "He's your father."

Koepp looks at her, expressionless. He leaps up and races to his room. Botalia and Tenebrant watch after him, curious as to what he is doing. Once in his room, Koepp opens his satchel and finds the letter. He retrieves it and runs back to the sitting room. He holds it out and Botalia takes it, reading what it says. She frowns.

"So, this is what you meant when you first arrived here," she says, pondering about the circumstances of Koepp's childhood as she rereads the letter. "Is this," she points to the letter, "the first time you've ever seen or heard of him?"

Koepp nods. Botalia doesn't know whether to be infuriated or unsurprised with his response. After a moment of thinking, Koepp adds, "Well, actually... I heard my guardians say the name 'Tanten' in arguments, but I never really knew who they were talking about." Silence. "Oh, and, before you ask, I don't know what contract he's talking about. I didn't ask before I left."

"Koepp, I was going to tell you I knew your father at some point, I really was. So please don't be mad at me," Botalia begs. Koepp appears shocked by her accusation.

"If you didn't tell me, you probably had a reason," Koepp replies. Botalia relaxes, handing the letter back to Koepp. He admires the letter, the key to his freedom, for a moment. He yawns. "I think... I think I'm going to bed now." Botalia smiles. "Goodnight," Koepp says walking away, "and to you, too," he directs at Tenebrant. Tenebrant grins and tilts his head.

Once Koepp exits, Tenebrant peers at Botalia, who stares at the ground. Focusing his eyes, he cannot decipher what emotion she is experiencing. Her aura wraps about her in a helix. Tenebrant can't recall ever seeing an aura look so impressive and powerful. He chuckles. Botalia lifts her head, surprised by his laugh. She smirks at Tenebrant and deeply sighs.

"Why is that people transform into those they hate most?" Botalia asks. Tenebrant's smile disappears. He glares at Botalia. Her gaze returns to the ground, and she lets out a laughing breath. "How did this happen to us?" She pauses before looking up again. "It's as if I'm sleeping."

"Is it a dream or a nightmare?"

"I can't decide," Botalia replies. She giggles again. "Why is this all happening now? Why not five years ago, or five years into the future? I'm so confused." The silence resumes. Botalia chooses to interrupt it again. "So, why did you do it?"

"Hmm?" Tenebrant locks eyes with Botalia.

"Take the path you did. I stay updated in the news and every time I see some heinous act committed, I cringe and hope my intuition is wrong. You embrace your hate of the world, using it as an excuse for your actions," Botalia remarks.

"Hate? As opposed to what?" Tenebrant snaps. "The world acted cruel to me first, I simply reciprocated. What I do with my life is no concern of yours."

"Back then, I felt we were the same. Targets for the world and yet strong enough to choose what's right. What our parents did was wrong-"

"Botalia-"

"It was immoral. But I hoped we would make it through, together, accomplish our wildest ambitions and prove to the world how capable we are-"

"Were." Tenebrant corrects. "Neither of us are any more than monsters now. And society feels the same way. Look where your good heart and innocent ambitions got you: exiled, completely eradicated from the world itself. The worst punishment for you, the one who wishes to save the world must now sit back and watch it suffer. You were naïve and childlike in your dreams. At least I accepted where society placed me, but you fought the mold."

The silence returns for a brief moment. They stare at one another, each picturing the other ten years younger. The past being their greatest weakness.

"I have no regrets," Botalia states. "I fought peacefully, proving myself capable rather than threatening and abusing others. You risk your life to prove a point. My parents would have never wanted me to live like that."

Tenebrant maliciously laughs. Botalia's expression turns to one of fury and she crosses her arms.

"You must not have known your parents at all," Tenebrant says. "They created you to be a monster, their greatest success story being their lab rat daughter-"

"No-"

"It was their dream to see their creation deal as much destruction as possible after their death. They probably laughed as you ripped that gang to shreds, coloring the ground with their blood, not hesitating to take the lives of those not even involved in the murder-"

"Shut up!" Botalia snaps, her fists clenched and her rage becoming uncontrollable.

"Unfortunately, they died premature and you had better self-control than they anticipated. Your parents probably never imagined after the monster was released you'd be able to suppress it again," Tenebrant leans forward, still smiling. "I know you felt being exiled was for the best. You knew your power far exceeded any force that would have been sent to restrain you had the monster escaped. Your parents created you to be an indestructible machine and they succeeded. However, they failed at filling your thoughts with their dreams. Geniuses in creation maybe, but amateurs in manipulation."

"Tenny," Botalia cries out in a shaky voice, her body quaking and tears streaming down her face. To relive the moments, to see it all on the screen once more. Botalia tried for so long to act as if it was a movie. Fiction. Didn't exist. But when Tenebrant recalls the events to transpire that night, the heated rage, the pouring sweat, the smell of blood, it all returns to her. She cannot deny that it happened. She was there. And she was responsible. "Please... stop." She pleads.

Tenebrant's smile transforms into a frown, as his jaw settles and his eyes look upon her with pity. Before closing his eyes, he observes her aura tightly encasing her body, forcing her life force to stay within its borders.

"You should get some sleep. I'll stay on guard in case anyone else invades. Please allow me this," Tenebrant says.

"Aye," Botalia replies.

She wraps her arms about herself and trudges to her room, thoughts still flooding her head. She doesn't want to argue with Tenebrant, but she doesn't want him to leave yet either. Botalia feels internally conflicted. She wants to believe the Tenebrant she once knew still exists, but since his arrival at the island, she's only been able to see a hollow frame. As she crawls into bed, she hums the lullaby her mother used to sing to her, the same lullaby she sang to Koepp when he experienced unpleasant dreams.

Tenebrant crosses his legs and places his hands behind his head. He thinks about the past, remembering what once was and is no longer. He remembers Botalia's strength of mind, body, and heart. Over the course of ten years, her mind and body increased exponentially, however, her heart seems to have weakened. To Tenebrant, Botalia appears strong but broken. He thinks the power she's gained by her immense life force may be the only factor keeping her alive.

"What was the cost?" he asks himself. "What does one sacrifice to attain seemingly infinite power?" After thinking about Botalia and her abilities, he remembers Koepp. "What is a Flynn doing here?" he wonders. "And it's not just him. Deducing from Botalia's reaction and Koepp's letter, Tanten must have visited this island not long ago. If that's the case, he must have wanted something from Botalia, and, judging by her expression while reading the letter, she refused, whether it be out of hate for Tanten or pure disinterest in the task."

Intuitively, Tenebrant feels Tanten is connected to Bysciw, whoever Bysciw may be. This thought strikes Tenebrant as odd. "Why would Tanten send his son to find Botalia if they planned to assassinate her? Maybe he didn't know of Bysciw's plans? Perhaps they are enemies... but the coincidence of Botalia and Tanten's meeting and the planned assassination occurring within such a small timeframe seems too perfect. Does that mean Bysciw and Tanten are on a team?" Tenebrant ponders this thought. He chuckles. The thought of Tanten being a part of a team amuses him.

Tenebrant and Tanten have dueled on several occasions back when Tanten served as a Council member. Tanten's job within the Magistrate Association included hunting high-rank convicts and serial killers, whether it be gangs or individuals. Tenebrant's lawlessness allowed him to ascend the criminal ranks at a rapid pace. He became infamous after his disagreements often turned into bloody scenes, always leaving behind his signature: a picture of a crescent moon drawn in his victim's blood.

Those in the underworld continuously try to recruit him into their ranks, however, Tenebrant prefers fighting solo. The only person he willingly joins is Naht. They don't consider themselves friends but allies, helping each other only when it benefits themselves. They met when Naht's mission entailed the assassination of Tenebrant. An exciting fight ensued and the mission ended with Tenebrant murdering the client, therefore, relieving Naht of his task. Once the client is dead, the designated assassin no longer has the obligation of completing the mission. Despite their relationship, Tenebrant often seeks amusement through his own means. His natural state is one of a hostile predator, always hungry and in search of prey. Though, in Botalia's presence, he's aware he's on the second tier of the food chain. She's a monster, and as such, rightly claims the position at the top.

Tenebrant looks around the sitting room. He examines the awards the Ultons won for their discoveries, theories, and proofs. The Magistrate Association held them in high regards. They turned their heads and cast an apathetic eye on the many corrupt and immoral experiments, so society only ever saw the good in "searching for the truth" or whatever strange tagline they chose.

"Who are the real monsters? Those declared so by their mutated DNA? Or those who strive after their own selfish desires, leaving everything else behind to disintegrate?" Tenebrant chuckles. "The answer is so obvious, it hurts."

Chapter Eight

Tanten sits atop the slanted, copper roof, oxidized from years of heavy rain in this coastal city. He stares down at the centennial brick house with wooden steps leading out the front door and wood paneled fence stretching from dirt to roof to block the view from the neighbors.

A woman hangs a rug from a metal cord nailed to the wood panels and beats it outside on the front step, the wind carefully taking the dust through the neighbor's open window. The woman, with hair contained in a net, yells inside to her husband, the subject matter insignificant. Tanten adjusts himself, trying to peer into the home through the front door, changing his angle to get a better view. Tanten only sees her husband inside.

"He appears to have left," Tanten glances at the ground following the garbage river at the side of the road. An odd sensation of worry and relief fill him. "Well, my work here is complete." Tanten pulls out his phone and looks at the time. "The assassination was meant to occur by now, but Atlas hasn't contacted me about the outcome." He dangles his legs over the edge of the roof. Tanten lets out a deep sigh. "I'm not sure I even want to hear the result." He gazes up at the sky and scoffs. "No stars."

He jumps off the roof and his phone vibrates.

"Atlas, what's the news?" Tanten asks.

"I don't think discussing this over the phone follows protocol. I'd prefer we talk about this face to face, so hurry back," Atlas replies, in a stern tone.

"Aye," Tanten responds. He puts his phone away and hurries to the base. A variety of outcomes fill his thoughts, the negative the only ones to echo in his ears.

The next morning, as the sun rises, Tanten arrives at the base. He enters the building, nodding to the members patrolling the entrance hall. He descends the stairs and opens the metal door at the bottom. Waiting for him in the corner of the room is Atlas.

Tanten rushes toward Atlas when he hears a loud commotion occurring in the common room down the hallway. Atlas acts uninterested in the noise, so Tanten proceeds forward. Tanten takes a seat across from Atlas, who has yet to look at him. The suspense of hearing the news tortured Tanten throughout his journey back.

"Well?" Tanten questions, exhausted from his night of spying and running back, yet eager for the news. He stares intently at Atlas. He hates relying on anyone, especially Atlas, for information, so he wishes the exchange will be brief. As Atlas raises his head, what appeared to be a solemn face to Tanten reveals a grin.

"What did I say?" Atlas smiles. "Never doubt an Ulton. They're monsters, the lot of them. The last remaining heir being no exception." Tanten releases a sigh of relief and laughs. Atlas raises his eyebrows, surprised by the degree of his reaction. Atlas knows Tanten dislikes Bysciw, but to experience such pleasure in the failure of an important mission truly signifies the level of loathing Tanten feels toward Bysciw. "And yet, Bysciw selects you as his second..." Though, perhaps there is another reason for Tanten's relief, Atlas thinks.

Another loud outburst issues from down the hallway. Tanten shifts in his seat, seeing if he can catch a view of what is happening. Atlas rolls his eyes. Tanten shakes off his curiosity and returns his attention to Atlas.

"Do you know any of the details?" Tanten asks. "Were there any casualties? Anything of note?"

"Why so anxious?" Atlas chuckles.

Tanten sits back and runs his hand through his unkempt hair, trying to display some semblance of a calm composure. One of the team members, one Tanten does not recognize, scampers out of the room where the commotion originates, he stumbles to the metal door and exits. Atlas and Tanten observe, Atlas shakes his head.

"Why do we have to work with such low lifes?" He asks sarcastically, though he knows Tanten would agree with no hesitation, even if asked in a serious tone. Atlas sighs. "To answer your question, I don't have many details to share. I talked to the lead of the group sent out there, the eldest son of the Kufuta family." Tanten's eyes widen out of fear, despite already knowing the outcome.

"You hired the Kufutas?" Tanten cannot believe Atlas sacrificed his relations with the family by sending them a failed mission. Tanten is well aware Atlas often hires professional assassins to do his dirty work, however, even Tanten knows Atlas treasures all of his connections and would stop at nothing to maintain those relations.

"They all survived, which is more than I expected of them. They moved as a group of three, though not even their combined experience compared to Botalia's strength and intelligence. The lead told me when they witnessed her aura, they immediately abandoned the mission, knowing they could not succeed. The boy sounded angry, maybe at their failure, maybe at me," Atlas responds. Tanten squints his eyes at Atlas. He perceives either Atlas or the assassin is hiding the truth, though he senses they both may be hiding information. Tanten remembers how simply setting foot on the island was enough to capture Botalia's attention. He knows the assassins could not have seen her without her noticing them in return. In fact, he knows Botalia noticed them before they could get close enough to set eyes on her, and she followed their every movement. The only question unanswered is whether or not Botalia and the assassins made contact.

"I suppose you were refunded," Tanten jokes. Atlas rolls his eyes.

"Getting my money back was the least of my problems from this failure of a mission. But who knows?" Atlas stands. "Maybe like you, my failures will entertain Bysciw."

Tanten, sensing Atlas's jealousy, replies, "I doubt it. Bysciw will have your head for this." Tanten smiles, Atlas returning a mischievous grin.

"Yes, well..." Atlas states as he begins to walk away. After a few steps, he turns to Tanten. "By the way, the fourth VIP showed up a little over an hour ago. They're in the room down the hallway, if you want a sneak peek at your competition. Ciao." Atlas exits the complex.

Tanten stands and decides he must introduce himself to the fourth chairman of their team, if only to size up this new leader. He marches down the hallway, once again hearing the loud commotion. Peering into the room, Tanten notices half of the men on the team gathered around who he assumes to be the owner of the empty chair. The team members appear to be acting strange.

"You don't have to stand outside the door. Come. Join us, Tanten Flynn," the voice behind the masses calls to him. Tanten laughs as he realizes why the situation is not as suspicious as he first expected. The team members part to give a direct path from Tanten to the person.

"I'll be honest," Tanten smiles as he steps forward. "I wasn't expecting a woman."

Sitting in the chair, surrounded by the team, is a middle-aged woman with wavy, long blond hair and blue eyes. She wears a black dress which, despite being full length, reveals quite a bit of skin. Tattoos, whether they be alchemic or ritualistic, cover her left arm. Her well-endowed figure catches the attention of the members who have been long away from the world. She licks her red lips as she examines Tanten, her eyes focus on his face.

"It's a shame the magnificent Tanten Flynn appears quite ordinary in person," the woman remarks. She takes a drink from her wine glass. "Even Atlas presents himself in a noble, stately manner. But you simply look like a filthy vagrant." The team members in the room laugh at her jest. Tanten glares at the woman.

"Can't say your appearance impresses me much, either," Tanten replies. "Though, I can see why Bysciw might have felt you to be... fitting."

The woman frowns and points to the chair next to hers. Tanten rolls his eyes, not wanting to begin a conversation. As he approaches, she shoos the team members out of the room. When the last man leaves, he closes the door as ordered.

The woman takes another drink of her wine and sighs. "Bysciw asked me to join the team, using your and Atlas's names as bait I assume. He never mentioned how miserable and hopeless the team members were. Sure, they possess unique and helpful abilities but not the brains or sense to wield them. Hopefully Bysciw keeps his word and allows us to invite our own troops into the team." She looks up to the ceiling, waiting for Tanten to comment. He silently observes her behavior. Focusing his eyes, he examines her aura. It flows like a stream. Tanten can tell by analyzing the movement of her aura the woman relies on her life force as a manipulation tool. He's seen similar auras in his work with the Council for it's not uncommon to have a strong manipulator on a team wishing for success.

Tanten says nothing, so the woman continues. "Allow me to introduce myself. The name is Syrenne Tyrney. I work under the Magistrate Association as a Toxicology Scholar. I perform a lot of research in the discovery and use of a variety of chemicals and unique compounds. Bysciw and I met when he became interested in the drugs I created. He desired to sell them in the underworld and give me some of the profit," the woman giggles. "I couldn't refuse."

Tanten tries to hide his contempt for this woman. He wonders why he must work with such corrupt persons. "This woman is starting to make Atlas appear as a saint..." Tanten thinks about what her intentions for joining the group may be. Tanten speaks up, "With the talk of the Schism, don't you feel strange as a Scholar working side by side with two Professionals?"

Syrenne laughs. "I have no interest in the Schism. It's such a petty fight but using it as a distraction is indelibly brilliant. I was concerned at first, feeling like I would be the underdog when compared to you and Atlas. However," she smiles at Tanten, "after hearing about your ventures and learning what you are capable, and incapable, of, I realize neither of you are a threat."

Her eyes pierce his, like she's reading him in the same way Bysciw did. But, Tanten feels her stare penetrates further than Bysciw's. Syrenne carefully examines his aura and life force potential. Her mathematically apt mind determines his strength with pinpoint accuracy. Tanten maintains his calm and cool composure, forbidding himself from appearing the least bit affected by her comment.

"Prove your worth. Did you come to relay a message or simply introduce yourself?" Tanten asks in a stern tone.

"No need to act so brash. And yes, I do have news, though, I'd like to discuss the details of your mission first," Syrenne states. Tanten shrugs.

"Well? What do you want to know?" Tanten questions.

"Why does Bysciw find interest in that beast child?" Syrenne asks. Tanten closes his eyes and sighs as he realizes where the conversation is headed. He can sense toxicity, or perhaps jealousy, in her voice. He decides to amuse himself given her weakness.

"What's not to be interested in?" Tanten begins, a smile covering his face. "She's intelligent, powerful in status and strength, and stunning. It's no wonder why Bysciw found her to be fascinating."

"But he tried to assassinate her," Syrenne replies, her face solemn in expression.

"He said it himself, if he can't have her, no one can," Tanten says with a matter-of-fact look on his face. He feels the anger and envy emanating from Syrenne. On the outside, Tanten appears serious, but on the inside he laughs at her.

She glares at him, noticing the change in his aura from the beginning of their meeting. "He's relaxed rather quickly. Perhaps he thinks I'm a joke. Ha. I'll show him," Syrenne thinks. "This is just a game to him."

"So, I told you what you asked for. It's only right that you reveal the news you've gathered," Tanten urges. She nods and takes a drink.

"I've been assigned to gather intelligence from within the Association and the Crusaders," she states.

Tanten focuses his eyes. The Crusaders pose as their rivals, the antagonists standing in their way from achieving glory and power. Though their mission is the same, they refuse to work with one another thus the competition begins.

"Both places require my attention in much the same way. A secretary of the Magistrate Association is a long-time acquaintance of mine, so getting information out of him is quite simple. As you all predicted, they began searching through files, looking for licensed magistrates to recruit. The Council inducted two new members in the past two weeks, bringing the total number of Council members to fifteen. Other possible candidates for the Council are still under investigation. For being broken, Azriel, who was elected as the Association's temporary Vice President, is pulling the Association together. She's doing quite an impressive job taming the chaos the Schism is causing." Syrenne pours herself more wine from the bottle sitting next to her and takes a drink. Tanten listens attentively, biting his lip to prevent himself from interrupting.

"The Crusaders aren't doing much of significance to report on. They're building their forces and constantly strategizing, but they have no clue what's going on in this war," Syrenne states. She leans back and sighs. "Well, any questions?"

"Yeah, plenty," Tanten begins. "But I'll go one at a time for you." Syrenne laughs, amused by his smug attitude. "Do you think Azriel can hold together the Association?"

He stares intently at her, expecting brief answers so he can get through all of his questions and leave. Though looking for amusement, his boredom becomes too titanic to ignore. He can't help but become tired when a conversation lasts longer than he intends or if he has no genuine interest in such matters.

"No. All she can do is prolong its demise. However, if an unaccounted-for factor joins the picture, things may change," Syrenne senses his impatience. Her hostility and hate toward Tanten increases slightly.

"Unaccounted factors?" Tanten asks, concerned.

"Whether it be an outside force or one of their own has an unknown ability which would act as their savior," she answers. She stares at the contents in her glass as she swirls it. "Next question."

"How long will it take the Association workers to reach Botalia's files?"

"If they continue at the rate they have been, they may never reach her files. The Association thoroughly researches each magistrate. They've created a ranking system to help them decide if they should recruit a person. They go through a list of traits and assign a number one through ten of the person's strength in the given field. The workers only move on after filing the rankings with the magistrate's files and then passing the folders on to the Council. The Council then decides whether the magistrate is worth recruiting or not. It's a time consuming and tedious process. By the time the real chaos begins, I doubt they'll have made it halfway through the files." Syrenne continues to look at her glass. She takes a sip.

"Concerning the Crusaders, how do their forces look?"

"As pathetic as yours," Syrenne laughs. "I swear, both teams have potential, but it's as if you've both scooped up those with little to no experience in exploration or combat. They may have very unique talents and abilities, I haven't been in either place long enough to examine the life force techniques of the teams, but focusing my eyes, every team member's aura is so unrefined. Though, I suppose there may be exceptions." Syrenne rises from her chair, adjusts her dress, Tanten averts his eyes, and she yawns. "Well, I guess I should return to business."

"Wait," Tanten says. "I have one more question."

"Fine."

"Who do the Crusaders believe you to be?" Tanten questions, gazing up to lock eyes with Syrenne. She seems a bit taken aback by the question.

"Well, they think I'm a team member," responds Syrenne, her explanation is cut off by Tanten.

"But what do you tell them to make them trust you? And what tasks do they assign to you? How-"

"I must be going," Syrenne interrupts. She passes by Tanten as she moves toward the door, ignoring the formalities. "It was a pleasure to meet you, and I apologize for not finishing our conversation. Perhaps next time we meet." She grins at Tanten and exits the room.

Tanten chuckles. He rolls his eyes, leans back, and puts his hands behind his head.

"Perfect," Tanten remarks sarcastically. "Now I get to work with three people I can't tolerate." He sighs and exits the room.

When he reaches the main hall, he realizes Syrenne has completely disappeared. The team members go about their tasks, researching and training, and Tanten takes a seat in the corner of the room, observing them while deep in thought.

"I can't believe I'm saying this, but, out of the three, Atlas is the best person to form an alliance with, though I'd prefer not to form an alliance with any of them. I assume Syrenne has Bysciw wrapped around her finger. Her life force concentration and aura combination signify she's a Professional Manipulator. It seems suspicious she didn't mention it. Though, if she's a Scholar as well as a Professional, that makes her particularly dangerous," Tanten thinks.

Being both a Professional and a Scholar means she has plenty of access to a variety of information and research data. Tanten ponders, "If she still works within the Association's walls, her information is invaluable to the team. However, the possibility that Syrenne isn't revealing all of the information is highly probable. I've never found a Professional Manipulator within the Association who is trustworthy."

Botalia comes to his mind. He smirks as he thinks how much better off he'd be if she accepted. He focuses his eyes on the training team members. Their auras and life force appear stronger and more controlled than before.

"But they're still helpless," Tanten thinks. He shakes his head. "If only I had the funding to do this on my own. Maybe I'll just have to round up a group of ruffians willing to follow me." Tanten sighs and closes his eyes. He smiles as he envisions how the assassination attempt might have looked. "Soon... soon the preparations will be complete, and I'll be able to make my move. Soon..."

Chapter Nine

When Botalia was younger, she remembers being strapped into a chair, bright lights shining in her face. Her parents drew her blood and examined her body, ensuring she was healthy and that no serious problems occurred due to her hybrid biology. After they received and recorded any and all results that could assist them in their studies, they would send Botalia to her room to rest for the remaining portion of the day. These examinations occurred once a week.

Once within her room, Botalia would peer out the window and watch the school children returning to their homes after a long day of classes. She always wished she could participate in public schooling like those children, perhaps giving her a chance to make some friends. However, Botalia's parents worried she may be bullied or neglected in a public system. They told her she was unique and deserved every last ounce of attention. They hired several tutors to homeschool her, providing her with an education far beyond what the children in the public schooling system experienced.

By the time she was eight, Botalia could recite several mathematical proofs and scientific theories and explain them in depth. She had even been able to focus her life force into her hands on command. Though she was eager to share her achievements with her parents, they were always busy with their experiments and research.

Her father, Chezland Costelloe Ulton, and her mother, Rhoda Anise Noble-Ulton, were considered elite Scholars. They performed many experiments in the name of the Magistrate Association and their sponsors. Chezland Ulton specialized in botany and chemistry while Rhoda Ulton specialized in physics and engineering. Together, their talents complimented one another, making them an incredible team. Their experiments often required exploration. Occasionally Botalia would tag along, but most often she would remain home, forbidden from leaving the house. Her parents brought back foreign plants and strange artifacts from their travels. They would bring gifts for Botalia from the ventures she could not attend.

Despite the lack of communication with her parents, Botalia admired their hard work and passion. She often attended award ceremonies and banquets where her parents were honored for their accomplishments and commended on their achievements for the betterment of humanity. They acted as her role models, her primary inspiration for succeeding in her schooling. Botalia wanted to be exactly like them: an intelligent and respectable magistrate everyone admires. She never once questioned their love for her. Botalia knew they treasured her. She never doubted it.

One day after a weekly physical, Botalia stared out the window, watching the birds peck at the crumbs in the street. She sighed as she saw the school children walking, running, and skipping down the street, but something seemed different than the other days.

A loud commotion started, and a crowd of students formed a circle. Botalia experienced a gut-wrenching feeling, and she shook as her impulse to run grew. Her instincts took over and she darted out of her room and to the streets.

When she arrived, more than only school children made up the crowd. Adults joined in to see the spectacle. Botalia's senses went into overload, so many sights, sounds, and smells. She pushed her way through the crowd. Once at the inside border, she realized what everyone had been staring at.

A fight broke out between a few of the students, however it was a couple of students ganging up on one individual who was left to single-handedly fend them off. He was bleeding from several cuts on his body accompanied by quite a few bruises. A gash in his eyebrow left by a punch to the eye left blood dripping to the concrete. He attempted to stand up, his position on the ground one of poor defense, but was never given the opportunity by the attackers. Botalia's eyes widened and a fear and wrath she never experienced before caused her body to tense.

Why is no one stopping this?

There were plenty of people, including adults, spectating, and yet no one intervened.

Why is this happening?

She clenched her fists as she watched the boy get kicked in the stomach. Tears filled her eyes.

As a group of boys were moving to simultaneously kick the boy on the ground, Botalia jumped into the arena. She pushed the boys away and leaned down to block the one on the ground. Her arms spread out in front of her in desperation. Everyone watching gasped and the boys who were fighting stopped and looked at her in disgust. Botalia was shaking, but she couldn't leave now. She made the choice long ago to protect those who couldn't protect themselves. Her parents did so every day and at that time it was Botalia's turn to prove her worth.

"Get out of our way," the boy she suspected of being the leader of the attacking group shouted. "I don't know who you are, but you shouldn't be saving that scum!"

"No, no," Botalia softly cried out.

"He's from a family that uses dark magic. Get out of the way!"

The boy goes for a kick, aimed for the target boy's head. Botalia grabbed his leg a moment before impact. Everyone around held their mouths agape with eyes widened. The boy who kicked expressed his shock, and he shook his leg in an attempt to retrieve it from Botalia's grasp. She didn't let go. Rather, a strange light glowed in her eyes, and she slowly closed her hand, crushing the boy's leg. He yelled out in agony. The scream brought Botalia back to her senses and she let go of his leg. The boy fell to the ground and slowly backed away, clutching the broken bone in his leg.

"You're crazy!" he screamed at her, tears forming in his eyes from the pain. "Protect that scum all you want, but this isn't over!"

His friends helped him stand and led him away. They yelled back, shouting rude comments and throwing pebbles at the two. The crowd dissipated, throwing out slurs and gestures of their own. Botalia closed her eyes, disappointed for snapping but she didn't regret protecting the victim of the attacks. She opened her eyes and saw him looking up at her. He sat up.

"Are you okay?" Botalia asked. The boy nodded, however, to Botalia's confusion, he appeared angry.

He grabbed his bleeding arm, experiencing a surge of pain.

"Here, let me help." Botalia pulled out a vial she always kept on her person in case of accidents. She poured some of it into her left palm and made a motion with her right hand. She then placed the solution from the vial on to his wounds. She grinned but he remained solemn. Her smile faded. "What did those kids want from you?"

"They wanted to prove their loyalty," the boy responded. "My family practices dark magic, so-"

"So they attacked you for being different," Botalia finished his sentence. He looked up at her in shock then chuckled.

"Yeah," he replied. The two stood up, continuing to look at one another. "But, it's more complicated than that."

"Complication is human nature," Botalia stated. "The universe is actually pretty simple if you just accept it for what it is." She smiled and extended her right hand. "My name is Botalia Ulton." His eyes widened for everyone in town knew who the Ultons were.

"Uhh," he hummed, slowly reaching for her hand. Botalia grabbed his hand and shook it. "Tenebrant. Tenebrant Mortu."

"It's nice to meet you, Tenebrant," Botalia responded. He tilted his head as a return to the compliment. At that moment, Botalia heard her parents screaming.

"Botalia, what are you doing outside?" her father yelled.

"You're meant to be in your room, it's dangerous out here," her mother stated.

They rushed over to Botalia, checking her over to make sure she was unharmed. Botalia rolled her eyes. She knew her parents were protective of her, but sometimes it felt like too much.

"Time to go inside," her mother commanded, holding on to her arm.

"Wait," Botalia said, her arm escaping her mother's grasp. "Here." Botalia held out a silver stone. "Maybe we'll see each other again some time."

Tenebrant accepted the gift and smiled.

"Yeah," he responded.

As Botalia and her mother walked back toward their home, Mr. Ulton examined Tenebrant with glaring eyes. Botalia's father returned to the house, an agitated march to his step, and locked the door. Tenebrant sighed as he rolled the stone in his hand and walked away.

That night, Botalia had a difficult time getting to sleep. She kept seeing the scenes from the fight, but from an aerial view. Below, she saw a monster tear apart the spectators and rip the fighters to shreds. The color red painted the ground. Her eyes shot open as the door creaked open. Her mother entered.

"Having a bad dream?" Botalia's mother asked. Botalia nodded. Her mother cuddled her in her arms and sang her a lullaby:

Close your eyes little warrior
Return to your dreams
Walk upon the red clouds
And sleep
Lu Li La Le
Feel the pain disappear
No need to fight on, fight on
The darkness draws near
Lu Li Lu La
Approach with gentle heart
Sense the monster's release
And sleep, and sleep
Sense the monster's release
And sleep
Lu Li Ly La Li Ly Le

AFTER THAT DAY, BOTALIA often snuck outside to sit on the stoop and watch the children walk home from school. She would wave at Tenebrant as he walked by, Tenebrant returning it. Sometimes, he would stop and talk to her. They would discuss their lives, both thinking the other lived quite oddly. She thought she may have finally made her first friend... she thought.

Botalia sits up in bed, being pulled out of her memories. She doesn't often reminisce, though, sometimes she enjoys the memories of the past. She sighs. Botalia hears Koepp already singing and dancing about in his room. She laughs.

As she exits the room, the bright morning sun, accompanied by the songs of the creatures, greets her. She prepares herself before going out to the sitting room.

Tenebrant sits outside on the back patio. Koepp runs down the stairs and rushes straight past Botalia to fix himself breakfast. He stops in an instant and turns to face Botalia.

"Good morning!" Koepp says, happiness in his voice.

"Good morning," Botalia responds. He must have had pleasant dreams, she thinks. Botalia looks around the room, observing her parents' trophies and certificates. She dreams of her own accomplishments becoming tangible with plaques and honors, but realizes her thoughts are only dreams. Although, she once believed having visitors was no more than a dream. But Botalia is starting to become accustomed to having others around. Koepp runs out of the kitchen and back to his bedroom.

"I forgot my notebook," he shouts as he rushes past Botalia. She is impressed in his perseverance of the homework she assigned to him. When they began his schooling a few days back, Botalia challenged Koepp to keep track of the creatures he encounters on the island. Every morning he eats his breakfast outdoors in hope of seeing a different species to add to his notebook. Koepp flashes back to the kitchen, notebook in hand, grabs his breakfast in the other and runs to the door. In Koepp's struggle to wrap his fingers around the handle, Botalia opens the door for him. Tenebrant turns to glance at his company before returning his gaze to the forest.

"Before you all came, a mother ranadune had just given birth to a beautiful baby," Botalia whispers, thinking back to the time before it all began. Koepp furrows his brow in trying to picture the creature in his head before hurriedly flipping through his notebook, wondering if he had laid eyes on one yet.

Tenebrant moves his gaze to Botalia. Her stare penetrates beyond the forest. Reminiscing of the meticulous care she kept of all on the island, a piece of her she lost since her past invaded her safe space. What was once tranquility to Botalia now kept her on edge. A constant state of paranoia and heightened senses consumed her seemingly infinite energy. Though her aura did not show it, the lines under her eyes did.

"Botalia," Tenebrant says, with a gentleness to his tone. Botalia slightly jumps as she is caught off guard. "Do what you need to do. We'll hold down the fort." He points at Koepp as he says this. Koepp smiles at Botalia. Botalia nods in gratefulness, slips on her shoes, and begins her journey about the island.

Tenebrant twitches as he looks into the wilderness, sensing the presence of Koepp to his right. He gazes at Koepp, but quickly looks away. He moves his eyes to the ground and closes them as he picks at his fingers in an anxious manner. His heart starts to race the more the thought fills his mind, knowing the boy is a Flynn acts as a catalyst.

As the urge seems too much to control, Tenebrant stands and walks into the house, Koepp watching him as he enters, not thinking much of it. Tenebrant moves to the front steps and observes the island from a different perspective. He trembles as he sits, but he knows he can't leave the island yet. He has yet to see Botalia's true strength, his curiosity being his main reason for staying. However, his withdrawal causes him to slowly descend into insanity.

"Tenebrant?"

Botalia drops down from above causing Tenebrant to jump, startled by her entrance. She tilts her head, focusing her eyes on his aura. She sees an unrelenting hostility, a bloodlust, and senses his life force compressing, like trying to fit a large volume of liquid into a small container, the pressure surpassing what it should. Botalia wonders how he's been able to hold it in, though she sees he's shaking from his effort. Tenebrant avoids eye contact with Botalia, his shame of what he believes a lack of self-control revealing a weakness. However, it's his self-control that impresses Botalia. "Hmm... Follow me."

Botalia stands and walks into the house. Tenebrant follows her. They go onto the back veranda and head toward the wooden door.

Koepp watches them pass and, in his curiosity, stands and follows them. The three descend the steps and enter the arena.

Tenebrant stops and shakes his head. "I cannot fight you," he says to Botalia. She laughs.

"I don't intend on fighting you, yet," Botalia grins. "Besides, I haven't finished my rounds on the island. So I'll provide you with a beginner's lecture to the real magic of this arena." Tenebrant follows her as she leads them toward the doors at the opposite end of the room.

She swings open the double doors to reveal another room. It appears like a database or laboratory, with a large monitor and a panel containing plenty of buttons and levers. In the corner is a tank of a phosphorescent, lavender liquid. Pipes lead from the vat and, with the help of a pressurized gas, are pushed into a machine. A series of tubes and pipes issue out of the machine and form a junction which rises into the ceiling and head in the direction of the gym. Botalia turns on the supercomputer, the screen lighting up. Tenebrant and Koepp drop their jaws as they look around the room. Botalia slides up a cover on the panel to reveal a sensor.

"Place your index finger in the center of the circle," Botalia directs at Tenebrant. He does as she says. "You'll feel a poke." Tenebrant turns his head to her just as he feels the prick in his finger. A needle. He looks up to the monitor and watches as the technology separates and analyzes his blood. A variety of stats appear on the screen. Tenebrant's shock increases as he reads through his personal data, noticing the machine is capable of quantifying his life force.

"Did you create this?" Tenebrant asks.

"Well," Botalia blushes at the accusation and scratches her head. "My parents began building the technology, the concept being a dream of my father's. When they died, I discovered the blueprints among their files and decided to continue it. I had to make some modifications to their original design. The system worked well, the largest problem became finding a reliable fuel source. Once I solved that problem, getting the mechanism to work seemed simple."

Tenebrant chuckles and Koepp continues to stare at the machine in awe. Botalia pulls up a different interface on the monitor. She pushes a few buttons, turns a knob, and flips a switch on the tank.

"We'll start you off with an opponent of lesser strength, though quantitatively not by a significant amount, and it will have a random ability, or abilities."

She walks out the door and into the gymnasium. Tenebrant and Koepp notice the liquid being pushed through the pipe and the machine. They follow her into the gym.

"Tenebrant, you stand in the middle. The second you reach the center your opponent will appear. If you're not careful, it will kill you. It will slowly adapt to your techniques, so try to discover its weaknesses and dispose of it as soon as possible."

Botalia and Koepp walk to the bleachers. Tenebrant pauses before passing the line of the force field.

He approaches the center of the arena at a steady pace, his heart racing. Tenebrant can only imagine what will appear. Perhaps a mechanized robot meant for combat will manifest in an instant, discovering his weaknesses and kill him on the spot. Tenebrant hesitates. He's never fought an opponent without knowing their skill set, without assessing their physical strength. Without understanding that probability of victory lies in his favor. He will be the first to admit he likes a challenge. But to fight when the odds are completely stacked against oneself would be no more than suicidal. Not to mention stupid.

Tenebrant swallows his fears. As he steps into the center, the presence of another takes form. Rising from the ground behind him, Tenebrant quickly leaps into the air, dodging the attack of his opponent. While in the air, he looks down upon his adversary and his eyes widen. His opponent takes no human form but rather resembles a monster.

Standing on two massive legs, nine feet tall, the maroon-colored beast, much like a minotaur, appears muscular and hostile. It holds a morning star in its left hand and a shield in its right. Tenebrant lands and the beast swings the morning star at him. He hops back and stares at the being, wondering what its weakness may be. Tenebrant notes the creature's size, sensing he can't beat the beast through brute strength. He will need to develop a proper strategy to achieve victory over the creature.

The monster charges Tenebrant with its tower shield. He jumps atop the beast's head, thinking the beast cannot raise its arms high enough. A moment later, the creature opens a second set of eyes, glowing red. Tenebrant leaps to the ground out of shock. The being swings his morning star, Tenebrant not worried because at the distance he stands from the creature, the head of the morning star will never reach him. However, the tip of the morning star illuminates and spikes launch toward Tenebrant, the centripetal force accelerating the spikes.

It's using life force.

Tenebrant thinks with clenched teeth, unable to believe the monster utilizes its own life force, transforming it into spikes. He dodges the spikes, the explosions of the spikes hitting the ground create a resounding boom. Flipping through the maze of spikes, Tenebrant realizes that the quantity of spikes increases but the quality of damage decreases. The sound of the individual spikes hitting the ground is not as vehement as the first attack. His acrobatics and agility prove quite advantageous against the monster. While strong, the beast cannot move as quickly as Tenebrant.

As Tenebrant closes the distance, he thinks of unarming the brute of its morning star. To do so will involve using his own life force, which for Tenebrant comes as a last resort when others spectate a fight he's in. Revealing one's abilities to a potential enemy is the largest mistake any practitioner of life force can make.

As he runs, he makes motions with his hands. In his right hand, a kris appears, a dark grey smoke rising from the blade. He aims to detach the beast's arm at the bicep. He knows he must wait for the monster to swing the morning star before attacking.

The monster sees him approaching from the ground and attempts a strike with his weapon. Tenebrant leaps up, holding the kris near his chest preparing for the slice. However, the creature uses the inertia of the morning star to rotate itself around. As it turns, it brings up its tower shield. Tenebrant, realizing he can't maneuver while in the air, collides with the shield, but uses it as a wall to jump from and onto the creature's head.

He peers into the creature's eyes and smiles. He raises the smoky kris above his head and pierces each of the four eyes of the beast. It yells out in pain, the screams deafening. Tenebrant jumps off the head. He decides to take his victory and plunges the kris into the beast's heart. The monster drops the morning star and shield, which vanish in a whirl of smoke as they hit the ground. The creature releases one last painful wail before collapsing into a pile of smoke which dissolves into the atmosphere.

Tenebrant breathes heavily, surprised at the extent of the beast's strength. However, he remembers the beast was tailored for him in accordance with his own abilities.

He turns to face Botalia and Koepp, who stand in the bleachers, applauding the fight. Tenebrant smiles. He exits the ring and approaches the spectators. Koepp appears in awe of Tenebrant and his abilities. Botalia shares a smile, glad to see Tenebrant genuinely happy. His smile is not forced nor derives from any malicious intent. Tenebrant's smile is one of pure enjoyment.

As they return to the main house for lunch, Tenebrant relives the scenes of the fight in his head. He realizes his bloodlust doesn't derive from a need to see others suffer, but it's a hostile state to prove to himself how strong and powerful he is. And in order to believe it, he must see results. Though he fought no living being, the beast offered a fight more enjoyable than any human he has fought for several years. He may even consider the fight with the monster to be on the same level as a fight against Tanten Flynn. Tenebrant chuckles. His eyes move to Botalia and focus. "I cannot imagine the demons she creates with that machine. But I would love to find out."

After lunch, Botalia and Koepp resume their lessons in the study. Tenebrant joins them and scans the book bindings, searching for one which catches his eye. His finger drags along the scientific and magical texts. Textbooks outlining the statics and principles of physics, chemistry, biology, botany, astronomy, geology, alchemy, druidic rituals, transfiguration, necromancy and... Tenebrant pauses. He looks around, paranoid someone may have spotted his hesitation. He remembers who his company is and slowly extracts the book, "Sacrificium Pro Potentia" (Sacrifice for Power). Tenebrant peers over at Botalia and Koepp. Koepp scratches his head while staring at his test paper. Botalia writes her report and skims through past files, checking for inaccuracies. Tenebrant sits at the table nearest to him and opens up the book.

"Is this the secret to her power?" Tenebrant asks himself. The text appears worn and some of the pages bend at the corners. A bookmark protrudes from the top of the book. He flips to the marked page. A transmutation circle is pictured, the rite labeled "Hymn of the Beast." He meticulously studies the pages, attempting to comprehend the purpose of such a rite. Numbers scribbled in the margin direct him to different pages, some annotations referencing other books.

"Aha!" Koepp screams, breaking Tenebrant's concentration.

He gazes up from the book. Two hours had passed in what felt like two minutes to Tenebrant. Had the tome locked him into a trance? Impossible, he thinks, inanimate objects cannot possess life force... He focuses on the old leather book and exhales in relief when he notices no aura signature.

"This is a great improvement," Botalia compliments Koepp, his smile expressing his joy. She turns to face Tenebrant. "We're going outside. You can join us if you wish." Tenebrant nods his head. As Koepp and Botalia exit the room, Tenebrant closes the book and places it back on the shelf. Before walking out the door, he looks back a final time to ensure he remembers its position among the texts.

As the sun sets, the three watch the world news in the den (a room down the hall from the sitting room). Koepp sits on the floor, reading his book. Tenebrant and Botalia pay close attention to the news, dissecting every piece of information.

"Breaking news," the reporter states, "a group who calls themselves the Arcane Allegiance stand outside of the Magistrate Association in protest. The leader of the group demands entrance to the Association. While protests appear peaceful at the moment, the inaction of the Association will lead to uprising, says one of the protesters. These protests are in reaction to talks of a Schism. The Secretary of the Magistrate Association refuses to comment at this time."

Botalia leans forward, squinting at the scene unraveling on the screen. She frowns.

"Other reports of rogue magistrates are popping up all over the nation. In our efforts to contact the Council, the Secretary requested our leave and told us the Council does not wish to comment at this time."

Botalia shakes her head in disbelief. Tenebrant catches a glimpse of her reaction.

When the news story changes to another, Botalia turns off the television. She stares at the black screen, thoughts flooding her mind from all sides.

"Looks like the Schism has begun," Tenebrant says. Koepp raises his head, deciding he would rather listen to their conversation than read.

"Koepp, can you go water the flowers in the greenhouse?" Botalia asks. Koepp nods, gleefully pushing his book away from him and jogs for the door. "Be sure to water near the base of the plant." Koepp waves back to acknowledge he heard and races for the greenhouse. She locks eyes with Tenebrant. "The separation began long before either side decided the issue was worth fighting over."

"Tanten asked you, didn't he?" Tenebrant questions. Botalia squints.

"How did you..."

Tenebrant chuckles his malicious laugh. "He invited me as well. But I don't enjoy fighting other people's battles. Nor did working with a Flynn amuse me." Tenebrant pauses. His face becomes serious. "Does he know about your abilities?"

"When he visited, he examined my life force and aura, but he cannot comprehend what I'm capable of. No one can," Botalia confidently responds. "Does that mean you're a neutral?"

He laughs again, this time in amusement of her question. "Botalia," Tenebrant starts. "Do you truly believe Tanten has joined a team to participate in the Schism?"

Her face expresses her confusion, but slowly the picture comes into focus. She recalls Tanten's slideshow of images, their conversation, and piece by piece the picture grows less blurry.

"They're using it," Botalia mumbles. "They're using it as a distraction." She slams her hands against her face. "I should have noticed earlier. I believed I over-analyzed his thoughts, but, uhh, how could I be so incompetent?" Botalia looks at the floor, attempting to brainstorm. Tenebrant continues to stare at her.

"Botalia?" She raises her head to look at him. "Did Tanten ask how you achieved such power? And if he did, did you tell him?"

She drops her jaw, lost for words as the thoughts create a barrier to forming logical sentences. Botalia wonders why these thoughts are surfacing when there are other issues of concern.

"Tenebrant..." Botalia starts, unable to make eye contact.

"Answer me," Tenebrant demands.

"No," she whispers. "No, no one knows."

"So, they have no way to attain a power parallel to your own?" he asks.

"I... I don't believe so," Botalia answers. "Who are 'they'?"

"Tanten and his 'team,' but anyone who knows Tanten understands he would never work with a team outside of his own necessity or desires," Tenebrant chuckles, remembering how disappointed Tanten looked when his troop would catch up with him on a mission, interrupting his and Tenebrant's duels. Hoping Botalia will get the hint, Tenebrant speaks one word, "Bysciw."

Botalia feels a shock. She recalls Naht mentioning Bysciw's name as he left, saying Bysciw was his client. Bysciw wants Botalia dead. She wonders why his name matters at first. However, thinking about the coincidence of Tanten's visitation followed by the assassination attempt, she understands they must be connected somehow.

"So, Tanten and Bysciw are working with one another?" Botalia mumbles, the thought racing through her head. She envisions Bysciw's appearance, realizing she's seen him. His picture revealed itself in the moment she touched Tanten's hand. *If Bysciw has caused Tanten suffering, why do they work together?* She closes her eyes and focuses on the audio and visuals of Tanten's slideshow. She spools through the memories of pain and suffering, searching for the man known as Bysciw. Tenebrant watches her, understanding the reason for her focus, her abilities becoming more intriguing. She finds a vivid memory and tries to play it, experiencing the situation through Tanten's eyes.

Just as the memory begins to play, an unknown force thrusts her out of her own head. Her eyes rapidly open and she feels an odd tug at her heart. Botalia does not stop to think because her intuition leads her to mortal fear.

"Koepp..."

Chapter Ten

"Koepp," she whispers, an immense fear fills her. She darts from the den. Tenebrant, confused by the sudden change in events, follows her. Botalia races to the greenhouse, her heart beats against her chest and sinks as panic overwhelms her. Koepp's presence from the island completely disappeared. Despite not being with him, she knows exactly what happened. No other presences appeared, his simply vanished.

"There's only one possibility... Please, Koepp, wait for me, please..." Botalia abandons all rational thought and acts on pure instinct, bearing no control over her actions.

They reach the greenhouse and Botalia instantly focuses her eyes. She identifies the plant with the heightened aura and runs to it, Tenebrant staying nearby. Botalia places her hands on the side of the plant pot and closes her eyes.

"Wherever he was headed, he arrived. Whether it's safe or not at the location is none of my concern," Botalia states. She feels a pressure on her left shoulder. She turns her head and sees Tenebrant's hand. Though short of understanding the situation, he wears a serious look on his face. "I need you to come with me. If Koepp is in danger, I may not be able to save him alone. Please," she holds out her hand and closes her eyes. Botalia prepares her state of mind and her life force swirls upward from the ground. Tenebrant grabs her hand.

Though her eyes are closed, a white light blinds Botalia. Her muscles tense and every fiber of her body experiences an agonizing strain. She wants to yell out in hopes of releasing some of the pain, but she lacks any control of herself. Botalia returns to her subconscious body in a fit, shaking, twisting. She feels like her insides are being torn from her, the pain unbearable. Her subconscious self squeezes her eyes shut, but an unknown force pulls her eyelids apart. The slideshow begins, a flurry of images and sounds attack her from every angle. Unlike any pain she has felt before, the worst suffering of all.

It's the suffering of one who continuously sees hope, a light at the end of the tunnel, only to be betrayed. Every time, all hope is crushed right in front of them.

How do they keep going?

The suffering continues day in and day out. In trying to change their fate of endless tragedy, they betray themselves. An endless cycle. The pain of knowing things will never change, that all hope is a lie. Yet, they somehow cling to the ideal while denying its existence all the while. They somehow extend their reach to the light in the dark only to watch it fade.

Does hope exist as an artifice or a weapon?

The worst suffering for humanity is one of inescapable betrayal. The betrayal of loved ones, of yourself, of the very world itself.

Does anyone care?

A magnet to all suffering and pain, attracting the negative to the positive. A contorted love takes shape, a dark emotion which succeeds by building up other's hopes only to devour them. A mechanism to defend against this level of suffering is just as deadly as the instrument itself. No compromises. Absolutes and ultimatums.

No one to suffer as so could be anything but broken.

She stops struggling and watches the slideshow, tears forming in her eyes. She experiences suffering every day. Her resolution which grants her power derives from the world's suffering. By lifting some of the weight off those in pain and with heavy heart, her strength grows, her power only increasing. She's felt the weight of the deaths of family members and significant figures, of natural disasters, and of war. At the start, the pain nauseated her, pushing her into an unconscious state at times. However, over time, she strengthened.

She was able to withstand the weight of suffering and pain while only developing a headache or jumping from a sudden jolt. The collective suffering of the world delivered to her through her vow became a pain she adapted to. She devoted herself, her body, her soul, her life, to lessening the pain of others.

She was naïve at the time, believing the suffering she experienced couldn't be surpassed. She could not comprehend, nor could anyone, the colossal supply of suffering the world experiences each day. Even accepting only a portion of that suffering could kill a person if occurring simultaneously. Being isolated for so long, she didn't realize the extent of her curse.

The moment she touched Tanten's hand and felt the sudden weight flow through her and attack her heart, she understood her mistake. When any portion of her hand touches another person's hand, her body accepts a fraction of that person's suffering, as well as gifts her with the sight to experience it. Her heart suddenly feels heavy, a pain she's accustomed to, and the other person suddenly feels lighter, as if a weight had been lifted off their chest. They don't forget their moments of suffering, but the painful emotions derived from such tragedies vanish.

Her vow to share the world's suffering created emptiness. Her resolution to take that vow filled the void, granting to her an ever-multiplying power. Expand the battery, the life force will follow...

Throughout those ten years of solitude, her memories were devoid of the emotions that were forced out. In ten years, she experienced the amount of suffering most wouldn't feel over three lifetimes. If she can prevent one tragic figure from following the path she took, she'll have succeeded. For this reason, she had to save Koepp.

A squeeze on her arm pulls Botalia to reality. Botalia gasps for air, her body collapsed on the ground. Tenebrant holds her arm, his guard raised from the strange sensations. He distinguishes the actions and results, though, he cannot quite comprehend the latter.

The first action being their teleportation to the location where presumably Koepp traveled. The tingling he experiences across his flesh as well as the moment of being off balance being the result. However, he pins the other effect to have been caused by their hands touching. Similar to what Tenebrant saw when Botalia and Naht's hands made contact, Botalia appeared in agony, though this time her pain seemed far worse than previously. Tenebrant remembers Naht describing the sensation of a weight being lifted off, and those are the only words Tenebrant finds to accurately depict what he feels. But what caused it? What happened in that moment of contact that he can't comprehend?

Botalia shakily rises, her first priority being Koepp. Tenebrant grabs on to her as she begins to fall.

"Thanks," she says.

He remains silent. Botalia moves forward, her eyes focus. Being in a foreign environment, her senses are enhanced, listening to every sound, feeling every vibration on the ground. The time difference means this area has already passed into the night.

The darkness looming in the wooded area, Botalia and Tenebrant follow the lit road. She extends her arm to the side, stopping Tenebrant from moving forward. Botalia leans down and places her hands on the concrete, closing her eyes. She smiles as she identifies Koepp's aura, however, there are others nearby. She counts seven auras total, not including Tenebrant. As she examines the auras, she recognizes another individual's aura. It's an aura she's felt before.

Tenebrant grabs her shoulder and points to the road behind them. The headlights from a vehicle approach. The pair leap from the road and into the tree line, all the time heading towards Koepp. As they move, Tenebrant senses the presence of the others as well. The two see a barn-type building up ahead. As they move closer, they notice people standing outside of the building. Botalia's eyes widen. Koepp is among them.

As Botalia starts to rush toward him, Tenebrant grabs onto her shirt and places a finger to his lips. He points up toward the roof of the building and then points to the vehicle which slows down to a stop in front. Botalia looks up to the roof, understanding Tenebrant's caution. The familiar presence is that of Nix Kufuta. This is an assassination site.

The men in front of the building stand in wait for the person or persons to exit the vehicle. They nervously glimpse at Koepp from time to time, unaware of how and why a child is at their rendezvous. They stand tall and broad, wearing black suits and bolo ties. Botalia thinks they may be members of the mafia, which would explain the suspicious activity.

The black SUV stops in the road in front of the building. Out of the front seat steps a tall, burly bodyguard in pilot shades. He steps to the back door of the vehicle and opens it. A man with a towering and intimidating presence places his feet on the pavement and stands. The five men who were standing outside of the building lower their heads, a sign of respect to their boss. A man exits from the other side of the vehicle and steps into the light. Atlas Lurio.

Botalia jumps up and Tenebrant immediately pulls her down. While her face expresses her shock, Tenebrant remains expressionless. He looks up to the roof and sees Nix watching from above, preparing for the attack.

"Use your life force to anchor Koepp into place," Tenebrant whispers into Botalia's ear. "He's far enough away from the men that he won't get hurt by proximity. The moment the assassination begins, I'll jump to grab Koepp. At that moment, release the life force and we'll jump into the tree line on the other side."

Tenebrant feels a pressure surround him. He focuses his eyes on Botalia. She struggles to control her aura, her life force pushing on it from the inside. If she can't control her strength, some of the men will surely sense her presence, he thinks. Botalia shakes, anger and nervousness filling every pore of her body.

"Can you control your life force long enough to go along with my plan?" Tenebrant asks. Botalia nods.

She closes her eyes, her aura taming itself in an instant, and places her hands on the ground. The life force flows from her hands and twists through the rocky soil and past every root. Koepp's heart freezes as he feels the force on his legs and feet. He can't move them.

As the boss approaches the members, he turns his head to Koepp and glares.

"Who's the boy?" asks the boss, in a northern Divesregio accent, his vowels accentuated.

One of the members responds, "We don't know. He just showed up."

The boss sighs, not satisfied with their answer. He starts to walk toward Koepp, but Atlas holds out his hand to stop him.

"I'll take care of this," he chuckles. "Head on inside so we can begin immediately." The boss eyes Atlas up and down, wondering why he should take orders from anyone. After a brief moment of thought and a cursory glance at Koepp, he nods in agreement and ushers his men to enter the abandoned barn.

Many events transpire over the next few seconds. Atlas approaches Koepp. Botalia shakes, instinct telling her to attack, but she knows she must follow Tenebrant's plan, for Koepp's safety. She focuses on her life force, ensuring Koepp cannot move. The moment the leading men step underneath the roof ledge of the barn, the young assassin drops down. A panic spreads across the mafia members. They pull out their guns and knives, but Nix moves too rapidly for them. One after another, members fall to the ground, blood spilling from their necks. As Nix charges, the boss shoots aimlessly at the assassin in a panicked attempt to save himself. Nix smiles and lunges forward. He extends his left arm, utilizing his life force to make the chop as sharp as the blade of a katana. He pulls up on the top of the boss's head with his right hand as he executes the slice. The boss's head falls clean to the ground, his body collapsing where it stood.

The moment the assassination began, Tenebrant took off from his position to secure Koepp. Botalia releases her life force the second Tenebrant grabs hold. Koepp's fear covers his face. Atlas who was previously approaching Koepp smiles in amusement as the scene unravels itself before him. Tenebrant and Koepp sit quietly in the tree line opposite Botalia, Tenebrant turning Koepp's face from the massacre presently occurring.

Once the boss's body hits the ground, Nix stops and shakes his left hand then wipes the remaining blood on the jacket of the mafia boss. His face appears disgusted by the sight of blood, however, his agility throughout the assassination showed he never hesitated. Knowing Koepp stood away from the group, Nix had no worries about completing his task. And if he did, Nix knew he couldn't show it, not in front of the client.

Atlas steps forward, applauding Nix's work. Nix looks around, wondering where Koepp disappeared to. Atlas smirks as he focuses his life force, searching for those attempting to hide.

"Wonderful work," Atlas says as he approaches Nix. Nix stops looking around for a moment and glares at Atlas, thinking he may have done something to Koepp. Atlas laughs., in a resounding, almost charming, tone. "No need to worry, your little friend is safe. It appears he's not the only one watching, in fact," Atlas closes his eyes and inhales deeply, "there are two others."

Nix and Botalia's eyes widen. Tenebrant glares at Atlas, his hostility burning in his eyes. Nix looks to the ground. Atlas moves to place his hand on Nix's shoulder, but Koepp breaks free of Tenebrant's grip, granted Tenebrant made no attempt to stop him. Koepp steps into the light.

"Don't touch him," Koepp commands, glaring at Atlas. Koepp does his best to avoid seeing the bloody sight adjacent to Nix. Nix gazes at Koepp, a slight smile sneaking through before his face grows grim. Atlas walks toward Koepp.

"Why, Little Flynn, you have as much tenacity as your father," Atlas chuckles.

Koepp feels this man's power surround him. Botalia focuses her eyes and observes his aura. His strength and control of his aura and life force leave her in awe. He hides his abilities well, though Botalia didn't expect anything less of him. After all, they don't allow simply any magistrate to become Vice President of the Association. She restrains herself, her fear of being caught begins to surpass her instinct to rescue Koepp. She knows if anything were to happen, Tenebrant would jump in, or at least she hopes.

"How do you know me?" Koepp questions.

Atlas maliciously smiles, with a lick of his lips, and closes the distance between himself and Koepp. Koepp remains frozen to the spot. Nix watches, too petrified to move. Tenebrant's patience runs out. He jumps from his spot and into the space next to Koepp. Atlas stops.

"Leave him be, Atlas," Tenebrant demands. Atlas grins at him. "Your business is finished. I'll take it from here." Botalia trembles as she sits in the tree line. She feels helpless, worthless. All she can do is sit and watch.

"I thought it was you I sensed earlier, rushing past to grab the boy. Are you here to kill him or protect him? You are aware this is Tanten Flynn's son, correct?" Atlas asks, subtly trying to provoke a hostile response from Tenebrant. Atlas senses Tenebrant's hostility and hopes if he can provoke him, the third person will make an appearance.

"You should leave now," Tenebrant threateningly states.

"You should honestly reconsider the offer of joining us, Tenebrant Mortu. Work with me and the tasks will almost certainly create amusement for someone like yourself." Atlas lifts his arm, as if displaying the massacre before them. Their eyes remain locked. "Not to mention, the opportunity to start your collection of pawns," Atlas says, pointing at Nix.

"Oddly enough, the need for that collection is fading, but I appreciate the sentiment," Tenebrant responds with venomous sarcasm lacing his tone.

Atlas glimpses at Koepp and chuckles. He looks around, hoping to see the final member of their team, knowing she remains hidden amongst the trees. When he exited the vehicle earlier, he felt her powerful presence. Botalia clenches her fists, fighting the urge to reveal herself, knowing her appearance to be exactly what Atlas wishes.

Atlas sighs. "Well, I should be returning,"

Atlas walks toward the vehicle, but after a few steps he stops and turns around. "Oh, and just a warning this time. But ensure she doesn't escape again, okay?"

Atlas grins, Tenebrant returning a scowl. Nix and Koepp show surprise, realizing who Atlas is referring to. He gets into the SUV and drives away. Once the car is out of sight, Botalia jumps out to join them. Koepp rushes toward Nix and they both share a smile with one another. Tenebrant walks onto the road and looks in the direction Atlas drove, shaking his head.

"Your self-control impresses me, Botalia," Tenebrant says. "Even I couldn't control myself. Though, I regret not fighting him. I bet his blood is a beautiful, dark shade of red."

Botalia places her hand on his shoulder, and he snaps out of his bloodlust. Tenebrant looks to the ground. He notices her fragile touch, and he senses the thickness of the air around him. Her life force is escaping and, though she releases it in a harmless manner, it acts of its own accord. Due to her control, the life force is unable to manifest itself. Her aura shakes, trying to return to equilibrium through any means possible, but Botalia restricts the energy from releasing simultaneously.

Botalia walks toward Koepp and Nix. "So, you really wished to see Nix, huh?" she directs at Koepp, who lowers his head and nods. Botalia expresses a half-hearted grin.

"I don't know how it happened," Koepp starts. "I was just watering the plants like you asked me to..."

"Koepp," Botalia leans down to look at him eye level. "I'm not upset. Honestly, the ability to access those plants' potential requires incredible concentration. I'd hoped you'd be more prepared before using them for such purposes." Tenebrant rejoins the group.

"What next?" he asks.

Botalia shrugs, looks around and a sudden jolt courses through her body. Her eyes widen as the realization hits her. Tenebrant feels her shift in emotions. "I suppose we are both fugitives now," Tenebrant directs at Botalia.

"Who's returning with me?" Botalia asks. Koepp and Nix turn to one another. Botalia sighs and looks up to the sky, only the brightest stars shining through the light pollution. "I'll give you ten minutes. But Nix probably needs to be returning soon as well."

"I have time," Nix mumbles. Koepp's wide smile forces Nix to grin. Koepp begins the conversation right away, and they sit themselves at the side of the road, backs to the barn.

Tenebrant chuckles. "Not exactly the ideal location for a playdate."

Botalia watches the boys. Their smiles and laughter are heartwarming, however, the time will come when those expressions disappear and loneliness returns. Being away from the island and knowing she is breaking the terms of her exile causes her head immense stress. Her entire body shakes. Though she knows she must recharge her strength if they are to return to the island, Botalia cannot tell whether prolonging their time in this location will rejuvenate her or destroy her.

"How did he do it?" Tenebrant questions.

"It's called 'potentia herba,' or power plant," Botalia forces a giggle. "It's a play on words. The plant produces an immense amount of life force due to its flexible aura. I've been working to strengthen them through selective breeding and genetic modification. Over the past nine years, I've been carefully tending to the plants, trying my hardest to improve them while not diminishing their integrity. You could call it an obsessed love, but I truly believe these plants could change the world for the better. They possess an incredible power, only accessed through the purest of intentions and desires due to its tranquil aura flow." Through her nervous shakes, Tenebrant realizes Botalia's pride and passion as she talks about the plant. She invests herself in her work, imprinting a part of herself on the things she values above all else. It's more than a love, it's a bond rooting her to life. Her care and love for her creations transcends the eternal pain and suffering she experiences. She clings to her humanity by a thread, the bond being that thread. Much like ions, Botalia finds stability through her bonds.

"If something were to happen to her creations, she would evolve into a monster in an instant," Tenebrant thinks, a familiar excitement returning to him.

Botalia continues, "He must have really desired to see Nix. It's the only explanation for how his wish became manifest through life force. Disassembling and reassembling cells in different locations is an extremely difficult task. Years of study and understanding, not to mention an immense amount of life force is required to complete such a feat. Tanten would be so disappointed to know he abandoned one with so much potential."

"No one ever accused Tanten Flynn of being brilliant," Tenebrant states.

Botalia glances around in a paranoid manner, her heightened senses still adjusting to the foreign environment. Tenebrant gazes at Koepp and Nix. Their conversation seems very dynamic from their arm movements and facial expressions. He glances at the bodies lying on the ground, but he must quickly look away due to a stir in his stomach. His life force dances on the tips of his fingers, ready for his command.

After several minutes pass, Koepp and Nix rise and march toward Tenebrant and Botalia. They stand across from them, their manner rather serious and nervous. The two appear like children who are ready to reason like adults.

"So, Nix and I have discussed a lot," Koepp begins. Botalia giggles at his formalities. "And we've decided it would be cool if... if..." Koepp's nervousness gets the best of him. Nix looks at Koepp and grins. Botalia sees a genuine happiness glowing in his eyes. Nix turns to Botalia.

"Will you accept me, Nix Kufuta, as your new apprentice?" Nix asks. Botalia feels taken aback, a surprised expression on her face. Tenebrant chuckles, the situation amusing him.

"Nix, I..." Botalia begins, shaking her head, before Nix interrupts.

"Please," he gets down on his knees, pleading. "I don't want to be an assassin anymore. I don't want to kill people."

A tear streaks down his cheek, more threatening to follow. Botalia is shocked that an empty vessel possesses human emotions and feels sympathy. Maybe she was wrong, or maybe he's changed since he first arrived on her island. Koepp gazes at Nix with a melancholic expression, upset to see his friend crying. His depressed expression hurts her even more. Botalia shakes her head.

"Nix, I can't take you with me," Botalia mumbles.

"But why not?" Koepp asks, confusion and yearning in his voice.

"Because... he's..." Botalia searches for the right words. She wants to remain honest but doesn't know how to convince the boy who carries Tanten's stubbornness in his DNA. She pauses.

"He's what?" Koepp insists.

"Nix has a family and a responsibility to them. I can't take him away from that," Botalia states.

"So, you're fine with me murdering people?" Nix questions. He points to the bodies on the ground. "You prefer me to live in a world like that?"

"That's not what I meant," Botalia starts, beginning to realize Nix may be equally as stubborn as Koepp. She sighs. "I don't wish you to live a life like this, but I don't know if I'm the one to help you escape. I feel sorry, but-"

"I don't need your pity," Nix snaps.

"Botalia." Koepp locks eyes with her. "I escaped my old life to learn from you, and you accepted. I didn't know if you were going to be worse than my guardians, but that thought never crossed my mind. I didn't care. I just wanted out. How is my situation any different from Nix's? I ran away from my job and my guardians in the hopes I could still change my future. I trusted you and wished upon the meteor. When Nix showed up, I thought it was a lucky one. But I feel lied to now."

Koepp looks to the ground, Nix staring at him. Tenebrant stands unmoving, expressionless, his eyes shifting between the three of them. When he glimpses at Botalia, he focuses his eyes and examines her aura. It appears weak and fragile, trembling. All of her life force focuses in her chest, rigid, like it's preventing some force or power from escaping.

"Nix," Botalia begins. "If I was a lucky meteor and I let you tell me one wish which I promised to grant, what would you wish for?" Nix gazes up at her, his resolve written all over his face.

"A friend," Nix answers. Koepp turns to him, a wide smile spreading across his face. Tenebrant chuckles. Botalia sighs.

"Well, we must return," Botalia says. Koepp and Nix look at her, unsure whether to express disappointment or anger. "I'll take Koepp first. Then I'll come back for Tenebrant and Nix." Koepp and Nix turn to each other, flooded with excitement. Tenebrant grins.

"But, how?" questions Koepp.

"The same way we got here," Botalia smiles. She extends her right hand to Koepp. "Are you ready?"

He nods and grabs her hand. Botalia closes her eyes and calms her mental state. She divides her mind into several focused partitions. Botalia concentrates, individually manifesting her thoughts into the partitions. One portion of her mind focuses on the villa, the sights, sounds, and feel of standing outside the front door. Another portion of her mind carefully deconstructs and reconstructs the human anatomy into individual cells then the form of an entire being. The last major fraction of her concentration is diverted to the flow of her life force. She establishes a current of her life force through her own and Koepp's body through the point of contact. Tenebrant focuses his eyes and watches in excitement as Botalia's life force flows through her and into Koepp. In an instant, they seem to vanish, no trace of them where they stood. Tenebrant and Nix stare at the spot in amazement. Thirty seconds later, Botalia returns.

"Are you two ready?" she asks.

Tenebrant observes her aura. Though hiding it on the outside, Botalia appears weak, barely clinging to consciousness. She controls her shaking and hides her fatigue, but she doesn't have the energy to disguise her aura.

Tenebrant and Nix slowly approach her, unsure what to make of what they just witnessed. Botalia holds out her hands but then quickly retracts them, her shock hitting her. Tenebrant deduces the situation. Botalia hasn't touched Nix's hand yet, the slideshow of his pain and suffering not revealed. She is unaware of the shock that will strike her when their hands make contact.

"Botalia, if-"

"I'm thinking," she snaps.

She knows the longer she thinks the more energy she'll lose. "If I attempt to make the leap from our current location to the island, and I pass out, the three of us will almost certainly die. The odds of our survival would be less than one percent in this scenario. However, if I have enough energy to stay conscious throughout the slideshow, the power I gain should be sufficient to get us to the villa unharmed. The odds of Nix's suffering being more potent than Tenebrant's is unlikely, about fifteen percent. Though, if the pain is over half that of Tenebrant's, the odds of me passing out is high... about seventy-five, no, seventy-eight percent. I feel myself fatiguing. The sooner we leave, the better."

"Botalia," Tenebrant urges. "We'll travel back the long way if the strain is too much. Use your life force reserve to return yourself. You've done plenty."

"No," Botalia mumbles. "I can do this," she says, her lack of confidence evident in her voice. She extends her hands and closes her eyes. "Trust me."

Tenebrant grabs Nix's shoulder. "Wait until I signal," he whispers to Nix. Tenebrant takes her hand in his own. She squeezes it, giving him an odd comfort. Tenebrant nods. Nix grabs her hand.

Without a moment hesitation, Botalia commits to the leap. She not only feels the pressure from the movement of the transport, but the blinding light returns. A pain stings in every portion of her heart. She feels her consciousness slipping away as her subconscious body manifests. Unlike every other slideshow she's seen, she notices Nix's suffering derives solely from his family.

He appears devoid of emotion, like his family emptied him out to fill him with traits and skills required to be an elite assassin. Killing people never meant anything to Nix, he never felt guilt or sympathy for his victims. Nor did he feel joy or satisfaction. He never hesitated, no matter the victim. The smell and sight of blood never disgusted him (though he wasn't fond of the sensation on his hand). Watching lifeless bodies hit the pavement never conjured up any emotions in Nix's mind. And that's why he hated his family. He wished like Neja he could find pleasure and excitement from assassination but trying to force an emotion made him feel emptier. His pain was a pain devoid of feeling, a confused pain. Numb.

Botalia watches the slideshow laid out in her subconscious mind, but also attempts to focus on her real body. She reconstructs every cell to its correct location and allows the current to flow to Tenebrant and Nix's cells. She feels the weight pulling down her heart, but she pushes the pieces back to their correct position. Every fiber, muscle, tendon, and bone of her body piece themselves together. She feels her blood flow and her heart beat. Her feet contact a hard surface, and she hears the excited scream of Koepp. Botalia opens her eyes. They made it.

Koepp's mouth continues to move as he rushes toward them. A deafening ring fills Botalia's ears. No other sound breaks through the barrier. A forceful motion shakes her from her shoulder. Tenebrant shakes her once more, his mouth moving but no sound.

Black dots fuzz her vision, and the ring grows to frequency she wasn't even sure she'd be able to hear. Her knees give way.

Everything fades.

Chapter Eleven

Tanten sits on a bench in the empty gymnasium. Waiting. He invited several of his comrades and other recruited, untamed talents, or as others would call them: ruffians. Criminals. Tanten thinks of them as self-serving liberals. They walk their own path. But that does not mean they cannot be tamed. That they won't follow one stronger than themselves. Whether out of respect or out of fear.

The first to walk through the door, telephone in hand, is one Tanten chooses to put his trust in. Not because the young man's strength overpowers all others, but because he excels in his field. Reece Horne, Tanten's disciple, practices technomancy. His aura takes a shape not far different than that of the Ulton girl. Not a common shape, but his aura aids him to move his life force in waves that mimic an alternating current.

Reece walks over to Tanten and takes a seat. He puts his phone in his pocket and turns his head to the door.

"They're coming, Mr. Flynn."

"Did they send you a message?"

Reece lets out a suppressed laugh and quickly tries to mask it with a cough so as not to disrespect his boss. Tanten understands his mistake. His disciple's phone does not work in that way. Reece moves his pointer fingers to his head, rubbing his temples.

"I thought we told them to turn off their phones once they entered the town. None of them listened."

Tanten smirks at the comment. Withdrawing his own phone from his pocket, Tanten checks to see if he's received any messages. One. Sender: Atlas Lurio.

His lack of desire drowns out all curiosity of reading the message. Atlas may still prove to be the strongest with which to form an alliance. However, Tanten's inability to trust and his knowledge of Atlas's inability to remain loyal means Tanten only has one choice: Try to form an alliance with Syrenne Tyrney.

The purpose of this training will serve to form a bond between their team members. And give advantage to Tanten should plans go astray. Fighting another life force user without knowing their field of study can prove dangerous. Once he analyzes their abilities, not only will strategizing attacks and formations prove easier, but also planning an escape.

"They've gathered outside."

"Well. Why aren't they entering?" Tanten asks, his irritation evident in his tone. From having peered at his phone no more than a moment ago, he knows they're at least one minute late to the training session.

"I can sense locations, Mr. Flynn. Not read minds. Though I'll practice if that would be of more use to you."

"Settle down, Reece."

Tanten focuses his life force and feels the presences of those standing outside the door. "What's going on?" Tanten wonders as he attempts to identify the auras. He recognizes a few of which he enlisted, the other aura's he assumes belong to Syrenne's team. Three of the auras flare, wisps of life force escaping. Wrath, Tanten reads. Whatever was happening out of the gymnasium, matters were about to turn violent.

"Children," Tanten whispers as he jumps to his feet.

With his hand raised, Tanten thrusts the doors open with his life force. The team members congregate around the action. A fight is set to occur. But not between the teams. No. All three men with auras flaring are Tanten's recruits.

With a hint of embarrassment, but overwhelmed by his ferocity, Tanten marches to the middle of the circle. Those gathered sense him before they see him, parting a path as quickly as possible. His aura consumes him as if he himself were the lava spitting from a volcano. And not one wanted to be a witness to his explosive eruption. These members did not know what Tanten was capable of, all they knew is if Tanten ever divulged his abilities to them, it would be discovered only shortly before their deaths.

Tanten eyes the ruffians, whose testosterone levels prevent them from being fazed by Tanten's anger. Tanten understands they may be too dimwitted and arrogant to detect a danger even when it's right in front of them. Here perhaps they saw no problem. But, this fault would quickly get them killed on their mission. "If that's the case," Tanten thinks, observing the battle-hungry men, "they're no more than weak links."

With care to conceal his life force so the others may not know of his abilities, Tanten plunges tiny, serpentine wisps of life force into the concrete. They feel the friction of the lifeless stone but it does not slow them. The serpents slither up the legs of the aggressors who continue to circle one another, cursing and spitting at the ground. As the serpents attempt to strangle their targets, a woman makes her way to the center of the ring.

"Now boys," Syrenne says, touching one man's arm while offering a subtle caress to the other's neck. "Let's filter our aggression into our training." She glides over to the third man and slides a finger down his arm. The three men drop their fighting form and stand up straight, arms limp at their sides. Their glossy eyes gaze at whatever it is they picture standing in front of them. Syrenne continues. "I think it would be more beneficial for *our* team if we focus more on our training than fighting one another." The three men nod, appearing no more than robots, and walk inside of the gym.

"Let's start the warmups. Quickly, as we're already late," Syrenne instructs, tapping her watch.

The others filter into the gymnasium. Syrenne's team members bow their heads to their leader, marveling at her extraordinary ability in manipulation. Tanten's men mumble to one another, glaring at Syrenne Tyrney.

"I was gonna handle it, you know."

"Violence isn't always the answer, Tanten Flynn."

Tanten hears the mocking tone with which she says his name. And then he wonders if she saw his concealed life force serpents. She is a team lead, after all. His life force attack would not have fooled Atlas for one second. And judging by her manipulation of three decent life force users, despite their control of their auras, Tanten deems Syrenne to be far more capable than she lets on. He had not hoped for her, of all people, to catch a glimpse of his life force signature. But he felt it would not be of much worth anyways. Sculpting is not his field of choice, and perhaps it better that Syrenne thinks it is.

Syrenne, not finished with her correction of Tanten's actions continues.

"Just as killing your problems does not always equate to solving them. But I sense that's a common theme around here, whether it works or not."

"Why change a strategy that works?"

"Killing a person that disagrees with you is not a strategy. It's the equal of a temper tantrum. A strategy always has a backup plan. What if you don't succeed in killing your target on the first attempt?"

Tanten laughs, shaking his head in disbelief. He wonders how deep he's dug his own hole in wanting to form an alliance with this supposed Professional and Scholar. Doubting in his abilities only proves her lack of awareness, her capability of sizing up the enemy. If she could do so with no significant error, she would realize how strong he is. Or perhaps her own self-conceit stands in her way.

Syrenne senses his arrogance. Her internal temperature rises as her temper bubbles up within her core. Does he truly think so little of her? Or does he truly think so highly of himself? Syrenne creates her own strategies. She does her research. And she longs for the day that Tanten will cower down, asks for her help. The day his luck runs out.

"So, you've forgotten you are not always successful on the first attempt?" Syrenne asks as she focuses her eyes on Tanten's aura. He controls it well, appearing as a calm flame. She wishes to witness the transformation. When the flame explodes into a conflagration. And perhaps her wish draws nearer than she thinks.

Tanten's humor turns to fumes. It's no more than a game to her, he thinks. He should have assumed any alliance with two leaders in control to create complications. After years of being the sole authority of the Magistrate Association's Bounty Hunter Department, Tanten gravitates to being in charge. He feels he is the most capable to give orders. Leading groups to the criminals. Hunting his prey. Closing in when he wanted the kill to himself. Not many life force users escaped Tanten's pursuit. And only one succeeded time and time again.

"Tenebrant Mortu," Syrenne says aloud as the name echoes in Tanten's ears.

Tanten looks to Syrenne. He wonders who her contact is at the Magistrate Association, a part of him wishing to kill whoever betrayed that information. Only an insider would be able to tell Syrenne that the Council voted to assign Tanten to the case. Tanten's job as lead of the Department involved assigning trackers and enforcers to the tasks at hand. However, with the Mortu case, the

Magistrate Association deemed the necromancer to be a high-level threat. The Council ordered Tanten to capture Mortu, dead or alive.

Deciding not to allow Syrenne satisfaction in her discovery, Tanten adjusts his expression. His eyes and smile displaying amusement once more. He released a maniacal laugh. Syrenne and Reece shared in their shock, Reece wondering if his teacher had finally gone mad. Syrenne opens her mouth, searching for words to form a response, when Tanten steps in.

"Mortu? You honestly think I couldn't catch of convict like Mortu if I wanted to?" Tanten grits his teeth while expressing a smile. "What if I didn't want to catch Mortu? What if I wanted to see what the necromancer would do next? What would that make me?"

"A corrupt bounty hunter," Syrenne responds with a straight face, not impressed with the lie nor the truth, for both lead her to the same conclusion. She partnered with insanity. "Or just lazy. I can't decide."

Tanten grunts as he disapproves of the latter title. Not wishing to waste more time, the conversation turning dull anyways, Tanten glances towards the door.

"Alright. Let's see what your team's made of."

"With pleasure."

The three enter the gym, Reece surveying the area before shutting and locking the door. The teams had divided themselves into their cliques. They stretch their bodies, warm up their muscles, and open their pores so their life force may flow freely.

Syrenne focuses her life force to her eyes. She examines the auras of those in attendance. While those invited by Tanten control their life force and aura, not allowing it to slip from their grip, the rigidity of their auras suggest a haphazard use of life force and demonstrate their disapproval in forming an alliance. Ruffians off the street refuse to trust in one another let alone strangers who practice the art of life force. Syrenne turns her head to face her team. Not rigid but their auras tremble, revealing their lack of control. However, Syrenne prefers their auras to be flexible, not stiff. Control can be taught. Changing consistency of an aura, however, takes time.

Tanten observes, viewing the difference between the team from the opposite angle. On one side, experienced fighters. His side. On the other side, wannabe soldiers playing around rather than training. Her side. Though they may be more intelligent than his lot, their brains are the strongest, if not the only, muscle they possess. Even the man with the broadsword appears out of practice. Tanten chuckles. What a miserable lot, he thinks.

"You don't see potential?" Syrenne questions after hearing Tanten's amusement.

"And you do?" Tanten asks, shaking his head.

"Life force takes time to build up. You didn't possess that great storehouse in one day."

"No. But I also didn't expect to join a war and win after my first lesson."

"They may not be the strongest, but they're far from the weakest."

"We'll see about that."

Tanten walks toward his group, observing their forms and the fluidity of their life force. The only team member of his that impresses him being that of his squad leader, an ex-magistrate. His license had been revoked two years prior for crimes the Magistrate Association chose not to forgive. He spent two months in prison before his escape. They call him The Ventriloquist, but Tanten finds nicknames a nuisance. As if the real name shouldn't be enough to draw fear.

"Jensen," Tanten calls him to attention. The man's aura acts as a steady wind about him, his serious face always a bit grim. "How are the troops looking?"

Jensen scoffs and glances at the team. When his eyes return to Tanten, they show as little hope in them as Tanten had expected. Tanten scratches his head.

"Is it that bad? Not even one person we can hone to our needs?"

"Mr. Flynn, they have so many years of incorrect practice and form, it'll prove almost impossible to fix at this rate. They've shaped their skills to their liking, not in a way we can easily improve or alter."

"But it can be done?" Tanten asks, knowing his squad leader will answer to his liking. After all, Tanten chose him to train the troops for a reason.

"I'm working it little by little. Too much and they'll catch on. Little by little."

Tanten focuses his eyes on Jensen's hands, noticing strings of life force so fine only a person looking for them would see it. The strings connect to several members of Tanten's crew. Jensen studied Manipulation and Emission. His own life force travels along the strings to each member, slowly changing the composition of their life force. Little by little. Over time, the life force is taught how to move more freely, faster. However, Jensen's ability is not only used for good, the prison sentence speaking for itself.

"Do it as you feel you should. You know your limits. Just don't disappoint," Tanten says with firmly connected eyes. Jensen understands the threat and nods, going as far as to salute his boss. Tanten looks around at the other troops. "Very well. Continue with your training."

Tanten watches Syrenne's crew. She walks among them and teaches form, pointing to their pressure points to teach not only effective attacks but necessary defense. Tanten smirks as they spar one another with their newfound knowledge. Training by sparring is no more than child's play, Tanten thinks. If they wish to learn, have their bodies truly adapt to fighting, they would need to fight as if their life depended on it. Not hitting the air, kicking to throw about no more than wind. They would need to feel their fists hit bone, their legs pushing against the body's resistance. Their minds need to learn to watch for their opponent's movements as well as recognize an opening. When caught in the heat of battle, the mind forgets the most basic of senses. Their breathing must align with the rhythm of their punches. Their eyes must never look away. Their ears must be aware of all around them. Their life force mustn't run low, or it's game over.

Tanten's thoughts wander. He examines every person in the room, no aura compares to that of the Ulton girl. And to think Bysciw wants her dead. What a waste of talent that would have been. He wonders what it would take for one to reach that level. Focusing on Reece Horne, Tanten watches how his aura moves. The tight circles around his body make his aura, or storehouse of life force, appear small. But rather than show a quantity, his life force compacts more so than a common aura type. Like a thick cloud surrounding him, his aura maintains its shape. The constant flow of the current keeps his life force in constant movement. That is why some doubt in Reece's ability. They believe all auras act as common type auras, growing in size as the storehouse grows. But Tanten quickly learned that wasn't the case in his first lesson with Reece.

Reece practices a field outside of Tanten's own. And while Tanten never studied technomancy, working alongside Reece transformed his thoughts about the field. In any team, a technomancer should not only be sought after but acquired.

Tanten observes the others on his team, mentally checking off the different types of life force users in their midst. He could see several manipulators, especially on Syrenne's side. They tend to focus their life force solely in their hands. However, unlike the sculptors who focus their life force in the same way, manipulators hold their life force tight to their skin, not letting even a wisp drift away. Upon examination, Tanten realizes many of the ruffians he invited utilize their life force to enhance their physical strength and speed. As Tanten looks around, he fails to find the rarest and most difficult class of life force user. An Elemental. If he had seen one on the street, he would have been sure to recruit the person.

Tanten rubs his chin and debates whether he should train alongside his men. Syrenne demonstrates to her group how she uses her abilities, hoping they learn possible ways to utilize their own life force. She has determined the powers she wishes her team to have and train them to her liking. Her strategy.

Syrenne created a file on her tablet that includes every member of her team. The more she learns of their abilities, the more she deduces how best to train them. Not only this, but Syrenne and her squad leader develop specialized attacks and think of necessary abilities their team may need in their mission. They assign these abilities to their members and further work with them to perfect it. Syrenne's strategy involves creating the life force users she desires rather than searching for them.

Tanten shakes his head at the idea. No human can coerce the life force of a person to act in a specific way. It moves as it pleases. Only that person will know how to best utilize it, and the special abilities will develop naturally. Many have tried to use a strategy much like Syrenne's. They call upon the strongest they know, decide who will utilize which class, and their plans always fail. One does not simply change their class of life force, not after years of study in one field. To become proficient, one must devote themselves to the field for several years. The desire to switch from one to the next will not make it so. Tanten can only think of one person who has ever succeeded in shaping others to their desire. Simply thinking the name puts a sour taste in his mouth. Atlas Lurio.

Tanten stands back and watches. Syrenne instructs all with the utilization of their abilities with the exception of the young woman at her side. She appears Botalia's age, her aura flowing like a river, calm and steady. Tanten focuses in, unable to identify her ability. The young woman notices Tanten analyzing her aura and glares at him before returning her attention to Syrenne. He figures the woman must be attempting to study multiple fields, the reason her life force flows so freely. Tanten wonders what Syrenne's plan is for her.

After all have viewed their file and begin to practice their abilities, Syrenne makes her way to Tanten. Her eyes glow with resolve and accomplishment. Tanten can do no more than shake his head.

"I would say all is going according to plan. At least on my side," Syrenne grins as she takes a place at his side.

"It doesn't matter what you think. You can think they're strong and talented, hell, you can think their demigods. But until we see them in battle, our thoughts are best kept to ourselves."

"Always so pessimistic? You don't wish to have faith in this team for even a moment, do you?"

"When and who."

"What are you talking about?"

"When," Tanten sticks up his pointer finger, "and who," he sticks up another finger. "Those are the two remaining questions. When will we need to be ready? When will it all begin? And who. Who exactly are we up against? And who among us will be ready when the time comes?"

"You and I have seen Bysciw's men. And I've seen what the Crusaders have to offer. We may be outnumbered but there is no way we are outmatched."

"And Atlas's men. What of them?" Tanten presses. While at the base, he rarely saw any of Atlas's team members. He doesn't know the numbers let alone their capabilities. And Tanten understands there is no way Atlas will stand along Bysciw until the final battle. He will have killed him before then. Tanten knows of Atlas's repulsion of Bysciw, but Atlas is far from unintelligent. Tanten finds Atlas irritating but cannot deny his genius. Tanten deduces it's of no coincidence that he failed to get a scope of Atlas's team. Atlas likes to be five steps ahead. Always planning. Always plotting.

"To be honest, I'm not sure. I don't recall ever meeting one of his team," Syrenne laughs, the thought amusing her. "I wonder what-"

Her hand flies up, swatting at something in front of her. Tanten blinks and looks around, admitting to the distraction of his thoughts. When Syrenne brings her hand up, a blade sticks from her fingers. No more than a trickle of blood appears where the blade sliced her as she caught it. Syrenne's eyes scan the room and stop on two members from Tanten's team. Tanten recognizes one of the members as an aggressor from earlier.

Syrenne flips the blade, the handle rests in her palm. Tanten sees the fire in her eyes and the hurricane shape her aura takes on. Her facial expression serious. Her muscles relaxed. But Tanten senses her rage. And though he would not admit it, her control of her life force impresses him. Not the tiniest bit escapes from her aura despite the whipping motions and speeds at which it travels. As she picks up her foot, Tanten throws his hand in front of her.

"Don't worry. I'll handle it."

She pauses and allows him the honor.

Tanten walks over to the ruffian. What a pain it is trying to train wild animals, he thinks. The friend of the aggressor worriedly glances at Tanten, warning his friend to back down. But the aggressor remains stolid, his fearless smile unwavering. His eyes attempt to pierce Tanten's aural armor. Tanten smirks, knowing the man wouldn't leave as much as a scratch if he tried.

"What's the problem here?" Tanten asks. Though his voice is low, all in the gymnasium shift their eyes, trying to get a peek of the action. Even those on Syrenne's team understand Tanten's temper. They hope to witness what the Professional and ex-Council Member is capable of.

The aggressor focuses his eyes on Tanten, appearing as if reading his aura. When his own aura doesn't change, Tanten assumes the aggressor was attempting to do no more than intimidate. For if the aggressor examined Tanten's aura, he would have shrunk back in defeat.

"Problem? There ain't one, boss," the ruffian answers with a smirk.

His gruff voice and stiff posture don't scare Tanten for a second. Tanten analyzes the man's aura. The ruffian focuses much of his life force in his arms and legs. He uses his life force to enhance his physical strength, Tanten deduces. The Professional lets out a disappointed breath, having thought he had better foresight in choosing team members. Tanten examines the ruffian once more and scratches his head.

"Well," Tanten directs at the man. He then points to the gym equipment and a punching bag. "Let's see what you've got."

The ruffian smiles, glad he's been given permission to use his full force. Tanten raises his eyebrows at the man's confidence.

"Grab some weights! Grab some weights!" the man yells to his friends as he walks over to the bench. Tanten squints at the man, noticing the bar is already full of weights. It had to weigh in the vicinity of seven hundred pounds. Tanten laughs.

His friends carry the weighted discs over, some with more difficulty than others.

"Clay, sticky 'em up."

The friend who had previously stood beside him, places his palms together. He concentrates his life force into his hands and slowly separates his palms. The life force hangs in between like a web. His hands shake as he moves to transfer his life force to the discs. Tanten shakes his head, noticing the man's nerves. The sticky life force slides onto the surface of the disc. A different ruffian grabs the ready discs and connects them to the bar. Tanten's expression grows serious, as he realizes the weight had surpassed one thousand pounds.

When they finish adding weights, the aggressor slides himself onto the bench. The bar itself appears twisted from such a weight. But the ruffian is not intimidated. Nor does he doubt his ability, as if he's done this time and time again. He grabs a hold of the bar, focusing his life force into his arms, and pushes up. The bar lifts from the holders. Many in the room gasp at such a show of strength. Tanten rolls his eyes. He glances at Syrenne, who also does not appear impressed nor has her anger dwindled.

The man lowers the bar back into position and rises from the bench, high-fiving his friends in celebration. His large smile expresses his assurance that he has impressed the Professional. The ruffian is certain if Tanten was not intimidated by his presence before that he would be now. However, when he looks at Tanten's face, he is shocked to see that Tanten appears bored. The ruffian finds himself getting angry.

"Is that really all you've got?" Tanten asks, hoping in his anger that the ruffian will show him something more. And the ruffian doesn't disappoint. He growls at the Professional and walks over to stone wall. Tanten tilts his head, knowing that the man is not about to attempt what he thinks. After all, this gymnasium had been built as a disaster shelter. Built by the greatest engineers the Magistrate Association had to offer to withstand any disaster, whether natural or man-made. Tanten grimaces, remembering that the plaque to honor the facility was marked with the name Ulton. The man stares at the wall, and Tanten knows at this point his words will not convince him. Even if the results are embarrassing for the ruffian, he will try anyways.

The ruffian closes his eyes in concentration. Once he focuses every ounce of life force into his fists, his eyes bolt open to lock onto his target. With a loud roar, he pulls back his arm and thrusts his fist into the wall. A sound similar to thunder rings out in the gym. Dust falls from the ceiling. But, as he pulls his hand away from the wall, no more than a small crack is left where he expected the damage to cause a cave in.

His shocked face offers little satisfaction in comparison to the breakdown Tanten hoped to see. Tanten starts to applaud the man, no one else joining in. Tanten sees the man used up all the life force in his storehouse and with such little results. Tanten stands next to the man and places a hand on his shoulder. The ruffian avoids eye contact, the feeling of defeat consuming his pride.

"I'm surprised you did that much damage," Tanten whispers, only the two and Reece, who has extraordinary hearing, grasp the words. Tanten shares a smile, and the man returns a gracious grin at the compliment from his boss. But his grin fades as the feeling of shock returns to him once more. His hand reaches for his neck, in it, a blade. Syrenne looks at her hands, having thought she had not loosened her grip. The blade was gone. The blood pours from the man's neck, the injury to prove fatal. As the ruffian falls to the ground, taking his last breath, Tanten bends down and whispers in his ear. "I would've practiced more religion than life force if I were you. At least one of them would have benefited you."

Tanten stands and wipes his hands on his pants. Those in the gym return to their practice, scared of what Tanten may say if they appear weak or distracted. Reece stares at his teacher. No one had even noticed that the Professional had attached his life force to the blade, leaving the string from his fingertip intact the whole time the ruffian tried to show off. No one saw the attack coming. Reece grins. He has much to learn from his teacher.

Tanten passes by Syrenne as he walks out of the gym, "Strategy. That's what it is. It's a strategy. And it works. Research that if you will."

Chapter Twelve

Tanten stands atop the tall building watching the city awaken. Though all business is conducted in the basement of the base, the other floors provide temporary housing for the team members. Many of the higher floors allow the members to keep look out, the best spot being on the roof.

Tanten enjoys the view from the roof. He thinks of it as observing the ants as they go about their cyclical life, performing work that makes them no more than robots. Often, he feels this is the true distance between himself and others. Sometimes, Tanten wishes the ants will fry in the sun or collapse of exhaustion. Other times, he wishes to be the one to squish the ants. Or perhaps their existence is far too insignificant to matter.

The door to the roof opens. Tanten turns to see Atlas, releases a disappointed exhale, and resumes his observation of the ants. Atlas walks over to him.

"You'll never believe who I came across a few nights back," Atlas grins at Tanten, but Tanten avoids eye contact, acting as though he ignores him. Atlas grows frustrated as Tanten acts uninterested in his news, but he decides to continue, knowing he'll catch Tanten's attention soon enough.

"Your son."

Tanten's eyes widen despite trying to restrict all expression. Atlas chuckles.

"I saw your son. Guess who was with him."

Atlas pauses, but Tanten refuses to move. Atlas glares at him.

"Tenebrant Mortu."

Tanten feels a heated sensation within him. He doesn't know whether to believe Atlas, but he knows Atlas has no reason to lie to him. Atlas would not benefit from creating a tale just to frustrate him. Tanten releases a nervous laugh.

"You're bluffing," he responds. Atlas continues to glare, irritated by the accusation of lying, especially from the likes of Tanten.

"Unfortunately, I'm not. Your son is in the hands of a thieving, murdering convict. How does that make you feel?" Atlas expresses a concerned face, though internally amused. Tanten realizes Atlas's desire to provoke him. However, Tanten returns to his calm and cool demeanor, whether genuinely or forcibly is yet to be determined.

"It's of no significance," Tanten answers. "The boy can choose his own path. Where he ends up is no concern of mine."

"But you sent him to Botalia as a distraction, correct? Unless you truly meant for him to learn from her," Atlas responds. Atlas knows he has the upper hand in this battle of self-control. He contains a massive amount of intelligence unknown to Tanten, not to mention his connections with individuals and organizations.

"I felt bad for her was all," Tanten replies, still avoiding eye contact. He peers down on the ants below, crushing each of them in his mind to release his hostility towards Atlas.

"You pitied her?" Atlas laughs. "You're the one who wanted to run experiments and tests on her." He chuckles again. "Your narrow range of emotions amuses me."

Tanten doesn't respond. Atlas sighs, bored by the stagnation of their conversation. Tanten escaped the conversation and returned to his imaginary world. Atlas steps toward the door but stops short.

"I almost forgot, I felt another's presence as well, a strong presence, quite threatening. Though, I could have been imagining things. Ciao."

Atlas leaves the rooftop. Tanten looks up to the sky and sighs.

Atlas descends the stairs and exits onto the top floor. He walks past the man standing watch, greeting him with a wave and a tip of his head. Atlas enters the elevator and pushes the button for the ground level. As he stands against the back wall, he closes his eyes and sighs.

After seeing Koepp at the assassination location, many questions spiral in his head: "Why was Little Flynn there?" and "What does Tenebrant have to do with Little Flynn?" Atlas hadn't the slightest idea of why the two were there, but what shocked him even more so was Botalia's, or what he assumed to be Botalia's, presence. Atlas wonders, "Is Botalia manipulating Little Flynn and Tenebrant, or has she somehow formed an alliance with them? She knew if she were to show her face, I would have recognized her. I am no threat, but perhaps the threat of her exile and the punishment should she break it continues to scare her. Hmm..."

Atlas looks up as he feels the elevator stop. Floor 27. A broad-shouldered, intimidating man steps into the elevator. Atlas grins as he enters. The man has messy, blond hair, a lazy eye, and tattooed arms. His appearance makes him look tough, but his intelligence is far superior to his combat skills. This is why Atlas chose him as general of his troops.

"Are the squads training hard, Keniph?" Atlas questions. Keniph leans against the wall next to Atlas as the doors of the elevator slide shut and withdraws a cigar from his jacket's chest pocket. The roll is labeled with the stamp of a famous, organic tobacco farm in Divesregio. The term 'organic' makes its origins seem innocent. But the youthful faces of the laborers say otherwise. Keniph offers a cigar to Atlas who turns it down.

"They're quite strong, Red. You really know how to pick 'em." Atlas rolls his eyes, as he's never liked the nickname derived from his hair color, but Keniph insists on using nicknames with everyone. "And I told you to use my alias if anyone is within a one-hundred-yard radius of us." The elevator halts on the ground floor. The two begin their walk out of the building.

"I knew they all had potential. Like diamonds in the rough, they just needed polished. How are their special abilities developing?" Atlas asks. He acknowledges the members in the lobby with head tilts and grins. Keniph searches his person for his lighter.

"They're certainly adept. I've got to say, with their mastered skills and teamwork, they'll be near unbeatable."

They exit the front door and stand outside of the building. Keniph lights his cigar, inhales, then lets out a puff of smoke. He sighs. Atlas looks around and Keniph continues.

"I was talkin' with Tanten's squad's lead, and he says their troops refuse to work with one another. Tanten picked skilled individuals sure, but their skills were already polished to their own standards. They have no desire to work with one another or let some guy boss 'em around. They're a rowdy bunch, thinking they'll never lose so they don't need to practice."

Atlas chuckles, "Seems they exemplify Tanten perfectly." A silence. "Time to head out. Don't expect to see me for a few days."

"Business?"

"Business," Atlas responds. "Keep up the good work. If anything happens, don't hesitate to contact me."

"Sir, yes sir, Red," Keniph places his large hand on Atlas's shoulder. "Don't get yerself into any trouble."

"Sometimes, it takes trouble to stop trouble," Atlas replies. Keniph laughs, a large puff of smoke issuing forth. "Stand tall, brother."

Keniph tilts his head and Atlas walks away. As he heads down the street, he feels the eyes of someone watching him, glaring at him with hostile thoughts. He laughs, knowing one day Tanten will regret his own disrespect and arrogance.

Atlas walks down the street and steps into a building with barred windows and a weather-torn awning. As he opens the door, the bell rings. An old, white-haired woman with a tan knit shawl enters the room. A shrunken head bobble swings from a chain wrapped around her ear. She steps behind the counter and brushes away any dust with her hands.

"Ah, Atlas... What are you up to this morning?" The woman asks in a raspy voice.

"Just a withdrawal, Lady Lucrum," Atlas responds, by force of habit he checks behind him before approaching the counter. He slips a paper onto its surface, and she grabs it.

"Another job, eh?" she questions, smiling.

Lady Lucrum hobbles into the back room and rummages around. Atlas surveys the area. He notices stacks of cigar boxes behind the counter, bags of a sage-colored powder piled at their side. He shakes his head and reveals a mischievous grin. Lady Lucrum stumbles to the counter and follows the direction of his eyes to her stash. Her grin mirrors his own. She slides him the money.

"Busy boy. Do you want some snacks for the road?"

"No, thanks. Besides, I wouldn't eat them for the fear of being poisoned," Atlas replies.

Lady Lucrum laughs until a nasty cough takes over.

"There should be two other clients stopping by today. What they owe is written on the back of that paper, no haggling. If any conflicts arise, threaten them with the terms of the contract." He looks at the money and puts it into his pocket. "Thank you, Lady Lucrum." Atlas heads out, the bell ringing as he exits.

"You keep me young, Atlas," she shouts after him.

Atlas pulls out his phone and checks the time. He sighs. He has ten minutes to get to the airship port located fifteen minutes away. As he rounds the corner, Atlas lets out an irritated exhale. The daily morning traffic jam. Walking is definitely the faster option.

Atlas focuses his eyes in front of him. His life force crawls over every pore, consuming him like a gentle, restrictive tornado. The pedestrians on the sidewalk blur past him, the air the only force of resistance as he moves forward. To him, everyone appears to be moving along in slow motion, and he simply rushes past them, despite walking at his usual pace.

He arrives at the airship port and checks the time.

"Hmm... I still have seven minutes. Not bad. Perhaps I'll get myself a snack."

When the airship lands at its destination, Atlas sighs a breath of relief. "Right on time." He looks around, expecting someone to be waiting for him. Near the entrance to the port, Atlas finds the one he seeks.

Sitting on a bench reading his book, his short, black hair and zipper hoodie give him quite the commonplace appearance, but Atlas recognizes him straight away. As he moves closer, Atlas realizes the book is about assassination techniques. He sits next to the young man.

"Clever, reading a book in public about a forbidden profession," Atlas says. The boy remains expressionless and closes his book.

"It's a classic. I've read it at least six times before," the boy replies. He turns to Atlas. "Shall we head to the manor, Mr. Lurio?"

"Just Atlas works. And yes, lead the way, Naht," responds Atlas. The pair stand.

"Yes, sir," Naht answers, leading Atlas to the vehicle which will take the two to the manor. When they arrive at the luxurious black car, Naht asks, "You know procedure I presume?"

"Yes," Atlas chuckles. Two guards step out of the vehicle, one from the passenger seat and one from the driver seat. Atlas holds up one of his hands to stop the one man from approaching him.

"I won't resist," Atlas states. Atlas closes his eyes. The other man focuses his life force in his hands and transmutes it into an opaque substance. He stretches his life force about Atlas's face. As Naht watches the procedure, he recalls his similar experience with Botalia. The substance allows for Atlas to be breathe, but it prohibits him from seeing or hearing anything that may reveal the external environment. Any visitor to the Kufuta residence must undergo such procedure for revealing the location of an assassin's training ground and homestead is the number one sin of being an assassin.

When they arrive at the manor, the man releases his life force from around Atlas's face. Atlas tips his head in thanks and follows Naht around a marble fountain to the front door. A residential butler opens the door and welcomes the two inside. Elegant tapestries line the exquisite dark oak walls. A great, blood diamond chandelier hangs from the ceiling, and a portrait of the founder of Kufuta Manor School for Assassins, the great grandfather of Naht, Nix, and Neja hangs on the wall in the foyer.

Atlas steps through the door and onto the lush, crimson red carpet of the hall. A second butler leads them down the corridor and to the family dining room where their meeting is to occur.

The two sit near the head of the table, cups of tea set in front of them. They sit in silence for five minutes until they hear the footsteps of another approaching. A middle-aged man with long, black hair and burgundy tailcoat enters the rooms. The majestic and kingly Aurelius Kufuta. Atlas and Naht stand as Kufuta and the butler cross the room. The butler pulls out his chair at the head of the table and Aurelius Kufuta sits. He nods and Atlas and Naht follow suit. He takes a sip of his tea and turns to Atlas.

"Atlas. It's a pleasure to meet with you once again," Kufuta says. His manner appears solemn, opposite of his usually cheerful self, Atlas thinks. Kufuta folds his hands, elbows on the table, and continues. "Before we start the meeting, there is a bit of business which concerns me. Naht tells me you traveled to the assassination site a few nights ago with the head of the target group. Is this true?"

"Yes, that is correct," Atlas replies. His heart rate slowly accelerates. He wonders, "Did someone else see what occurred?" Atlas glimpses at Naht who sits straight up with his eyes closed.

"Did you stay until the mission's completion?" Kufuta's stern face expresses his seriousness.

"Yes, sir," Atlas responds. Naht sighs and Kufuta closes his eyes. He leans back in his chair and wipes at his brow.

"Is something wrong?"

"Nix never returned."

Atlas squints, attempting to hide the intrigue in his eyes, and picks up his teacup. He examines Kufuta from over the brim of the cup. Never has Atlas seen Aurelius Kufuta as anyone more than a head which supervises his assassins. Killing is in his blood, it's what he lives for. Assassination is what it means to share blood with the Kufuta clan. Devoting one's livelihood to killing means sacrificing their own life and humanity. Aurelius Kufuta knew this, yet feels concern when his own son doesn't return. Is the concern based in being his father or being his boss? A concern for himself and his business or Nix? Atlas cannot decide as he analyzes Aurelius Kufuta.

Kufuta continues. "We'll move on, but if you have any information regarding Nix's whereabouts, it would be greatly appreciated. I'm not asking you as my client, but as a noble ally."

"I wouldn't think of concealing any information I have," Atlas responds. He vehemently exhales. "Unfortunately, I know nothing of his location." The three of them look from one to another and simultaneously drink their tea.

"Onto business," Aurelius Kufuta resumes his folded hands position. Atlas pushes the money to him. Kufuta nods and the butler steps forward, placing the money on a silver platter before concealing it with a lid and exiting the room. After hearing the door close behind the butler, Atlas slides a list towards Kufuta. He examines the list of names, nodding, and hands off the paper to Naht.

"Looks like you want to add fuel to the fire," Kufuta laughs. "Are these orders direct from Bysciw? Or orders from elsewhere?"

Atlas laughs. "No orders from anyone. Simply looking to the future."

"The future? With the dates you requested for each target, the world will be in total war in four days' time. So Bysciw doesn't know of these plans?" Kufuta questions, curiosity and excitement evident in his voice. Atlas chuckles.

"Serving Bysciw was mere child's play. He chooses Tanten as his second, despite Tanten's arrogance and lack of respect towards everyone. Neither of them take our mission seriously, and if they think they do, they lack all intelligence and abilities for being successful," Atlas states. Naht looks up from the paper. Hostility glows in Atlas's eyes when he mentions Tanten and Bysciw.

"So, you intend to lead your team to victory?" Kufuta asks. Atlas takes the last sip of tea and shrugs. "Well... Looking at your list, it won't be easy, especially if Nix doesn't return. However, we will assist you in your plans. As our alliance stands, I expect a portion of wealth from your victory," Kufuta locks eyes with Atlas, "for I do not expect you will fail."

"I won't accept failure, especially at the hands of Bysciw or Tanten," Atlas responds. Aurelius Kufuta stands.

"I expect you're a busy man," he begins. "I'll let you leave, so you may prepare. Naht, fit our assassins to their tasks. I won't allow another failure for our loyal client."

"Yes, father," Naht replies, bowing his head and exiting the room.

"As always, I am honored to call you an ally," Atlas directs at Kufuta. They shake hands and a butler leads Atlas from the room. Aurelius Kufuta watches as he leaves, laughing all the while.

When Atlas arrives at the port, he looks at his phone. One message. The voicemail is from Keniph.

"Hey Red, it's Jet. Great news. Targe was able to hold her life force for more than ten minutes today without shaking. Her conjured wall has about a twenty-five-foot radius from her body and is indestructible. We shot multiple forms of explosives and life force projectiles at it, but nothing could break it. You said that was our signal the time is approaching. Just send over orders. We'll keep training until then."

Atlas laughs. "No one will be able to stop us... I almost feel sorry they've wasted so much time and energy simply to be defeated." Atlas looks to the sky and sighs. "History is made by the victors and our names will live in glory for eternity. Tanten and Bysciw... you played well, unfortunately, I was your opponent." Atlas calls Keniph.

"Hello?" Keniph answers.

"It's Red. Tell the troops to move out at six this evening. We'll meet up in the predetermined location. When you're leaving, cause some chaos however you see fit, a coup of sorts. I'll meet you all tomorrow morning," Atlas commands.

"Sir, yes sir," Keniph replies.

"And Jet, don't get caught by the enemy."

"You got it, Red."

"Stand tall, brother."

Atlas hangs up the phone and returns it to his pocket. His next order of business presently seems irrelevant. "Perhaps a visit to the Magistrate Association?" he thinks. He shakes his head and looks around, observing the people as they pass. He thinks of Tanten and the joy he will feel when he sees the look of defeat upon Tanten's face. Atlas isn't material in nature, he does not desire what it is the group seeks. He never wished to win the race, he simply didn't want to lose. But the prize for winning, the failure of the others, proves irresistible to him. Atlas chuckles.

"Match and set."

Chapter Thirteen

Tanten sits in the basement of the base, playing poker with a few of the team members. Normally after losing several times, Tanten grows irritated and storms away. However, on this particular evening it seemed his luck had changed. He internally grins as he looks at his current hand and board, three-of-a-kind kings. He raises the bet, sliding his chips into the center of the table. A queen and a ten is drawn to the board. Tanten eyes his opponents and feels confident.

At that moment, one of the squad leaders from Syrenne's team rushes into the room toward Tanten, holding a phone out.

"Mr. Flynn, Syrenne requests you speak with her," the squad leader shouts out, panic in his voice. Tanten holds up his left hand, his right hand almost pushing his cards into the table.

"Wait a moment," Tanten replies.

"But, sir, she-"

"Wait for the end of the hand," Tanten orders.

The squad leader expresses his shock at Tanten for being so careless. Tanten doesn't break face but keeps his head in the game until the hand is completely played out.

"Are we ready?"

The men sitting around nod and reveal their hands. Tanten clenches his jaw as he sees the hand that beats his kings: A straight flush consisting of king, queen, jack, ten, and nine. Tanten throws his hand to the table in frustration and stands. He extends his right hand, glaring at the squad leader for his slow reaction time. Tanten takes the phone up to his ear.

"What do you want?" he questions, already impatient.

"Who did it!?!" Syrenne screams. Tanten moves the phone from his ear and glares at it. "It's one of you, I know it's one of you! Is Bysciw there? Did he order this?" Her voice fades as she talks to those in the background, "It should be in the back room, next to the boxes... Call him immediately." She returns to screaming at Tanten. "It's too early! What is Bysciw thinking!?!" The alert in her tone and the commotion in the background lead Tanten to deduce they are in a high emergency state at the moment. Her questions confuse Tanten as he tries to reason through them.

"First off," Tanten begins, "calm down. I can't understand you when you're yelling questions at me. Second, Bysciw's not here. He hasn't been since before I met you. Third, where are you? What's going on?"

"I'm at the Crusader's base. They're running around in a panic upstairs. The elite squadron, the Crusader's first regiment, was brutally slaughtered not long ago. We're guessing it happened around 5:30, but we're just estimating," Syrenne states. Her voice starts to calm, but the racket in the background remains constant. "One of the members stumbled into the room, the entire squad lying in a pool of their own blood."

"Assassins?" Tanten asks.

"I assume that's the case. Whoever it was entered their quarters and killed the bulk of them without being seen or heard. I can only think whoever did so was a professional hunter of sorts. Not necessarily a magistrate, but definitely capable of life force manipulation," Syrenne sighs. "The chaos has caused the leader to grow discontent. If someone knows this location, the Crusaders are looking to move out right away."

"But we're not ready," Tanten responds. "Is there any way to stall them?"

"They're all in a panic. There's no way for me to reason with any of them, even the leader. Until we find the culprit, I'm sure tensions will remain high," Syrenne replies. "Who else could possibly know of the location, let alone the existence, of the Crusaders and desire their demise?"

"Stop talking for a moment," Tanten orders. He taps at his temples and remembers squashing the ants, and finally squashing –

"Damn ant... Syrenne," Tanten begins. "I think I know who it is."

"Who?" Syrenne begs.

"Atl-"

Tanten falls to the ground as an explosive force pushes him down. The phone slips out of his hand. Several explosions occur. Smoke fills the room. Gunshots bang around him and the screams of the team members. Tanten focuses his eyes and sees the outline of everyone's aura in the room. As members die, their aura fades away.

He ducks behind the chair, staying out of the way of the attacking force. Tanten extends his right arm and supports it from beneath with his left arm. He focuses his aura to his right hand and projects his life force toward the group of belligerents. His life force takes the form of a missile, a strong concentration of power within them. It stops short of hitting any of the attackers, the explosion small and contained.

"A shield?" Tanten questions.

The group moves toward the stairwell.

"They're leaving? But that means they've gotten what they want or accomplished what it is they set out to do... A betrayal?" Tanten's eyes widen as the name reaches his lips once more. "Of course. He doesn't need assassins to trek here when the weapons are readily available. Atlas..."

Tanten leaps from his position as a body of one of the members is thrown in his direction. He recognizes the burnt face of his squad leader. Rage fills him.

When the metal door to the stairs opens, the smoke filters from the room. Tanten rises and assesses the damage on an instant. Ten dead and twenty-seven injured. Some others move from their hiding places, looking around and rushing to the aid of their friends. Screaming and explosions can be heard coming from the ground level above them. Fear and dread fills the air. Tanten's anger takes over and he rushes up the stairs, skipping steps in between his long strides.

All those who were standing guard or relaxing on the ground floor lay in a bloody mess. Tanten shakes his head in disbelief. He creeps toward the entrance and peeks around door into the outside. All appears normal. Quiet. A dreadful tranquility. The regularity of the outside environment adds to his rage. His breaths become short and shallow. Losing sight of the traitors he never fully saw in the first place irritates him to no end. For a mere second, he feels weak.

"I don't need to see them... They were Atlas's men, I know it... They did this, traitors, vermin..." Tanten shakes his head, scratching and pulling at his hair. "Scum, the lowest form... Atlas and the rest of them." Tanten reenters the building and heads for the stairwell. "I won't let you win, Atlas. I will defeat you. With my own hands I will squash you from existence."

Tanten descends the stairwell and sees the injured being attended to by the trained medics, a few of which survived. Tanten looks at his watch. Quarter after six. He's paralyzed. Stunned. Unaware of their next move. Atlas knew they didn't have a plan yet. Reece Horne walks over to Tanten, a cut on his face where a life force arrow narrowly missed him.

"We lost, boss," Reece says to Tanten. Tanten nods.

"I know," Tanten squints and focuses on the floor. "Gather the remainder of the troops. Not just ours, but Syrenne's and Bysciw's forces as well. We need to examine our strengths and weaknesses and come up with a strategy. The belligerents were probably only the beginning. I expect absolute chaos by midnight, and not just for us. Go."

"Yes, Mr. Flynn," Reece salutes and heads off to inform the survivors of the plan. Tanten knows he's second-in-command, but he also knows not many of Syrenne's and Bysciw's forces respect him, despite having tried to ally with Syrenne. If they don't listen to him, he risks Syrenne's and Bysciw's rage, especially if assassins turn up like they did with the Crusaders. Tanten predicts this scenario is highly probable.

"Total war is coming. No doubt Atlas deployed multiple groups of assassins. Some to distract the Crusaders and our own group, but also others to fuel the civil war within the Magistrate Association, the Schism. He's no longer a simple spectator in this game. Atlas is a contender." Tanten chuckles. "Atlas is too naïve. He doesn't know what my team is capable of."

Reece returns, notepad in hand. Others march into the room, naturally dividing themselves into their leader's group. Tanten's forces stand before him. Reece hands him the notepad. Tanten examines the numbers he has to work with:

Flynn Troops: 25
Lurio Troops: 0?
Tyrney Troops: 16
Bysciw Troops: 32
Total Troops: 73

TANTEN CHUCKLES AS the numbers affirm his belief of Atlas's forces being responsible for the attack. He realizes the numbers include the injured so, subtracting from the given number, the present total of usable troops drops to forty-six. Tanten sighs.

"We're waiting for your orders, Mr. Flynn," Reece states.

Tanten thinks through the possibilities. The most difficult factors to surpass are Atlas's knowledge as to the whereabouts of their other bases and the strength of each of their members, seeing as Atlas maintained the records for all on the team. With Bysciw and Syrenne absent, Tanten remains unsure as to what moves he should make, despite knowing which moves he would like to make.

"Listen up!" Tanten shouts, the crowd silencing themselves. "I'm aware not all of your loyalties lie with me, but, for the sake of our mission, I ask for each of your cooperation."

"And what's your strategy, Commander Flynn," a man in the crowd shouts sarcastically. The others in his group laugh.

"You're one of Bysciw's men, aren't you?" Tanten asks.

"Yea and we won't take orders from the likes of you," the man replies. The others in the group shout in agreement of his statement.

"Please be patient!" Tanten yells, nearing the limits of his own patience. "I talked to Syrenne before our base was attacked. She said the Crusaders also faced an attack, however, they experienced an entire regiment wiped out by assassins. Our forces are a target. That is certain. Whether it be by the will of Atlas or another is insignificant."

"Insignificant!" another of Bysciw's members screams. "Atlas knows everything about us!" The tension amongst the crowd increases. The team members suspiciously look from one group to another, distrusting of anyone outside of their forces.

"How do you plan to contact Bysciw about the change in location? Or about any of this?" Bysciw's man asks.

"Silence!" Tanten shouts, his rage grows at receiving disrespect from the troops despite being the second. "I'm not about to fight with any of you. If you wish to stay here, I won't argue. I expect those who trust in me to follow my orders without question. If there is any doubt in your hearts about my intent, don't follow me. I'll give you all five minutes to decide where your loyalty lies but know one thing. Whatever happens next will be hell. Our mission began when we were attacked and betrayed by our own. That was the first of many trials to come. You all knew the nightmares that awaited you when asked to join our forces. Five minutes. If you can't decide your path in five minutes, we don't want you. Anyone who wants to walk out now can, I won't stop you."

A thick silence fills the room. They stare at Tanten, awe and shock on their faces. After a few seconds pass, some of Bysciw's men walk toward the chairs and sit themselves down. Tanten closes his eyes yet feels relief knowing he and Bysciw can fight as enemies when the time comes.

The room segregates into the predetermined forces, Bysciw's creating distance between themselves and the others, Tanten's standing fast, ready to follow their leader, and Syrenne's look from one another in confusion about what they should do. After the first walks over to join Tanten's group, many of the others follow with two walking opposite to sit with Bysciw's men.

Two minutes have passed and as Tanten opens his eyes, he notices the resolve on each of their faces. Twenty-three soldiers stand before Tanten, ready for war. Tanten grins.

"Let's move out," Tanten commands his troops. "We'll leave in small groups and head in different directions. We'll meet up at the large rock in the glade outside of town. From there we'll decide our next move. Try not to draw too much attention and remain alert. Assassins may be waiting for us outside, so never let your guard down. Our mission has started. Grab your belongings and form your groups."

Tanten turns to Syrenne's team members. "Once we arrive, we'll try to contact Syrenne. I don't intend to abandon her, for your sake." They nod at him in thanks. "Get to it."

The members head up the stairs to pack their belongings. Tanten waits for the last one to enter the stairwell before he follows. As he exits, Bysciw's men glare at his back, and Tanten cannot help but laugh. "In due time, they'll be sorry they chose Bysciw. For soon, Bysciw will be dead, and I'll hold the power in my hands."

Tanten stands in the lobby. The room slowly fills with the team members ready to move out. Tanten sends them out in groups of four. He senses the nerves in each of them, but he can also feel their excitement.

"The situation is not ideal," Tanten thinks, "but that's half the fun of this game: utilizing half-configured strategies and mediocre troops. Atlas, you know how to entertain me. The real treasure may be the look on your face when you're begging me to kill you."

The last group forms in the lobby. Tanten joins the group of three, and they head out. Tanten appears confident and excited. He checks his watch. 7:42.

Upon exiting the building, Tanten feels no eyes examining him. A good sign. This means that Bysciw's men have chosen to let them leave without the paranoia of being followed at a later point. Tanten listens carefully, taking in the sounds of the environment around him. He hears nothing out of the ordinary. The evening seems suspiciously normal. This realization creates stress within Tanten.

As the group rounds the corner, they notice a crowd of people gathered around an electronics shop. The televisions in the window are tuned into the news. The group stops in hope of a look at what is causing the crowd. The headline reads: Breaking News, Separatist Groups Fight Near Magistrate Association. The footage on the screen shows fire and explosions. Focusing his eyes, Tanten can see the use of life force causing plenty of damage. Bodies lay on the ground. The scrolling news line at the bottom of the screen reads, "Vice President of Magistrate Association, Azriel Vayl, states Association is working hard to calm the aggressors. Council Member and Lead of the Magistrate's International Security Forces, Rhys Champney, has stationed troops around Association building and in streets surrounding the battle that rages."

Tanten shakes his head as he watches the chaos unfold. He starts to walk again, the three others following him.

"Looks like the Schism has begun," Reece says, as his eyes watch the unfolding chaos on the screen.

"The Schism began long ago. People knew it existed yet ignored its ever-growing presence. This is no longer simply a schism, but a civil war tearing the Magistrate Association apart," Tanten responds. "But that is no concern of ours. We need not get distracted from our mission."

"Atlas and Bysciw will compete no doubt, but do you think the Crusaders will join in?" Reece asks.

"The Crusaders aren't going to let a small-scale assassination scare them away. Their leader is probably motivated by the event. It's certainly worrying though. Before, only two teams were in competition. Now there are four..." Tanten thinks about the probability of his team winning. He shakes his head and decides he'll assess the group once he arrives.

"Tanten," Reece starts off, a nervousness in his tone. "What are the odds there are other groups?"

"I presume..." Tanten stops in his tracks, concentrating on the question. "The probability of other unknown groups with the same mission is exceedingly low. Now that the Association is dealing with the war, their eyes won't return to this project for quite some time, leaving them out of the count, though we never included them to begin with... The odds are extremely low."

They resume walking. The group enters the forest, following the stone path. As they climb the hill, their heads peek over the top, and they see a group of people gathered in the glade. Tanten notices all but one group have arrived. He looks around, down the hill, toward the city, but sees no signs of the group. He looks at his watch. 8:52.

"There's still a group missing," Reece states. "What should we do?"

"They have until nine..." Tanten responds. He feels the nerves beginning to crack through his calm composure. "After that, we start the meeting."

One of the team members rushes over to Tanten, phone in hand. Tanten knows who it is.

"Syrenne," Tanten starts. "Meet us at ten. Tonight, we strike. The altar piece will be ours."

Chapter Fourteen

Botalia slowly opens her eyes. She lays in her bed, the room illuminated by the sunlight. Her muscles ache, every breath a chore causing her heart to accelerate. She looks around. Her head feels light, and the environment gives off a different aura.

"Something's not right," Botalia whispers.

She attempts to get out of bed but is paralyzed. Her muscles won't listen. Rigid and heavy, her body lays there, as if she no longer controls it. Her heart accelerates. She stares at her right hand which lays at her side, hoping for just one finger to twitch. Nothing. She sighs in despair.

The last time she remembers being in such a state, she woke up after lying unconscious for four days, and she couldn't move until two days later. Her body was weak, her head empty of all thought.

"But that was... ten years ago."

Though she has often tried to forget, she remembers that day well, though the events leading to her collapse remain blurred and distant. Ten years ago, when she was no more than an empty vessel, devoid of all feeling and rationale, she abandoned her humanity...

Botalia recalls what led her to barren waste.

DAYS BEFORE THE HAPPENING, Botalia went to the site of the Magistrate Assessment. Her nerves and excitement hit her in a flurry that added to the glow of her aura. She had studied and trained consistently, day to day adding to her strength in both mind and body. Her dream of following in her parents' footsteps could come true over the course of the next few days.

As she looked around, she noticed the competition seemed incredibly competent and combatively strong. However, focusing her eyes, she noticed none of the others had honed their auras and life force. Her parents informed her a while back that not many people ever learn to utilize their life force before becoming magistrates. Their teachers would later instruct them how to do so should they choose the path of a disciple to a Professional. Practicing life force without proper instruction was dangerous and could possibly kill the user who wields it without caution and respect for the universal energy. But Botalia figured those desiring to be magistrates would have followed similar procedure to her own.

The first test was just that, a test. Like taking exams in a school or university, not that she would know what either was like, the competitors took seats in a hall filled with thousands of desks. Botalia, like many of the more humbled competitors, sat cross legged against the padded walls, insufficient seating within the space. And the seats were quickly taken by those most proud.

The exam covered scientific method, basic laws and principles, mathematical questions that any chemist or engineer should have no problem answering, and much more. The questions grew harder the further into the exam they got. Questions that were once applicable to many branches of science turned to questions that perhaps only those with years of study in a particular branch could answer. Her parents had told her not to worry if she was unsure of an answer. They instructed Botalia to continue on through the test, as the information needed to answer earlier questions would appear later. And they were not wrong. Not simply an exam of knowledge but of critical thinking was what separated a simple student from a magistrate.

The second trial was no more than a physical with a test of strength and flexibility. Botalia wondered why they must do this. Her parents had mentioned life force users changing their appearance, or others' appearances, but this seemed all the more reason to make the one responsible a magistrate. Or so Botalia thought. News broke a few years later that underground organizations disguised members in hope of getting them a license, granting them access to coveted information and connections which they otherwise might not have had.

When the doctors, no more than informants by the look of their auras and the time it took to perform the most basic tests, examined Botalia, they turned to one another with wide eyes at the results of her pulse and body temperature. They told her to remain in her seat whilst they spoke with a proctor, often a highly regarded Scholar or Professional searching for students among the examinees.

They stopped at a man who appeared quite young, red wavy hair framed his face in an almost regal matter. He looked at the results and then to Botalia. A smirk grew as he focused on her. Botalia shifted her eyes. He waved away their concerns and Botalia was promptly allowed to the next stage of the trials.

The third test involved brain puzzles, riddles, and deductive reasoning. To Botalia, it seemed more like a quiz show than a test as one could not move to the next question until correctly solving the first one. She took a minute from her thoughts to scan the room. The numbers had dwindled. Some had been forced to leave due to cheating, others left when they understood their dreams of being a magistrate lingered beyond their grasp. Botalia took a deep breath and concentrated, refusing to surrender.

The fourth trial was an obstacle course designed by a group of highly acclaimed Scholars and Professionals. To arrive at the finish, one had to overcome challenges of physical, mental, and emotional strength. Even before beginning, Botalia noticed the life force woven throughout the course to achieve such challenges for the competitors. This trial lasted the longest as only one competitor, chosen at random, could enter at a time. After four hours of waiting, Botalia finally got her chance. She finished in swift timing and arrived at a door at the end of the final labyrinth.

She entered the room and was met by a panel of the judges, five Professionals and five Scholars. They applauded her victory. Botalia gulped as she realized she stepped into the final trial.

After no more than a few seconds of examination, one of the men, clearly a Professional, spoke.

"You are trained in life force, correct?"

"Yes."

"Show us."

Botalia focused her energy, bringing her life force to her hands. She bent down to touch the ground and a figure sculpted itself in front of everyone. It was a tall, wispy figure, like a man in a cloak several sizes too large. Botalia struggled to breathe, exhaustion setting in, as she had never sculpted a full figure before. But the familiar form gave her comfort. Her parents sculpted their servants in the same way.

The panel clapped and without further comment dismissed Botalia to await her scores.

Botalia remembers her happiness upon receiving her marks. They far exceeded all others taking the test at that time. At the end of the third day of the assessment, Botalia held her head high as she departed with her magistrate license. The suspense of wanting to show her parents her accomplishment tortured her on her journey home.

On the train ride, many people called her wishing to hire or sponsor her because now she was a magistrate (though her last name may have added to her popularity). She glowed in her excitement because for the first time in her life, she knew she possessed the power to make a difference. There were no longer any excuses about why she wouldn't be able to help someone. Yet a pounding in her heart, one she hoped was no more than an excess of energy that resulted from her excitement, knocked and knocked at her chest. A sudden rush of heat caused her to sweat. She thought it was homesickness, as she had never been away for so long.

"We're almost there," she whispered to herself, a hand on her chest. "We're almost there."

When she approached the front step, she placed her ear on the door, listening intently. To her disappointment, she heard no one inside. Botalia creaked the door open and looked all around before entering her home. In her hopes to still surprise someone, she placed her hand on the wall and closed her eyes. She sent a pulse out of her hand using her life force. Any obstructions to the pulse and she'd know if someone were home. Botalia felt nothing.

She trudged to the kitchen, hoping her parents left her a hint as to their whereabouts and when they would return. She found no note but did find herself a nice snack. Once up in her room, Botalia decided a nap was the best way to pass the time.

When she next opened her eyes, she saw a haze before her. Figures in black outfits moved through her room, crawling like shadows across the floor, weightless. She felt a pressure on her chest, like the monster inside trying to force its way out.

A dark figure approached her drowsy body. It placed a cloth over her mouth and nose, its hand holding it firm in place. Botalia's heart raced as the panic of the nightmare set in. Her vision drowned in a black sea at the absence of air. She hoped this was the end of her nightmare, that now she could wake up. She learned later it was no dream.

It was the catalyst. Once the reaction began, it could not be undone.

When she awoke, the house was as silent as when she first arrived earlier that day. The time was approaching 10:00 pm. She looked around. Not all was as she left it. She panicked, like being caught in a nightmare once more. Though she began to think none of it was a nightmare. It was not in her head.

Botalia slipped out of bed, a shiver sent down her spine. Her eyes remained half-closed as she moved toward the door. She creaked it open, her intuition warning her something was wrong with the balance of the environment. The scent of smoke and blood hit Botalia. She trembled as the realization of her nightmare set in. She wanted to run, but her legs wobbled underneath her and she could barely stand. Botalia forced herself to commit to a fast walk.

She approached the steps and caught of glimpse of the horrors that awaited her.

The sliced body of one of the friends of her parents lay on the steps, their blood covering the wall. Botalia squeezed her eyes shut, holding her breath as she passed, the scent of iron too strong.

As she turned the corner at the bottom of the stairs, she realized the sight of the mangled body was simply the prelude. The sight she experienced at that moment appeared more terrifying and gruesome.

Act one of the real performance was only beginning.

The smell and sights sent her body into a petrified state. She continued moving forward, for if the colleagues of her parents were here, her parents must be around somewhere. That thought made her heart race even faster.

"But they're strong... and smart. There's no way they'd-"

Botalia saw the opened, blood-stained door to her parents' laboratory. She reluctantly descended the stairs, half-knowing, half-denying the sight she was about to see.

The laboratory lay in shambles, broken glass and machinery strewn about painted red with the blood of the victims. Among them were men and women dressed entirely in black. One particularly gruesome body had his head exploded. Through her tears, Botalia managed to focus her eyes, knowing her parents wouldn't let anyone win, even in death. Written on the wall in her mother's life force was an address. Directly beneath it a note was written, still her mother's life force, but with a shakier hand and incomplete. "We lov..."

An immense pressure weighed on her chest again, not that it had ever really stopped. She fell to the ground, her fear and anger streaming from her eyes in the form of tears, her heartache transformed into loud screams into the night, straining her burning throat. She became blind, physically, mentally, and emotionally. She found no strength. Only emptiness. A feeling she had never known. She never realized how full she was until she saw nothing left. Until she realized all she loved had been taken from her, unrightfully stolen, destroyed, and something that could never be repaired.

A strange sensation coursed through her veins. A comfort issued forth by one who felt Botalia's pain, a support for her broken heart. It held her in its arm like she had regressed into an infant. The stream of tears slowed and her heart calmed. Her eyes no longer glowed scarlet with despair but with wrath. Botalia placed her hand to her chest.

"Please," she begged to the being within her. "Please, they can't get away with this."

A jolt shocked her body, a collection of charged particles forcing its way out. The being crept out of hiding, where it sat unmoving for so many years. Botalia released the chains imprisoning it. Whether it deceived her or not, this being was the only one who could mend the situation. It was the only one Botalia trusted. Because it was a part of her. And had been, since the day she was born.

Botalia let go of the controls, willingly handing them to the monster. Her vision faded and she felt herself forced into the dark room. The monster's habitat became her temporary home. Every once in a while, when she closed her eyes, she would see images that appeared all too real. She couldn't decipher whether they were dreams or if she was viewing the world from the perspective of the monster.

She saw the brick wall labeled with the address seen earlier. She watched as a band of men wearing black ran in fear after realizing their life force utilization could not defeat their enemy. She witnessed their heads being ripped from their bodies, despite their efforts. She saw their blood cover the ground. She heard the screams of pain and despair. She listened apathetically to their pleas and apologies, making their deaths all the more satisfying.

As the last one lay dying in a pool of his own blood, she saw her parents' mangled bodies, their heads cut open. Their brains had already been removed, placed in jars with some form of preserving liquid. She shook, trying to force her eyes open to avoid the sight seen by the viewer. Her subconscious form managed to open her eyes. In front of her stood the form of the beast. The monster gently handed the controls back to Botalia, a sympathetic look in its eyes. Botalia trembled as she attempted to grab the controls. She held them shakily in her hands and watched as the monster curled up in a corner, unable to face her. Botalia took control of her body.

She caught a glance of the sight, the smells, the sounds, before collapsing to the ground. Unconscious.

When she awoke, the location around her had been taped off by the police. All the bodies had been removed, except her own.

Botalia felt pains and aches surging through her. She attempted to rise, but her body would not allow it. She was paralyzed.

Approximately an hour passed before an investigator came along and saw her awake. He picked up her unmoving body and carried her to his car. He placed her in the passenger's seat and drove her to the hospital. The investigator never asked questions, he didn't interrogate her nor did he attempt to coax her into talking. The only words to leave his mouth were, "I'm glad you're alright."

Botalia remained in the hospital for two days, finally leaving when she was able to move again. The investigator visited often, bringing food and flowers to her side. She would later learn he was on the Council of the Magistrate Association, his name Cefni Medina. When she was released from the hospital, she didn't know where she should go. Cefni approached her and said he was to take her to the Magistrate Association building. She agreed to go, though she was rather hesitant. However, she felt she owed this man who selflessly cared for her. If the other Council members were anything like him, she wouldn't have a problem. Unfortunately, they weren't.

She stood before the Council members. As she focused her eyes, she was in awe over their tremendous life force and smooth auras.

The door to the meeting room opened. The Council members rose from their seats. Two men entered: the President and Vice President. They walked to the opposite end of the room from Botalia and sat themselves down. The other Council members followed suit. Botalia remained standing.

They began their discussion, gazing up at Botalia every few seconds. Throughout the discussion, Botalia noticed certain trends. Some of the Council members always agreed and some seemed to love arguing with one another. One particular person who stuck out was the Vice President, who seemed to consistently play Devil's advocate.

Botalia remained silent throughout the majority of the discussion. As they were finishing the President looked up at her, the first time he had done so. He squinted his eyes and smirked.

"Ms. Ulton," he began, all eyes in the room now on her. She felt the nerves begin to settle. She locked eyes with the President. "How do you feel?" Such an ambiguous question. Botalia could interpret it any way she pleases, but only one answer crossed her mind.

"I have no regrets," Botalia replied. She knew that was all she was able to say.

The President laughed at her answer. She felt shocked by such a response. The Vice President grinned, and the other members responded in a variety of ways.

"If you'll excuse us, Ms. Ulton," the President said.

Botalia left the room, a pit in her stomach. The discussion concerned her, so her curiosity got the better of her. She placed her hand against the wall and closed her eyes. She could hear every word they said. Her jaw dropped and her eyes watered when she realized they were discussing her exile, throwing about the terms "dangerous" and "monster." She couldn't believe it. She thought she had lost everything, but they were stripping her of her humanity.

She dropped her hands, not wanting to hear any more. Sounds of shouting and table smashing escaped the room every so often, the argument clearly heated.

After several minutes expired, Cefni opened the door, a solemn look worn on his face. Botalia followed him into the room. Everyone appeared rather serious, one Council member, Tanten Flynn, had his eyes closed and arms crossed. The Vice President, Atlas Lurio, appeared angry, his head resting on his hands, his stare menacing. The President rose, his arms open at his sides.

"Ms. Ulton," he started. Botalia's body shook uncontrollably. She closed her eyes, awaiting her inescapable fate. The President sighed, realizing she understood what was about to happen. "I'm most sorry to inform you that, for the safety of the general public and yourself, as a group of elected officials who aim to protect and progress our society, you are forthwith exiled from Dominia."

When the sound of the final word reached her ears, tears flowed down her face. She couldn't feel angry about the choice they made, she would have done the same if faced with a monster like herself.

They handed her two papers: one for her signature and the other the minutes of the discussion along with the vote. The Council felt they should not hide the reasoning for their decision. Botalia stared at the numbers: 17 For, 2 Against.

Cefni extended his hand. Botalia didn't move. He sighed and walked out of the room, Botalia following him. They got into a car and drove to the docks located the next city over. They arrived at the island around sunset. Botalia recognized the location as her parents' isolated vacation and research home.

"Ms. Ulton," Cefni began.

"Botalia is fine," she stated. His jaw sat slightly agape as he stared at her. She had remained silent for the majority of their time together. He exposed a slight grin.

"Botalia," he restarted. "Please, don't do anything rash."

Botalia gazed toward the setting sun. She shook her head.

"I won't do anything. How can I when I have nothing? ...I'll do nothing."

Cefni was about to respond but stopped when he observed the emptiness in Botalia's eyes. She no longer suffered nor felt pain. There was nothing in her. No hope. No motivation. No life.

But hiding in the corner, curled up, waiting for another chance, lived a monster.

Once Cefni left, Botalia slowly marched the forest path to the villa. She listened as the birds and other creatures of the island sang her lament.

Chapter Fifteen

Botalia returns from her memories, still unable to move. She wonders how long it will take for someone to find her awake. A few minutes pass, and she hears footsteps in the hallway. The door cracks open and Koepp pokes his face in. A smile explodes across his face when he sees her eyes open. He rushes to her side.

"I've been checking in on you all the time," Koepp starts in a frenzied tone. "But every time I checked, you were still sleeping. I'm so glad you're up." He turns to the door. "Nix! Tenebrant! She's awake!"

Koepp hops onto the side of her bed, his cocoa eyes shining with the luminosity of a white dwarf star. Botalia smiles, knowing it's the most she can do to express her happiness. She hears the footsteps quickly ascending the stairs. Nix races into the room, a smile across his face. Botalia returns it, amazed at the difference a change in environment can make on a child long devoid of happiness. Tenebrant leans against the doorway, wearing a solemn expression.

About ten seconds pass before Nix's smile begins to fade. His eyes move to the floor, avoiding Botalia, realizing the truth of the situation. Koepp's expression changes to confusion, as he notices the transformation of the air in the room. His jaw drops when he notices Botalia's unmoving person.

"Koepp. Nix," Tenebrant begins. "We should let Botalia rest."

The boys nod their heads and hop from the bed. Botalia watches as the three head toward the stairs. She closes her eyes, embarrassed about how weak and fragile she is.

Botalia sighs as she wonders how she managed to pass the time when she was last in this state. At that time, her mind was empty, she thought of nothing. Presently, she cannot stop the many thoughts racing through her mind. She wonders which is worse: thinking of nothing or thinking of everything. She decides to think through her experiments as well as theories she has developed. She ponders the different methods of manipulating life force, considering the efficiency and strength of each method. At some point during her thinking, Botalia dozes off.

A light shines in the distance, the sounds of explosions surrounding her. Life force missiles combined with artillery and dynamite. The smell of gunpowder fresh in the air. She runs forward. Titanic figures rise from the ground, their faces indistinct in the haze. She reaches a set of stone brick stairs, stopping in her tracks, unaware if more dangers await her at the top. She turns her body one-hundred and eighty degrees, fully grasping the nightmares that lay behind her. Bodies of fallen soldiers lay on the ground. A host of shadow monsters feast on their bodies, growing stronger with the nourishment. The Titans, in their ragged armor and carrying rusted iron weapons, continue to walk toward her. Botalia cannot see any survivors among the rubble and devastation.

She hurriedly ascends the stairs. She looks down and around her and feels as though she's making no progress. The stairs seem to move under her. She pushes her hardest, continuing to run the seemingly infinite staircase. A blinding light explodes and fills the area.

She trips and lands on a flat stone surface. Before her, she sees an altar, lined with gold and sapphire. A yew staff, curved at the top, protrudes from the altar. She feels its strength of presence. Not only is the staff mystical and awe-inducing, but it awakes fear or desire within all who gaze upon it. She focuses her eyes. The power, the immense power contained in the staff, far surpasses her own. Any who possess this staff could use its power to fuel their own life force, making them stronger than any in the nations. A staff of the gods, held sacred upon this altar. Though called by its beauty, she takes a step backward, her fear of the staff's power overtaking her desire of it. The floor under her crumbles and she falls into the void.

Botalia jumps awake. A cold sweat moistens the sheets under her, and Botalia releases a breath of relief. She looks to the door and sees Tenebrant staring at her. Botalia, who has regained control of movement, props herself up to a sitting position, her energy consumed by that simple movement draining faster than normal. Her body is sore, her life force reserve only beginning to build up once more. Tenebrant leans against the doorway.

"Nightmare?" he questions.

"I'm not sure..."

Botalia analyzes her hands, lifting them up and rotating them.

"How long have I been out?"

"It's been five hours since Little Flynn found you awake," Tenebrant states. "Before that, you were unconscious for about two and a half days."

"Not too terrible, I suppose," Botalia responds. Tenebrant chuckles and shakes his head.

Botalia swings her legs over the side of the bed. While still feeling stiff and weak, she manages to stand up. She figures its hunger that makes her limbs shake, as she fights to maintain balance and not pass out.

"I can't imagine I've missed much."

Tenebrant smiles.

"Prepare to be surprised at the amount of chaos that can ensue over the course of two days."

Botalia's eyes widen. The boys stampede up the stairs. Koepp rushes into the room and wraps his arms around her. Nix stands beside them, his straight face twitching as it thinks to smile. But

Botalia maintains eye contact with Tenebrant, confusion spelled on her face.

Botalia descends the stairs with the help of Tenebrant and heads straight to the den. Koepp and Nix enter the room, carrying plates of food they prepared for Botalia earlier, when she had initially awoken hours earlier.

Botalia turns on the television, believing it to be on the wrong station at first, only to realize it was not a movie.

Smoke spiraled into the air. Birds and beasts sculpted of life force took to the cities, some quite majestic, others collapsing the further they got from their caster. Armies of informants, some with their Scholars, some without, took to the streets looking like military units with odd new weapons in their possession. Professionals and their disciples threatened entry to the building they deemed as anti-peace. From Dominia to Juhm. From Collephlox to Froslow. Universities constructed by the association pictured with broken windows and graffiti. Labs and work sites demolished or up in flames.

The chaos. The war. The Schism. It was all real. It was happening.

And it had been happening over the last two days. The news called it 'The War of Science versus Magic', the Magistrate Association pinned as the enemy for never mending the separation between the groups. Hundreds of innocents reported missing. Hundreds of others, civilians and magistrates alike, reported dead.

"I don't understand," Botalia mumbles, more so to herself than the others. "The Magistrate Association is all about peace, prosperity, working together. But this is..."

"Devastation? Absolute, unfiltered evil? Sounds like the Magistrate Association I'm familiar with."

Tenebrant leans back in his seat and places both hands behind his head. His expression shows no sign of shock nor horror. Rather the images of flames, broken glass, and blood painted streets pull a chuckle from him.

Botalia takes a bite of her food, steaming hot on the outside and chilled in the middle. She forces herself not to spit it out despite the burning of her tongue. The center of the potato chunk cools the burns while the salsa stings the entire way down her throat. She offers a smile of gratitude at Koepp and Nix before returning her attention to the television.

"Are they really so committed to tearing the Magistrate Association apart?"

"I won't lie. It is odd. I don't see any profits in this for Atlas unless a nation paid him to stir up trouble. As for the other," Tenebrant glances at Koepp and smirks. "There's absolutely nothing to gain from this war. Unless they both wholeheartedly hate the Association. They're both Professionals, they'd be fighting on the same side. Which, to be honest, is even more strange."

Botalia stares at the ground in front of her. Perplexed. Indecisive. She bites her thumbnail while lost in her thoughts. This island. Her family...

"I'm an exile. Why do I feel so strongly about this? About defending them?"

"Your loyalty exists outside of your own well-being. You pledge yourself to the Association's mission, one most members don't take too seriously to begin with. Their mission does not reflect their most powerful leaders. They've been built upon a foundation of manipulation and greed. You're naive. And you'll get over it in time."

Their eyes connect for a split second before Tenebrant darts his away. He bites the inside of his bottom lip, his fists clenching. The sorrow and pain in her eyes tug at him. He finds himself slipping. But he would never join a fight to save the Magistrate Association...

"This pounding in my chest. Whether it's the beast or the monster, I don't think it matters. Maybe it's fate." Botalia pictures her house in Dominia. Growing up may not have been an exciting experience, nor one she would ever wish to relive, but the faces of her parents shine across the screen of her memory. A slight grin leaves her. "I'm still a magistrate. I won't let the Association fall if I can help it."

Botalia stands and grabs the remote, turning off the television. She shakes her head to organize her thoughts. Her heart screams at the pain and suffering of the victims, of the innocents.

"They think they know me. They think they know what I'm capable of. They have no idea. Well, I'll show them. We all will."

Chapter Sixteen

After finishing supper, Botalia leads the others to a storage shed located behind the greenhouse. Tall grass grows up around the unit. The sage green siding appears faded from sun, the roof missing shingles in some spots. The overgrown path leading from the garage door disappears not far from its departure.

"Sorry," Botalia states, as she struggles to kick down the grass in front of the man-door while fidgeting with the keys in her hands. "There was never a reason for me to come here because... well, you'll see why."

She turns the knob to open the door, but it doesn't budge. Tenebrant gives the gesture for Botalia to move away. Pushing his weight to his shoulder as he turns the knob, he thrusts the door open. As he steps through the entrance, he flicks the light switch on the wall inside.

The light illuminates all within the garage, shining off every cobweb and waking some spiders and other small critters from their slumber. Moths that had been silently sitting on the aluminum sided walls begin to buzz the light bulb. A large object sits hidden under a tarp in the center of the garage, covered in dust.

The boys explode through the door, a new playground for their adventurous spirits. Botalia grins, leaning herself against the door frame as she feels her legs shake under her. For the ten years she lived on this island, she never once opened this shed. She felt no need to. She tried her best to erase the thoughts of what lay within, knowing she could not leave.

Koepp and Nix approach the large object and attempt to peek under the tarp, as if seeing the object is prohibited. Finally, Koepp turns to Botalia, his curiosity brimming.

"What's under this blanket? A car?"

"No," Botalia giggles, the thought of having a car on the island amusing to her. She bites her lip to stop herself, realizing the seriousness with which Koepp had asked. "It's not a car, but something much more exciting. Want to see?"

Koepp and Nix vigorously nod. As Botalia goes to lift the tarp, Tenebrant applies pressure to her shoulder, her physical form still weak. Their eyes connect and she gives a thankful nod before stepping back. Tenebrant lifts the tarp to reveal a luxurious, yet compact expedition motorboat. A small, roof covered cabin with entrance below deck proved the perfect size when her parents went on their voyages from island to deserted island. Seeing the boat brings back memories of watching her parents deep-sea dive for bones and metals, of watching her parents sail off into the horizon without her.

At the sight of the motorboat, the boys gasp in excitement. Tenebrant's eyes meet Botalia's, whose blank expression proves she's lost in her thoughts.

"This is your plan? Cruising a boat over to Dominia?" Tenebrant asks, a strange fire in his eyes.

"Unless you have a better plan." Botalia rubs her forehead to bring herself back to reality and help with the headache derived from her body's exhaustion. She senses Tenebrant's hostility growing by the second, forcing her to stay on edge. Koepp and Nix distract themselves with the boat, having already climbed inside and inspecting the dashboard. Tenebrant shakes his head and closes the distance between himself and Botalia.

"Why have a plan at all? Why do we need to go?"

"I'm not forcing you to go, Tenebrant," Botalia says in a lower tone, an edge in her voice as she says his name. He looks at the boat and then back at Botalia, his aura swirling about him like a violent tornado.

"This isn't our war. These people never fought for us, so why should we help them?"

"It's not about who we're helping. It's about doing the right thing."

Tenebrant rolls his eyes and starts to turn away, but Botalia grabs him by the arm to prevent him from doing so. He restrains his usual reaction to such an act, his heart accelerating and his muscles tensing. His life force bolts to his hands, ready for the attack. He grits his teeth and takes deep breaths. Her sympathetic eyes meet his and look further into him.

"You don't have to go, you know. But it will be a chance, our chance, to stop them from getting away with this."

Tenebrant thinks about the 'them' that Botalia refers. She speaks of Bysciw, Atlas, and-

"Tanten..." the word brushes Tenebrant's lips, a vengeful smirk grows across his face and his heart accelerates once more, this time with excitement. While helping the Magistrate Association would disgust Tenebrant, the thought of challenging Tanten Flynn, one on one, no interruptions, may just prove worth it.

Tenebrant chuckles.

"I can't believe you talked me into it," Tenebrant says, a smile spreading on Botalia's face.

"We arrive in Dominia, make our way to the Association building. Find out where they are. When they'll attack. We'll be there, and we'll be ready for them. I promise, we will find them. And we will bring them down."

Without another word, Tenebrant nods. Botalia feels relieved and whistles to get the attention of the ever-curious boys. They turn to face her, their faces spelling out their worry of being in trouble.

"Let's wheel this motorboat to the dock and get going," Botalia says, her smile cracking as the weakness turns her legs to jelly once more. She trembles and shakes yet uses her energy to appear as though nothing is the matter. After all, these are the consequences when one does more than their storehouse of life force should allow. Even in an adrenaline rush, even with the surge of the curse, why would Botalia ever think it alright to perform so many atomic shifts within a one-hour increment? Life force users, those new to the craft and masters alike, know when their reserves begin to take from their physical body and not only the life force that creates the aura that it is time to stop and rest. Otherwise, the consequences could be deadly.

Botalia shifts her weight to the stronger of her legs, understanding her mistake while feeling frustration all the while. The echoes of her weakness, of her fragility, shout at her. And her refusal of letting it show is what drains the energy from her. She doesn't use her life force to hide it, for in Tenebrant's examination of her, he understood her still to be incredibly weak. But if her smile can help mask the worry from Koepp and Nix, showing them that she is strong and capable, more than any other mentor they could possibly hope for, the drain will have been worth it.

The garage door creaks open and, grabbing a hold of the hitch, the team wheel the motorboat down the path leading to the dock. Botalia whispers to the forest, not knowing if these goodbyes will be her last to them. After all this time, she will return to Dominia, the land of her childhood. The land of her experimentation.

Once they arrive at the lonely dock, Tenebrant and Nix use their life force to enhance their strength. They push the motorboat from the trailer and into the water from the shore. A smirking Nix, seeing an opportunity, splashes Koepp with the saltwater. Koepp jumps at the surprise and prepares for the leap until he feels the glare from Tenebrant. Koepp understands and peers at Botalia, whose eyes are shut. He grabs her hand. She feels his warmth and tightens her grip.

The group board the motorboat and begin the journey to Dominia, the journey to the Magistrate Association. Tenebrant sits at the wheel, using no more than his life force to lead the way. Botalia and the two boys relax on the embedded leather couch at the side, the boys peering over the rail and into the deep blue waters. Botalia watches the island disappear over the horizon. With eyes closed, her head turns to the sky. A strange conglomeration of emotions fill her. Worry. Anxiety. Fear. Freedom.

She bites her lip, digging her teeth in to feel the pain. As she opens her eyes, as if trying to wake from any dream she may be having, as if thinking she will still be in her bed, she sees nothing but the waters of the Aldarion Ocean around her. The tranquil waves replace the torrential rapids in her head. She remembers when the boat traveled the other direction. She remembers feeling cold even as the sun beat down on them from high above. Grief washed over her. The loss of her parents, the only family she knew she had. Gone. She had nothing. And at that time she was travelling to her cage. Her punishment. Her exile.

Botalia looks around her. She finds her strength to her side, Koepp and Nix, giving power to her heart. Never before did she understand how important it was to have others by her side. Something she can protect. Almost as if that is her sole purpose.

"Look at that!" Koepp screams, the joy of discovery in his voice causing a smile to spread across Botalia's face.

The two boys race to the stern of the motorboat. In the wake, a school of cotinga fish fly up through the warm waters. The bright scarlet and turquoise colors display themselves on the scales of the magical fish. Some burning bright like fire. Others glistening like ice in the sun. The boys, with mouths agape in awe of the species, watch as the fish flip through the air, jumping up to ten feet from the water. As if soaring through the air, propelled by fins that provide an unusual strength, the cotinga fish perform for the group. Botalia focuses her eyes and realizes the fish utilize their life force to reach such heights. Their auras, though no more than a thin line extended from their bodies, flow like calm waves.

Koepp and Nix watch, mesmerized by the sight, never having witnessed anything the like. After a few minutes, the fish slow their jumping and lose themselves in the deep once more. The boys continue to discuss the spectacle, debating which color fish flew higher. The discussion lasting for no more than two minutes, their conversation finding a distractor that leads them in a different direction.

The sun begins to set, and the stars reveal themselves in the thin curtain of darkness. The lights of the port city of Mercuria shine in the distance. Nine hours after their journey began, they arrive.

They dock the motorboat, Tenebrant tying it to a post and handing the key to Botalia. The salty, summer air brushes against their cheeks. The commotion of the others on the docks catches their ears, their talk of the Schism, their voices laced in fear.

"Once we finish loading up, we're heading to Thyll."

"But I hear they got the same problems over there."

"It can't be worse than here. Where her parents are at ain't got much problems there."

Botalia and the others make their way up the pier, the lampposts illuminating their way. Many people scurry about the port, even at these late hours, for the group see many flashlights and lanterns moving about. The four near the group they overheard at their arrival.

"These crazy magistrates keep running about and there's no one to control them."

"Yeah. Ever since the president of their association died, they all went nuts."

"Peace and prosperity my a-"

A loud explosion fills the night sky with colors of fire and smoke, the sound and force shaking all within its radius. Screams cry out, children and adults alike. Botalia examines the distance, about two miles northeast of their position. As she focuses her eyes, she sees the residue of life force.

The Schism.

Koepp and Nix stare in awe at the sight, wondering what could have caused it. Tenebrant, having deduced it was the result of an attack by rogue magistrates, shakes his head and smirks. A rush of air breezes past him and Tenebrant turns to see Botalia no longer stands with them.

"Botalia!" Koepp calls after her. "Where are you going?"

Tenebrant looks ahead and sees the frame of the little girl he met on the stoop years ago. The one that leapt into action at the sight of violence. Her instincts may lead her, but its her heart that calls her to action. Its her heart that calls her to protect.

The young necromancer follows in pursuit of his once friend. At the moment, he didn't feel scared by the demons at his feet. He only feels the weight of the silver stone in his pocket, pulling him in her direction. How can she be so ready to protect when she had failed before? How can she be so sure she won't fail again? Tenebrant wonders, his own failures filling his head.

As he turns the corner, the smell of sulphur and cherry blossom meets his nose. His eyes forward, trying not to lose sight of Botalia, Tenebrant halts mid-stride. The silhouette of another takes her place. A young girl, beckoning him to follow. Tenebrant, no longer in control, races in her direction, the silver in her hair glittering in the city lights. She turns the corner, and he hopes not to lose her. As he makes his way around the building and down the street, he notices the girl, frozen in place. The flames reach from the ground and consume her, the screams deafening. Tenebrant covers his ears and falls to his knees, gritting his teeth in anger. And guilt. He closes his eyes to erase the images, but the bloodlust grows within him. A pressure on his shoulder forces his eyes open and he jolts his hand to grab the attacker.

As he turns, he finds himself face to face with Botalia, water, forming tears, lining her bottom eyelid. Tenebrant feels every tremor of her body as his tightened hand holds to her arm. But she does not pull away. Botalia remains calm.

The boys race toward the two and pause before reaching them. His aura reaching to the sky like someone added gasoline to a fire, Koepp takes a defiant step in their direction.

"Let go of her," little Flynn says, the growl in his voice reminiscent of his father's. Unfortunately, with this, the bloodlust within Tenebrant magnifies. He attempts to control himself but feels his aura slip from his grip. Nix pulls Koepp behind himself and bares his teeth. Tenebrant releases Botalia but stumbles as he takes his first step.

"It's alright," Botalia's calming voice like a sweet lullaby to their ears. "There's still some aultiatus gas in the air. It's a hallucinogen. It must be affecting him."

Botalia puts her hands side by side with her palms facing the environment around her. A gust of wind whisks the smell of sulphur and cherry blossom away.

Silence encapsulates them until another explosion sends them to the ground.

Reality strikes and Botalia and Tenebrant jump to guard the young boys.

"Get behind me," Tenebrant says to Botalia, her aura visibly trembling. She shakes her head, ready to defend until the death.

The soldiers of the resistance draw near. Life force users. They use their tricks to intimidate, knowing full well that Scholars and informants don't often study life force to a broad extent, especially after becoming magistrates. Professionals and their disciples study specific branches of life force within the Magistrate Association, just as a Scholar would a branch of science or humanity. And now, they square off against one another in the battle of science versus life force, or as the new stations claim "magic."

Botalia focuses her eyes just as the leader sends another life force missile into the air, though she sees its no more than a collection of photons the user wielded from a street lamp not ten feet away from himself. It's like fireworks without the sound. No more than a light show.

"You think that's impressive?" Tenebrant shouts in their direction, not a hint of fear or confusion in his voice for the fighters to feed on.

Some of the approaching group turn their heads to the leader, wondering why their intimidating tactics have no effect. As they marched the streets earlier, the townspeople ran in fear, begged to allow them time to grab their families and escape. Of course, these were people with no knowledge of how life force operates. Unfortunately, Tenebrant, Botalia, and even Nix, are not inexperienced with life force. The leader of the resistance group smirks.

"What about this?" he says, throwing his hands up and emitting two bright flashes. The flash forms an orb that flies upward and explodes into thousands of other orbs. These light orbs head straight for the four of them.

"It's a stunning trick," Tenebrant says. "Close your eyes."

Botalia understands and holds Nix and Koepp behind her, gently squeezing their arms. A pulse radiates from her chest and through her body. Not now, she thinks. She expands her aura and waits for the disappearance of the orbs, sensing as they draw nearer the three of them.

"Wait... three?" Botalia questions. Koepp and Nix remain behind her, but Tenebrant's presence has disappeared from her side.

Like a shadow, Tenebrant makes his way for the party of amateur disciples before the orbs explode. The group stand in excited tension, waiting for their attack to frighten the unsuspecting group. However, when the flashes cast a blinding light directly in front of group, they hear no screams. No sounds of confusion. No pleading for their lives.

A member of the resistance taps the leader on the shoulder.

"Man, I just focused in on their auras," he says, his voice beginning to shake. "And I think they might be-"

"Life force users?" Tenebrant asks in a soft tone, located behind the group. "Stronger than you imagined?"

They jump in shock, not one of them having noticed his movement. Not one suspecting that he'd closed in on them. Like prey discovering too late that the predator lurks behind them, the group stands frozen, with the exception of the leader. An expression of wonderment on his face, the short of stature man, no older than thirty, steps toward Tenebrant.

"Are you a Professional coming to our aide?" he whispers, in a tone suggesting a prayer being answered.

Tenebrant chuckles. He raises his eyebrows and grabs a hold of the cloak worn by the amateur magician, lifting him several inches off the ground. The playful smile turns to an expression of fury and wrath.

"Do I look like a piece of Association trash to you?" Tenebrant asks before using his life force to propel the leader into the middle of their new battlefield. The army watches from one side, Botalia, Koepp, and Nix from the other.

Tenebrant approaches the scared leader as he scurries to stand from his position on the ground. His aura flows about him like water in a glass that's been overfilled. There is no control. His excess life force, the life force he should be able to utilize, pouring away into nothingness. In contrast, Tenebrant's aura appears like a contained tornado. Harmless, if he so chooses for he has absolute control. But no doubt powerful.

Botalia closely watches Tenebrant's aura, noting the bloodlust radiating from him. She prays he does nothing rash, especially in front of the boys, though Nix has probably seen worse. Tenebrant can handle these resistance fighters, Botalia is certain. She finds comfort in not having to fight the battle. Though no longer shaking from being weak, Botalia does not want to push herself with exertion of life force before arriving at the Association building. Despite the length of their travels, she finds her life force still to be only a fraction of her storehouse. If she wants to appear convincing, and impressive, in front of the council, she will need her aura to be unwavering, strong, and full of energy, even if not at full capacity. Anyways, she knows her interference in the fight would only seek to infuriate Tenebrant.

The sly necromancer continues circling his prey. His life force creates an ashy smoke which encapsulates his hands, hiding any movements his fingers may be making. The group of disciples watch in horror, terrified to defend their leader, but also knowing the shame it would bring if the leader were not capable of defending himself in a fight against a non-magistrate. After all, if he was not a Professional, they could not see how Tenebrant would be able to defeat a skilled disciple. But their doubts only grow with every second that passes.

The leader stands at long last and gathers his life force into his hands. Botalia understands him to be the disciple of an emitter with the constant focus in his hands and the knowledge of sending the manifested life force from his person. A powerful ability when mastered, but no greater than any other form of life force training when still learning.

"I'm warning you," the leader states, concentrating the flow of life force into his hands. "I don't want to have a casualty outside of the ignorant informants we seek to annihilate."

"The only casualty would be in the form of a dim-witted disciple who thought he was capable," Tenebrant retorts, not even looking at the leader. He closes his eyes and takes deep breaths as another surge of his bloodlust hits him. "But capable of what? Changing the world? Resisting the unjust ways of the Association? Might I add the Association has never been just or fair, or promoted peace, or we wouldn't be here, would we?"

"You dare speak ill of the sacred Magistrate Association?" the leader says, his anger billowing as his pride, exaggerated like hubris, consumes him. "That is why my men and I fight!" The resistance fighters agree with their leader, their shouts echoing in the night. "We fight to restore the Association to its practices of old! Exploring the ways of life energy should be our purpose! Those informants killed our President and now it is their turn to pay!"

"Your president was as corrupt as the Association he ran-"

"Traitor!"

"How can I be when I was never on your side? That's the secret. Self-preservation. I'm on my own side."

His words are calm, almost chilling. The high-tension environment does not affect Tenebrant. If anything, it excites him. He waits patiently for his chance to pounce when the opportunity seems the most satisfying. However, he knows he can't try his old tricks, not in front of Botalia. The body will remain as no more than a body at the end. No attempt at resurrection. No attempt at creating life from death. The scenario bores him, disappoints him. His bloodlust fades away, his enemy too weak to be worth his time.

The leader prepares his attack, creeping up behind Tenebrant as he stares into the night sky, searching for the light of the stars. The pure white life force in his hands changes intensity as a scarlet red light takes its place. The light transforms into flames, licking at the disciple's arms but causing him no pain.

"No wonder he's the leader," Botalia thinks. "He's an elementalist."

Tenebrant feels the heat prickling his back and chuckles.

The leader opens his palms ready to emit the inferno upon Tenebrant. The resistance army stand in awe of their leader's power. The flames dance about, the oxygen fueling their hunger for Tenebrant's flesh. If the disciple does not remain focused, the fire will extinguish, or worse, escape his control. With a steady hand and swift movement, the flames roar for their target, the leader letting out a cheer of triumph that his attack not only appears effective but powerful. However, the flames travel through the thin veil that was Tenebrant. Their contact points swirl like an ashy mist for several seconds before reforming into the shape of the necromancer. The manifested form of Tenebrant disappears and screams of pain from the group fill the night.

The leader turns in terror as his men drop to the ground, rolling to and fro. Some tear their shirts off and swat at their own backs. Their eyes water, the sensation of burning the cause to their madness.

Tenebrant steps from the shadows behind them, a smirk worn proudly on his face.

"What have you done to my men?" asked the leader, a pleading in his voice as if begging Tenebrant to stop.

"Only what you wished to do to me," Tenebrant replies, stepping away from the moaning group, who are no longer in panic, only pain. "It's a curse, you see. Your men have felt the effect of your flames, the ones you sent through my sculpted life force. The pain you wished to inflict upon me they would feel, and they have."

"Are you trying to teach us a lesson? That we should have empathy for our enemies?" the leader asks, as if the truth finds him.

"No, I just wanted to see if it would work. I'd never executed this combination before. It was just a little bit of... practice."

At that moment, a large bird of prey in the sky screeches into the night. Botalia focuses her eyes as the bird lands upon the ledge of a building, watching them from above. A strange aura surrounds the bird.

"It's made of life force. Someone's sculpted it. But it's not from another resistance group, no..." Botalia wonders.

"Run, boys!" the leader of the group calls out, hoping his soldiers will stand. "They've heard us! We need to hide!"

The men stumble to their feet and disperse from their current position. As they head for the docks, their talk fades into the distance. The life force bird takes off from the ledge, pursuing the resistance fighters, the gold in its feathers flickering in the lights of the city.

"We need to go," Tenebrant warns the others, his voice monotone. They nod. "The Magistrate officers can't be too far behind."

"Can you mask your aura?" Botalia asks as they begin their way down the street. She directs her question at Tenebrant, but to her surprise, Nix nods. After all, he is an assassin, blood shared with the great Kufuta clan.

"You worry about your own," Tenebrant orders Botalia. He looks to Nix. "Same with you. I'll cover myself and... the Flynn."

Though Koepp appears taken aback, almost scared by the thought of Tenebrant helping him, Botalia releases a slight grin. It must have taken every fiber of his being to accept the responsibility to protect Koepp, and even more to say the words out loud. Though he hides deep within the hollow shell, Botalia understands the Tenebrant she thought she knew may exist yet. But those words continue echoing in her head. Self-preservation. What did he mean by that? Was every act a selfish one? Did he only seek to serve himself in aiding Koepp, knowing Botalia wouldn't let him far from the group? Knowing that with any slip up the Magistrate officers may find them, two boys, a forgotten exile, and a criminal? But he would abandon them surely... if the officers caught them, Tenebrant would waste no chance to escape. Self-preservation...

The four find their way into an alley, hiding in the shadows. The sounds of explosions echo in the distance, the battle ongoing in this city without sleep. According to the news, many of the innocents had evacuated. But those who stayed remain indoors at almost all hours. All offices closed. The city appears abandoned, light rarely escaping from windows in the night.

"Let's find a room in the nearest hotel and stay for the night. We can travel to the Association building come dawn," Tenebrant says, his eyes constantly focused on their surroundings.

"But how do you expect us to pay?" Botalia asks, the innocence in her voice causing Tenebrant to chuckle. He shakes his head, smirking all the while. Botalia understands the reaction and says nothing. It wouldn't be the first law she's broken. After all, this is her second time on the mainland since her exile. If caught, her crime could be punishable by death.

The four find their way to a dark hotel. No lights appear in the lobby and the door is marked by shrapnel ricochet and the carbon waste left by a fiery life force attack. No one waits to attend them inside. Rather, the place appears entirely abandoned. Tenebrant jumps behind the counter and grabs a set of keys. Waving them in Botalia's face, he leads them to a room.

"Nix and I will find food," Tenebrant says.

"Just be careful," Botalia instructs, seeing the visage of the boy she once knew, bruises on his arms and cuts on his face.

Tenebrant rolls his eyes before he and the assassin exit. As they walk up the corridor to the cafeteria, Nix swiftly slashes the air in front of Tenebrant forcing him to stop. Nix stands with his arm blocking Tenebrant's path, life force enveloping it.

"There's a hostility in your aura. In its vibration."

"Yes..." Tenebrant whispers, wondering why Nix would wait until they were alone to point it out. His bloodlust had waned, Tenebrant understood as much. But Tenebrant feels a different pulse in his heart, harder, darker, and denser. The beat of a tribal drum echoing within him. It plays the song of a hunter chasing its prey. Steady... steady. But growing more ominous every moment. Tenebrant wonders if Nix hears it, if his assassin ears had been trained to detect the song of the hunt. Or perhaps, Nix's heart plays along to the same beat.

"I'm warning you now," the ex-assassin starts, his eyes staring down the hallway, as if he catches the movement of every shadow. "If you hurt my friends, it's the last move you will ever make."

Tenebrant licks his lips and takes in a shallow breath. His fists clench as his temper rises. The act of being told how to behave never a favorable one to Tenebrant. The statement made by the young assassin surprises him, but not as much as his restraint.

"Don't tempt me."

Chapter Seventeen

Syrenne stands in the middle of the circle of teammates. She repeats the plan and their objectives, assigning roles accordingly as she sees fit. One of the members creates orbs of light to illuminate the glade as the darkness thickens. The group's paranoia reveals itself in their auras, ribbons of life force slipping from their grasp and focused stares on the shadows beyond the light's reach.

Tanten and Reece position themselves close enough to hear the plan but far enough to mumble to one another without detection. Tanten huffs as Syrenne provides her team with the offensive, most of Tanten's picks titled as guards or backup. From their joint training, Syrenne understands his members' capabilities. Yet, her lack of trust in their ability to take orders make them undesirable picks for the mission at hand.

"She even put Jolcob on lookout," Reece mutters, shaking his head. "Syrenne must really trust her team if she's leaving the better life force users for defense."

"It's fear," Tanten says, eyes squinted at his supposed co-captain. Despite his disagreement, he makes no comments. Out loud, that is, for the insults fly rampant in his head. "The woman who is both Professional and Scholar trembles at the thought of her precious Magistrate Association catching her. The plan paired with her picks to exercise utmost caution and to prevent any members from being caught. I say everyone's responsible for hiding their own face and covering their own tracks. Hmmph. What do I know..."

"More than her. And I say that with certainty," Reece responds with eager voice. Tanten smiles, as he always enjoys the affirmation of his disciple. "Time is of the essence. We don't know what Atlas is planning. They could be moving for the Association as we speak."

"No," Tanten murmurs with a slight chuckle. "I may not understand Atlas, but I know him more or less. No doubt he's already heading for Qoterra. He knows someone else will steal the piece for him. That way he doesn't get his hands dirty with the authorities. Though I'd say the deck's already been stacked against him. He's left too many prints."

"You're right. The rebels aren't talented enough to win against the Association's forces nor loyal enough not to betray his name when interrogated. But I'd say he already knows this and has his alibi."

"He always does," Tanten mumbles. He scratches his head, wondering how Atlas manages to do it all while consistently building his alliances. As if the rumors of his filthy deeds and constant instigation never reached the ears of another. Tanten saw the man behind the mask from the moment they met. Atlas the austromancer, loved by many and to become the youngest Vice President in the history of the Magistrate Association. Atlas' gusty aura, swirling about him with a confident ferocity, sucks all within it without them ever realizing his games. How he builds such trusts without ever revealing information about himself shrouds Atlas in mystery. And yet, only Tanten would ever view him as a traitor.

Finished with her speech, Syrenne approaches the two, expecting to hear their complaints the moment she stops at their side. The team warm up their bodies and life force for the mission ahead, Tanten's ruffians doing so begrudgingly at best. They murmur to one another about their disagreements on their placement. Angry glances meet Tanten, wondering why their captain made no comments in their favor. Tanten ignores it, not caring what they think. For in the end, he knows Reece and he could accomplish the mission by themselves. And no matter Syrenne's qualms, they will do so.

"Could you wipe that glum look off your face for ten seconds to not dampen morale?" Syrenne asks Tanten, arms crossed and gazing back at the team. "They already have their fears and doubts. The last they need is the knowledge that their leads are not confident in the plan."

"I'm confident we will succeed in the mission. Whether or not the plan works does not rest on my shoulders," Tanten responds, placing his hands behind his head and closing his eyes. Syrenne glances at Reece who averts his eyes, not wishing to get in the middle of their argument.

"We developed this plan together."

Tanten shrugs.

"I know you'd rather work alone. But you're a part of a team now. A team." Syrenne emphasizes the word. Tanten opens one eye to observe her expression before closing it again in his disinterest. "Teams work together, using everyone's individual abilities to multiply the power of every individual. You may not need us for this mission. But for the mission ahead you'll need all hands on deck. Better to train them now than to expect they'll be ready in the instant you require their assistance."

"That is why I suggested finding strong life force users from the beginning. But no. Syrenne knows best. Let's search for people who are good test takers, kind hearts with experience in the library or laboratory," Tanten sarcastically mocks, closing the distance with an intimidating stare. His voice remains low, but their expressions prove enough to draw the attention from the team. "What they need are abilities in which they are confident, well trained, and experienced in the battlefield. We don't need scientists. We need soldiers."

"So now this is a competition, is it?" Syrenne questions, amusement spelled across her face. Tanten hates when she finds enjoyment in his rants. "Then let's make it high stakes. If your team steals the altar piece successfully, the staff of the gods will be your claim when the time comes. And if my team-"

Tanten turns his head to mask a breathy chuckle. Syrenne bites her cheek to refrain from cursing.

"If my team steals the altar piece successfully, the staff is mine. Agreed?"

"While the stakes entice me, making it a competition between the teams may create division or some hostility for the one that loses. Similar to, oh, I don't know... Like a schism?" Tanten remarks. Syrenne rolls her eyes at his comment, knowing he'd always play devil's advocate when it came to her ideas. Reece understands the Professional often manipulates the terms of agreement to benefit himself more, however, he lacks to see how Tanten could desire anything more than the staff.

Tanten uneasily glances at his team members. It was enough that Syrenne attempted to direct them, in the least he wouldn't have to worry about the ruffians. But the thought of having to work as a team alongside them to fit Syrenne's tricky terms benefits her moreso than it does him. Even so, the prize tempts Tanten as they had never discussed who of the two would claim the staff. Tanten wonders if the winnings outweigh the cost. Either way he looks at it, he only needs her team as long as he sees them a necessity on his way to the staff. If at any time he decides them to be no more than a burden, he will continue the mission as he sees fit.

Syrenne reads Tanten's body language. Knowing the stakes, and the possibility she could win the prize of claiming the staff for herself scares him. But his arrogance and confidence feed his calm composure, preventing him from changing expression. She imagines he thinks himself good at poker, manipulating the table with his expressions. But she sees through the act. She's trained to. Yet he continues to underestimate her.

"If you wish to set the terms or have ideas for a new plan, I'm all ears," Syrenne says with a smile. Tanten realizes they play the same game and wishes to waste no more time.

"We need to move out. The sooner we get there, the better."

"So? Which plan is it?"

Tanten, with back to Syrenne, bites his lip, undecided whether or not to take her bait with a competition. He knows the Association building like the back of his hand, but her connections may have provided her with crucial information as to the storing of the altar piece. Perhaps settling on teamwork for the time being may be to his advantage. He'll finally get to see what this team's capable of.

"Everyone's already got your plan in their heads. Better to avoid confusion by not changing it now," Tanten replies.

Both Syrenne's and Reece's eyes grow wide. But Syrenne quickly deduces his reason to be one he refuses to admit. Tanten doesn't wish to risk losing the staff to her. Not that he would honor the deal, but in losing the others may see him as weak or lesser. Syrenne knows he lacks the abilities to coordinate a team, always relying on the individual to do their job and follow his lead. He doesn't wish to train rather find those capable and competent enough not to slack. He's found himself in over his head with this group of ruffians.

"Well then. Let's move out. I'll get the team together. You just do..." Syrenne pauses and takes a deep breath. "Just do whatever it is you do. Reece, start listening for transmissions. We don't want to walk up on Magistrate officers in their hunt for rebels. It'll be obvious we're life force users."

"Yes, ma'am," Reece mutters, eyeing Tanten to see if he permits his disciple taking orders from another. Tanten's expression remains unchanged, so Reece focuses to intercept what signals he can.

"The city's full of forces from the Association. Wouldn't be surprised if Rhys Champney's troops protect the Magistrate Association building," Reece whispers as Syrenne walks away. Only

Tanten hears him. With eyes closed, the technomancer raises his hand like an antenna, sending out life force waves at different frequencies in hopes of picking up on the channels of transmission.

"This plan will fail miserably if we don't step up now. None of her group have the strength to outmatch Rhys' troops. And there's no way I want to see his smiling face with what would be an easy victory for him," Tanten says as he shakes his head. He peers at his members, their disgruntled expressions proof they do not intend to follow Syrenne's plan.

With an angered expression and nudge of his head, he urges his men forward. They sigh in resignation and split off down paralleled roads. Despite their size, their footfalls land quietly in the all but silent night. Sirens blare along with warning horns, those often used to warn of storms and hurricanes, now being used by the military to force those in the capital to evacuate. The magistrate watch dogs, their hearings and sight magnified by life force in the night, linger not too far from where they stand. The streets crawl with life force users. Not all with good intentions. Tanten and crew are no exclusion.

Syrenne leads the group. Every intersection they pass, members slip off down adjacent streets. Tanten follows Syrenne at a distance, never taking his eyes off her. Not that he suspects she'll slip away, but he wishes to see the true limits of her life force. Enchanting power attempts to root with every step she takes, displaying her apprehension. Tanten's chest huffs as he silently chuckles.

Reece jumps as if hitting an invisible wall. His fingers curl inward and he tilts his head to the side. Those who remain in the group do not appear to notice, concerned about watching out for a possible enemy. Tanten notices Reece's reaction.

"If the team had any paranoia about being watched, simply watching the technomancer would be enough to either ensure or deny their suspicions. Their trust in those more powerful lacks," Tanten thinks.

His eyes focus in the direction of Reece's hand. Acting as an antenna to send out waves at different frequencies, it must have met interference. A searchlight from an overhead helicopter passes at the right angle. The faint glimmer gives away his position. A sniper.

At the sound of the helicopter blades, the members of their team duck behind vehicles and flatten themselves to the walls of the buildings lining the streets. Reece takes his place behind a streetlamp, his hand raised all the while. Tanten, who refuses to show fear, steps out to the center of the road. He squints his eyes, focusing life force within them, to get a better view of the sniper.

It appears the marksmen's weapon aims to the south, perhaps noticing the movements of a separatist group. Tanten lifts his arm in a straight line and points two fingers at the higher levels of the apartment complex. It was a great position as a corner lot with wrap around balcony, no doubt belonging to a wealthy politician. The complex also sits at an intersection. Tanten closes one eye and adjusts his arm to ensure pinpoint accuracy. With a careful exhale, pulling as much life force into his fingers as possible, he fires his pellet shaped life force in the direction of the military sniper.

"He'll neither see it nor feel it until it is too late," Tanten thinks as a smirk crosses his face. He knows the country's military sent defenses not well practiced in life force nor associated with the Magistrate Association to protect themselves from possible disloyalty. With confidence, he knows they will never determine him to be the killer. The better of the two snipers.

The life force remarkably holds shape until it hits its mark, but only after a shot rings out. Tanten's eyes widen to follow the trajectory of the bullet, but he loses sight as it continues along the back of the buildings up ahead. The team duck further in their hiding places, others throwing themselves to the ground. Reece covers his ears with both hands, gritting his teeth with the ringing of his sensitive ears. Tanten's eyes turn back to the lifeless form of the sniper. He sprints to the intersection, hoping to see the victim of his fatal shot.

"Tanten Flynn! What are you doing?" Syrenne yells in her whisper of a tone. She jogs after him.

Reece shakes his head, hoping the ring to go away, before raising his antenna once more. His palm turns toward the helicopter. Not ten seconds later, the helicopter spirals overhead. Interference directs the controls every which way until it crashes into the top floor of the apartment complex, leaving the bodies of those within and the sniper on the balcony no more than a pile of ash. Tanten's confidence far surpasses his own, with cleanup not always being a necessity but a definite precaution.

Tanten turns down the adjacent street and ducks behind a stationed delivery truck. Syrenne who follows not far behind, hears the explosion above her head and throws herself to the pavement. She wraps her life force about herself in a protective shield. She wipes the loose strands of hair from her face to look above, fire engulfing the top of the complex, shattered glass and metal fragments raining to the ground. Others from the group rush to Syrenne's side to ensure she sustains no injuries.

"Check if Ms. Tyrney is okay," one of the sculptors of the group says as they construct a barrier of life force to protect from falling debris.

A young woman holds out her hand to her leader to assist her up.

"She's fine," the woman states with a smile. "You think something as measly as that is going to take out one of the strongest life force users in the world?"

Syrenne shares a grin, grabs a hold of the offered hand, and stands to her feet, brushing any dust or dirt from her clothes. Syrenne peers down the intersection to see Tanten has stopped running.

He stands in the middle of the street with his fists clenched. His aura wraps about him as a fiery twister about the eye. Forceful. Menacing. Syrenne gazes down the street and notices a large lump in the road next to a vehicle. Blood pours from a bullet hole in the forehead, pooling onto the street with a river streaming from it and into a nearby sewer drain. It's one of Tanten's ruffians.

Sirens draw near, their blues and whites glittering in the night. A life force hawk flies overhead and lands near the lifeless body. Rage overcomes Tanten. With the squeeze of a fist, a steady and near undetectable string of life force wraps about the sculpted bird of prey and chokes it to the point of dissipation. Its user will never receive the message. With another twitch, the body of the ruffian splits into several pieces, steaming as the skin corrodes, leaving him unrecognizable.

Tanten returns to the group but stares at the ground.

"No one knows. And no one will ever figure it out. Our respect is all he will need," Tanten says before laying his gaze on the illuminated Magistrate Association building. He struts forward, not looking back. Reece runs to meet his teacher, hand raised all the while. A grin spreads across his face. Syrenne and the others gaze at one another before following behind.

Tanten pauses as they approach the next intersection. He turns to the right and notices a small group of shadows creep through the intersection the next street down. The Professional shakes his head at his own team's inability. The barking of patrol dogs sound in the distance behind them. A flash of light erupts into the air.

"Separatists calling attention. Either a perfect distraction or a costly one."

Tanten crosses through the intersection at a quick sprint. He conceals his aura all the while they traverse the city, not wishing to be noticed by another life force user scouting for auras. A scream echoes and a show of lights enters the sky above.

"An emitter. And with awful aim and concentration. Life force flying everywhere. Such inexperience..."

Tanten steps with confidence, not afraid though uncertain of what lies ahead.

"If I see that bloody Rhys Champney, I'd love to swipe that head right off his stupid neck," Tanten mumbles with a malevolent chuckle. "Or perhaps Atheas... I'm not picky."

Quick steps behind alert Tanten to turn around. Reece rushes toward him.

"Mr. Flynn, sir. Move along the wall. Let the shadows consume you. A magistrate officer has sent out bats. I hear their screeches and they seem to be heading this way. I can alter frequencies, but probably not for everyone at the same time."

"Do what you can, Reece. If the bats sense one of us, that person will be forced to run in the opposite direction to lead the bats away. But the bats can't go far if they're directly connected to their conjurer."

The team following behind rushes through the intersection, firetrucks with their sirens blazing down the street to the site of the flames which lick at the sides of the apartment complex. Syrenne takes a deep breath and gazes behind. She prays no one to be within that building when it eventually collapses. Her heart quakes, as if the consequences of all her life choices rise to meet her. Syrenne blinks away the threat of tears and jogs down the street.

Tanten smirks as he peeks around the corner at the illuminated Magistrate Association building. The ivory stone stands tall with white lights hitting the metal letters presenting the building to the world. A fine green lawn lined with flowers of many origins occur in patches with mosaic walks in between. Tanten walked this path many a time before, but never with such caution. Guards stand watch by every entrance, one with a sculpted earth golem nearby. Their eyes search the dark streets for any sudden movements. For any signs of attackers.

His eyes search for cause of a distraction. Certainly his own life force could go undetected, despite this lot having more experience than many on their team. Tanten goes to take a step, but Reece pulls him back by the shoulder. Tanten's initial reaction to turn and swing at the force is cut off by a howl in the air. A stray puddle in the road demonstrates the vibrations of a heavy object shaking the earth. All in their group freeze and listen, utilizing their life force over their senses to understand the shape and position of the object. But not only one exists. Tanten releases a breathy chuckle. The armored weaponry steps in time, synchronized down to the steps it would take to arrive at the building. And it comes from all directions.

"Good, they're doing it for us," Tanten smirks, looking behind and focusing his eyes to see a mechanical armored beast.

"It's not bad engineering," Reece comments while focusing some attention to the design. "Not perfect, most definitely some electrical flaws that they'll discover when they attempt to use the attachments."

"It may be to our advantage that they provide somewhat of a distraction," Syrenne whispers.

Tanten jumps, not having noticed she moved so close. He squints at her in his disgust. Her facial expression responds, and she steps back.

"The problem now is that the forces here will be hyper aware, drawing more forces near. If these are no more than amateurs, they won't do us much good."

"But we've still got a trick up our sleeve."

Tanten pats Reece on the back, sending a shiver of pride through his disciple.

The team huddle in the doorway of the corner shop and wait. Every step that draws near shakes the glass and vehicles in the streets. Sirens approach and then turn away, as do helicopters who wish to do no more than visualize the attack from the sky. Tanten recognizes some of the vehicles to be news outlets, doing all they can to snag the next story from other outlets. However, others belong to Dominia's special forces. When they notice the aim of the attack will be focused around the Association building, they leave, knowing it is not their fight.

The first rocket launches past the team members blending into the shadows of the corner shops of the intersection. They fear the rocket's flames will illuminate their faces, but this fear fades as the magistrate officers focus fully on stopping the rocket. The smell of burning fuel fills the air, smoke following the rocket in its wake.

One of the magistrates steps forward, lithe and slim, with a stylish pixie-cut. Her hands clap together and then pull apart at great speeds, a web like that of a spider's forming between them. Life force bursts from her palms, travelling to the left and right of her, expanding the web as large as her life force allows.

The rocket hits the web, stretching it to its limits, the nose poking at the window of the second floor before coming to a complete stop.

A tall officer with small, circular glasses, removes a cloth from their pocket. It expands with the life force that flows to it from their hands. They throw the cloth over the paralyzed missile, wrapping it up neatly, as easily as a present. Snatching the corners and bringing them all together, the cloth shrinks to its original size.

They hand the captured missile, now one-thousandth its original size, to a bulky man at their side. The man, built like a lilac-maned gorilla, places the cloth in his gargantuan palms. His life force concentrates in his hands, and he squeezes the cloth. An explosive boom resonates in the night, sounding as if the rocket collided with its target. The man separates his palms and several plumes of smoke escape. A satisfied grunt leaves the man.

With better understanding of their opponent's strength, the Scholars and informants command their attack vessels forward. Throwing strategy out the window, the chief makes a signal to fire from all sides, a last-ditch effort made by a chief not at all confident in their success.

Tanten focuses on the rockets flying at the Magistrate Association from all sides. His hands spring in front of him. He may not have the abilities built up by Atlas, but Tanten has his own way to shape time. The life force bursts from his hands, shifting the consistency of the air in some places. More friction in some places, less in others. The rockets all set to converge and make impact at the same time.

"Come on!"

Tanten rushes forward to the warzone, Reece hesitantly running behind as he understands the strategy Tanten employs but fails to see how they will make it inside the building alive.

The officers focus their life force on the oncoming attack, not concerned at all the blurred figures running toward the building. Their sole purpose: protect the Association building at all costs.

Tanten directs a finger pistol at one missile then another. He releases a concentrated burst of life force. The officers prepare to catch and deflect the missiles before they explode upon contact. Little did they know no contact would be needed. The tall officer with the cloth notices too late, as he senses the life force bullet fly past him.

Self-preservation takes control.

They wrap themself in the cloth before the flames of the explosion lick at them. The lithe woman cries out as her webs deteriorate, able to hold back objects, not fire. The hulky man attempts to split his life force across his entire body in hopes of protecting it. Unfortunately, he does not see the rocket aimed for his back, thanks to Tanten's misdirection.

Screams of triumph can be heard from the Scholars and informants as they close in. Celebration soon turns to panic when they come to learn the officers in front of the building were not the only threat. The shadows were also alive.

Tanten and Reece arrive at the front doors of the Association, masked in the smoke of the attacks. Reece trembles, fear overtaking him. Tanten connects eyes with his disciple and nods. The technomancer returns it and, with an exaggerated gulp, holds his hands up and releases a strong burst of energy in order to fluctuate the electromagnetic field about the building. In an instant, the lights about the Magistrate Association, from those within, to those shining upon the lettering on the outside, black out. Having studied the map of the Magistrate Association several times in their recent training sessions, they focus their attention and power through the doors.

The objects that had been slid in front to prevent entrance fly in all directions. Tanten's eyes meet Reece's. Their silent accord, one decided upon earlier should the situation come to this, has reached its prerequisites to be accomplished. A series of deep barks fill the halls coming from the back entrance of the Magistrate Association. Tanten smiles. The ruffians have arrived.

Bangs, booms, and screams erupt as chaos ensues. Those working in the front office of the Magistrate Association scatter from their workstations. The few who have been trained in the use of life force attempt a defense so others can escape. Tanten chuckles, absorbing their fear like a refreshing ray of sunshine after sitting in the breezy shade. He taps Reece's shoulder, who's become engulfed in the chaos of the room, covering his ears to prevent a break down. The two run for the elevator.

Syrenne watches as the ruffians scare the workers of the association. She squints and focuses on their attacks. None aim to kill their targets. Stun. Intimidate. Distract. This is not to plan.

A metallic clunk occurs in front of her and the sphere rolls to her feet. Before she processes what is about to happen, Yasmine yanks her arm to pull her away. Syrenne peers behind at the metal sphere, which twirls as a sickly fog whirs out. Her hand rises to her mouth, understanding the gas to be of the deprivation variety. It won't kill but deprive a person of the oxygen necessary to maintain consciousness.

"Of course they did," Yasmine mutters.

Syrenne starts to nod in agreement when her eyes meet Yasmine's face. Her ally's eyes do not look behind but ahead. His image flashes before her, the elevator door closing in front of them. Her aura flares in her rage, consuming her like a typhoon. Syrenne propels herself forward and slams her fists against the metal barrier. A whiff of the gas reaches her and the two run for the stairwell.

A locked door blocks entry to the lower levels. A locked entry means nothing to a practiced Professional. In the next moment the generator kicks in and the lights return. Yasmine emits an icy dart of the camera aimed in their direction, causing it to fall from its stand and hang by the cables. Syrenne places her hand on the door and allows her life force to flow through her. It works its way through the circuits and triggers the emitter to click the locks. With a swift push the door flies open and the two rush downward.

Tanten smiles to himself as he replays the shocked expression on Syrenne's face over and over. Reece focuses with a hand pressed against the wall of the elevator, sensing where the exits lie and examining which one they will take. The elevator clunks as the power returns.

"Damn it," Tanten says, pounding a fist against the wall.

"No worries, sir," Reece says, eyes squeezed shut as if in pain. "I disabled the cameras the moment I heard the generator click on. They won't have a single frame of us, I promise, Mr. Flynn."

Tanten, trusting in his disciple, taps his forehead in thought. His life force stems out in many directions. Examining the auras of those near, Tanten's confidence grows.

"That altar piece is ours."

Reece attempts a smile, but his nerves and focus make his expression appear squeamish. The elevator door opens, and Reece releases a large exhale followed by an equally deep inhale. Tanten jumps from the elevator, pulling Reece by the collar behind him. Reece hits the floor in shock of Tanten's quick action. The chill of the concrete embraces his palms and crawls up his arms, sending a shiver down his spine. The doors to the elevator close as Reece relinquishes his control of it to begin his focus on the journey ahead.

Several cameras, sensors, and other detecting devices surround the entire facility. The technomancer twitches as he thinks of what the holding chamber may include. His life force inches forward, curiosity taking over. His aura spins about him, the speeds picking up. And then... a wall...

"Uhh, Mr. Flynn-"

"Not now, Reece. I need to focus."

"But Mr. Fl-"

A throwing knife surrounded by a cloud of smoke cuts through the air between them. Tanten rushes forward.

"I trust you'll deal with the electrics," Tanten screams back as he charges the cloaked guard, wondering where the others hide. "Time to study more physics," Tanten says to the guard whose invisibility shielding loses form. Tanten directs his life force into his fists and punches the guard in the gut.

Reece sends out a strong electromagnetic pulse and triggers the breaker in the nearest fuse box. A strange reverberation of the electromagnetic field returns to him. The high field causes him instant nausea, not uncommon for one of his profession, and a sharp, passing headache, especially not uncommon.

His eyes focus and he emits a small, concentrated pulse. It reaches the metal door down the hall and bounces back. But it does not deflect from the door itself. The door was constructed to coincide with the natural shield, not the other way around. Then again, this entire level was constructed to protect this artifact. And they stand so close.

Tanten swings his leg outward to hit the man in the head. The hood falls from the guard's face. He focuses his life force into his hands but not quick enough to beat Tanten. An uppercut surprises the guard, sending him backwards into a steel wall with pipes leading from the floor to the ceiling. He winces as the scalding heat of the pipes radiates through his clothes.

Tanten steps forward to deliver a swift blow, his life force dancing on his fingertips. The sound of a footfall behind him sends Tanten spiraling 180 degrees. A blade of focused energy flies from his fingers in the direction of the interrupting stranger. Tanten's eyes widen. Another guard.

His fists clench as he watches the second guard dodge his attack. The blade dissipates before it can make contact with the exposed cables against the wall behind.

Tanten had not sensed this one.

The one he had sensed remains hidden behind crates by the emergency escape stairwell.

The guard motions his hands as if weaving spider webs in front of him. His life force knots about itself forming a net. The guard chuckles, obviously not recognizing the ex-Council member. Not realizing the heavily disproportionate battle about to ensue. Tanten smirks.

The life force net flies towards him. Tanten swings his right hand behind his back and sculpts a scimitar of life force. He holds his stance, releasing a steady exhale to time it right. Closing his eyes, Tanten rotates his shoulder and commits to the neat slice of the air.

The net fades away about him, fine remnants brushing against his cheek. He twists the blade about, cutting the distance between them. The guard wraps his life force around his forearms, believing it sufficient to shield the attack. However, his eyes spell out a different fear. Before the scimitar makes contact, his form falls to the ground.

Tanten pauses mid-motion in shock. The scimitar disappears like dust blowing in the breeze as he analyzes the guard.

An exposed dart plunged through his neck. As Tanten reaches down to grab it, the dart dissipates into raw life force particles, reentering their cycle in the universe. Tanten looks to Reece, who has made it to the metal door leading to the chamber. Reece stares in front of him, as if able to see what lies beyond without actual vision of it. Tanten's eyes search the room, and they fall upon the door to the stairwell. Two forms fill the once blocked doorway.

The first guard squirms behind Tanten, as if reaching for a weapon. Tanten's aura turns malevolent, sending heat waves of fury into the air. The man, sensing his powerful aura, freezes.

Tanten takes a deep breath, not wishing to appear as if he's not calm and collected. Syrenne approaches but Yasmine remains in the stairwell.

"The jig is up. We take the altar piece, regroup, and try to forget about all this bullshit," Syrenne says in the most patient, motherly tone she can conjure. Tanten hears the annoyance and nagging in her tone, forcing him to roll his eyes.

"That sounds about as brilliant as your other plans." His sarcasm shines through with the agitating, blinding light Syrenne's grown accustomed to.

Syrenne takes a step towards him, and he holds up his hand to stop her.

"Don't take another step."

"Tanten-"

"I said don't take another damn step. Reece! Open the blasted door and let's finish this."

"Yes, Mr. Flynn."

His trembling hand finds the handle and he pulls back. The aura hits him with an explosive gust. Awe overcomes him. Sitting in the middle of the chamber in a glass case is the altar piece. The broken piece of marble, carved with intricate details on the smooth sides, glows like the flame of a candle in a dark room. An odd disk shape receptor connects to the top of the case. A large cable runs from the top of the cap to the ceiling where it splits into several cables and heads in different directions.

"It's an energy mill..."

The life force of the altar piece paralyzes him. He fears its power. A shove pushes him to the side. Tanten slips past, angrily muttering.

"Reece! Have you shut off the cameras?" he asks as he paces to the middle of the room.

"There are none, sir. There's nothing. No traps. No gimmicks. It's just the altar piece inside an ordinary glass container."

"Well, then."

The container explodes into a million glass shards at the snap of Tanten's fingers. It's aura, which exceeds the radius of any he's ever seen, pushes back against his own. He smirks at its attempt. For as much as it pushes him away it pulls him in. His desire for such power consumes him. He unfolds a drawstring bag kept in his pocket and slides the altar piece within. The weight, not enough to deter a seeker, pulls down on the fabric of the bag. Tanten swings the bag about his back and utilizes his life force to lighten the load as well as mask the aura of the altar piece. The latter proves difficult.

With a grunt to get his momentum going, Tanten marches from the room. His eyes meet none, focused only on the door to the elevator.

"Come," he orders, Reece knowing the authoritative voice to be aimed at him.

"Yes, sir."

"And you," Tanten starts. He pauses in his tracks but does not turn to face her. "Wipe their memories."

Syrenne scoffs, a nervous quake escaping through her vocal cords.

"I'll just manipulate them, create conditions."

"Wipe. Their. Memories. Tonight, yesterday, their entire damn existence. I know you can do it. You're capable. So just do it. Do it!"

All jump at his scream. The injured guard against the pipes and the other in hiding gulp down their fears, thinking of their personal plans for escape. They realize their optimism to be futile. In the least, they will escape with their lives.

Reece enters the elevator alongside his teacher. Fear and an odd sense of pride swell within him. Tanten notes the tremble of Reece's aura and chooses to ignore it. The kid will learn. One day.

The elevator door closes as Syrenne approaches the man by the pipes. She holds out a hand and shakes her head in disapproval, while understanding her own reputation to be at risk should she fail. A heated glare comes from Yasmine, staring at the ex-Council member for the monster he is.

Tanten chuckles.

"Perhaps I am a monster. A monster for now. But soon, I'll be a god."

Chapter Eighteen

Koepp and Nix lie in bed, tucked in comfortably at the request of Botalia, despite the heat encased in the room. They tried to turn on the air conditioning unit, but the electrical outlets did not work, which would explain the lack of lights in the hotel. Koepp breathes calmly as sleep envelops him. Nix stares at the ceiling, he's in bed only in obedience to Botalia. Tenebrant sits on the other bed, legs extended in front of him and hands behind his head. His eyes are closed and a steady stream of life force flows about him like a gentle breeze with several channels. It stretches out on all sides but entirely within his control, able to be pulled back in a moment's notice.

Botalia sits on the ground by the glass door to the balcony. She drew back the curtains to get a view of the city below. Lights and traces of life force fly into the sky all around. Her eyes trace the skyline. A tall building constructed of ivory stone looms in the distance. A shiver rises up her spine and a force pushes against her chest. Her heart races.

Botalia clenches her fists.

"Calm down," she mumbles to herself, though more the being inside of her. "We're not doing anything wrong. We're doing what's right. It is right. Stay calm."

She pulls her knees in close and rests her head upon them. Her jaw chatters and a tear falls from her cheek to the carpet.

Tenebrant opens an eye to glimpse at her broken form. In his frustration of her fragile emotions, despite having such a store of life force, he wishes to scream. Rather he bites his lip and shuts his eye.

Her eyelids slide down, blocking and blurring her sight. Fatigue and drowsiness wish to pull her into a deep sleep. But her nerves keep her on edge, forcing her stay awake every time the threat returns.

"You should get some rest," Botalia mumbles to Tenebrant. Whether to keep her own self awake or cover her guilt of dragging him along, she fails to decipher. Her voice proves her emptiness. Her hopelessness.

"What about you? You're practically sleepwalking at this point."

"I'm not tired."

"You're also not a liar. Right?"

Botalia releases a breathy scoff. She rubs her eyes then slaps her cheeks simultaneously. As she opens her mouth to respond, her lips push together. His words sink in. A slide from the show of images burns into her mind. She shakes her head. Guilt, an ever-looming emotion, presses down on her back.

"Listen, I get it. But we can't change the past."

"Despite how much it's changed us?" Tenebrant asks. Botalia turns to see him staring at her with a laser focused glare.

"Yeah..." Botalia peers into the night. The streetlights illuminate buildings which cast their shadows on those behind. Shadows darker than those around them move through the streets. Botalia pulls her legs in a little bit closer. "We have changed a lot, haven't we?"

"So is life."

Silence falls between the two. As much as Botalia feels the thread bonding them to one another pull and tug, she can't help but wish to let go. Rid herself of the memories and the heartache. Echoes circle her mind. Inability to help. Inability to save. Despite having the power, she'd never be capable. Her exile stopped her from nothing. She would always be her own roadblock. Her own shadow.

A helicopter zooms by the building at incredible speeds. A searchlight angles toward the street below. Botalia's eyes pop in alert. She quickly disguises the auras of all in the room, hoping she isn't too late. Nix jolts up and looks to the window.

"What was that?" he asks in a panic.

"Nothing to worry about. It was just a helicopter, probably after someone, or multiple people. It's fine. Everything's-"

An explosion occurs a few blocks over. The sky turns crimson as the flames kiss the clouds. Koepp jumps awake and all stare out the window. Botalia's jaw drops. A pain hits her in the chest. She clenches her fists and punches the ground.

"I'm not sure what they're hoping to accomplish with this Schism," Tenebrant says with an eyeroll. "Wiping an entire city off the map isn't exactly helping their cause. Not only is the Magistrate Association after them but the Dominian National Guard."

Botalia rises from the floor, places her palms against the cold glass pane, and gazes at the burning apartment complex. Blue and white lights from the emergency vehicles rush from all sides of town to the complex. The sirens barely reach her ears through the glass.

"Not sure why they'd even waste their time," Tenebrant says. "The only ones left inside of this cursed city are the rebels and magistrates too proud to leave."

"And us," Koepp whispers, the comforter of the bed pulled up to his chin, his fingers seen clutching the fabric.

Tenebrant chuckles.

"And us..."

Several minutes of silence pass. Botalia slinks to the floor, stroking the sleek wood panels beneath her.

"Little friction," she mouths without allowing her voice to escape her mind. She brings her palms together into a praying position before separating them in front of her. Her eyes focus to see the spiderweb like life force hanging between her hands. With a deep breath, she places her palms on the floor.

Her life force travels like an excited pet hearing the call of their owner. Botalia smiles, joyous to experience the tranquility of her life force connecting with the earth. Her life force finds the concrete and, as a spring when reaching its limits, it retracts itself in an instant with elastic force. Botalia jumps. She bites her lip in frustration and wipes at her brow.

"How do you do it?" Koepp's hopeless voice sounds disembodied in the quiet room, as if no more than a thought wishing to make itself known. "How are you not scared? Why did we want to come to this bad place?"

Botalia peers at Tenebrant, who raises his eyebrows at her as if she alone should answer.

"I'm not really sure," Botalia says, her voice barely passing a whisper. "You and Nix probably shouldn't be here. This is my fight, really. It was selfish of me to involve you all in this."

"You didn't force us into this," Nix states in a bothered tone. "Our parents did. We never had a choice. Since we were born it was sure we'd have to choose a side at some point. You saved us from being on the wrong side."

Tenebrant rolls his eyes but chooses to make no comment. Botalia stands and walks to their bedside. She places a hand on Koepp's head and rubs his shaggy, black hair back. Unkempt and dark as obsidian. Just like his father's.

Botalia tries to blink away the memories, their memories, as they flash through her head. Koepp's past trauma felt as heavy as Tanten's during the time of the slideshow. But their age difference... father and son. *And yet father put son through hell for his own pride... pure narcissism.*

"Nix, I appreciate the sentiment," Botalia states, swiping her hair back and sitting on the edge of the bed. Nix squints as the meaning of her word passes by him. Koepp glances at his friend and is relieved to find he's not the only one who doesn't understand Botalia all the time. "But I'm not sure you want to be on my side. No one ever was." Tenebrant rolls his eyes yet again and bites down on his lower lip in a grimace. "And no one ever should be. I'm an exile for a reason. Believe me, they made no mistake in their decision. Maybe that's why I wish to help. I know their intentions are good-"

"The Magistrate Association is a large conglomerate of people from all over the world," Tenebrant interrupts, a venomous tone taking over. "To say they all have good intentions isn't only naive but complete stupidity."

Nix's head jolts in the direction of Tenebrant, a scowl revealing itself to the necromancer.

"Shut up."

"Excuse me?"

Tenebrant and Nix glare at one another.

"Believing in good isn't stupid."

"But no one is wholly good. Not you. Definitely not me-"

"Then they can't be all evil either."

"Stop fighting!" Koepp screams in a whisper, fear crawling through him for the ongoing war outside. Botalia reaches out to grab Koepp's arm but her hand springs back as if static shocks her. His aura leaks in his fear and anxiety. "Don't you understand. We're supposed to be here. Together. We all have good and bad in us. But we want to stop a bigger bad."

"Your dad?"

"Tenebrant," Botalia snarls through barred teeth.

Koepp grips the blanket in his hands, squeezing the life from it. He releases a shaky exhale, the word yes almost forming from the breath to pass his lips.

"I'll tell you one thing that's certain," Tenebrant sits up and pulls his feet together in a butterfly position. "If it is Professionals versus

Scholars as they say the Schism is between, the science side stands no chance. Tanten is a Professional with not a scholarly bone in his body. He's on the strongest side, as per usual. He hates losing. The Magistrate Association created this monster by dividing the sides and not forcing its members to be skilled in both a science and life force area of study. Being classified as a Professional attracts those hungry for power through the need to feel stronger than others. That's what learning life force does. It turns from wishing to utilize a supernatural power to the desire to use its abilities to cause fear and demonstrate power."

"Not everyone uses life force for violence and war," Botalia says with a pleading in her tone. Her own intentions in learning life force and her limits with it were never attempted with ill will. Her heart trembles and a shiver finds its way up her spine. "Some of us want to help."

"And look how quick the Association exiled you. Not two days after passing your exam and they filed you away as a monster. And funnily enough not the type of monster they wanted."

"It was because I was a danger. Not because of my intentions."

"And your parents were highly regarded Scholars-"

"Tenebrant..."

"No doubt someone in the Association felt intimidated by the power they possessed. Is it odd that after you pass the exam, proving how powerful a trained hybrid can grow and at such speeds, your parents wound up dead within days? They learned that day that Scholars possess a power they would never be capable of. Creating a biological weapon. One with sentience. One that can grow exponentially faster than humans."

"Tenebrant," Botalia says, staring at the blanket on the boys' bed, unable to face him. "Please don't talk about me as if I am a monster."

Tenebrant focuses his eyes. Botalia's life force centers on her chest, pulsating with an angered intensity. The creature wants to play. It wants to protect.

"Being good with life force doesn't make her a monster," Nix interjects, his irritation obvious. "And wanting to be good at life force doesn't mean you have bad intentions."

"Says the boy who's been taught life force for the sole purpose of killing others."

"You two need to stop ripping at each other's throats." Botalia makes eye contact with Tenebrant for the first time since their conversation began. Her vision blurs behind the wall of tears threatening to collapse. Nix turns to her in defiance.

"He's had the aura of a killer since we got here." Nix sticks his arm out straight as he points at the necromancer. If his arm had been longer, Nix would have sliced through Tenebrant's neck. "I know you sense it," he says as his aura forces Botalia to look at him. It swirls about him like a twister hugging his body, defending him from outside influences of power.

"Botalia," Tenebrant whispers. "Do you never wonder who sold your parents to those traders?"

Botalia swallows the lump in her throat, tears refusing to form in her eyes. In her ears, she hears the racing of her heart and behind it a low rumble of a growl. Fists squeezing the life out of the nothing in her palm, Botalia attempts to control the life force slipping from her grip. It drips in wisps and tries to manifest.

"I-" Botalia's voice falls off, her breath unable to push words forward. She bites her lip and looks out the window of the balcony. The sudden warmth of Koepp's hand finding her own gives her comfort. The pounding on her chest calms and she takes in a large breath.

"You killed the organ traders, sure," Tenebrant continues. His eyes look past the point where the wall meets the ceiling, as if no longer speaking with Botalia but to himself. His thoughts take form and cloud the air, hanging there above all their heads. "But what sort of closure does that bring? Is there any satisfaction in killing if no answers are unearthed?"

Botalia's head darts in the direction of Tenebrant with his self-revelation she's certain not even he realized. Her jaw drops as if wishing to speak but words fail her.

"There's no point in always thinking about the past," Nix states, his tone never wavering as he speaks. He masks his emotions, taking a serious tone, never allowing any into his head. "You can't change what happened. No one can bring the dead back to life." Nix's voice takes an odd turn with his comment, the venom targeting the necromancer.

Tenebrant releases a breathy chuckle with the semblance of a pained grin appearing on his face. He raises his eyebrows and, with a lick of his upper lip, admits defeat in his resting expression. He extends his legs and places his hands behind his head as he closes his eyes.

The weight of the room crushes Botalia. She stands and walks to the window, placing her fingertips on the chilled glass pane. Botalia closes her eyes and mumbles a prayer. She's never considered herself religious. But when the dark closes in on her, sucking up all the light, the belief that something bigger than the universe exists calms her mind. Perhaps this omnipotent being does not need life force. Maybe it created life force. Botalia lets slip a pained grin.

Flames build up in the distance. The grey clouds mask the indigo sky. Botalia imagines the damage to be done if that elementalist in the rebel group was skilled enough to control the fire. It's no more than luck that the groups partaking in the Schism had not already caused mass destruction. One advanced in life force, near a similar level to Atlas or Tanten, would have no problem destroying the capital of Dominia were they actually involved in the civil war. Botalia squints, the thought striking her as odd.

Tenebrant may be on to something...

Most high-level scholars are above such petty fights. However, high-level Professionals are often fueled by pride and a thirst for more. But more what? A Professional could easily dismantle the tactics of a Scholar, life force better equipped for battle than machines, as the greatest sculptors could create such weapons but to a greater power.

Botalia opens the glass door to the balcony, her hair blowing back with the breeze. She listens. Sirens. As she lifts a foot to step forward, she hears loud screams and the sound of an explosion. Several blocks over, darkness wipes out the lights of a section of town. Botalia slams the glass door shut and slides her back against it.

"It's been a long time since I've been here," Botalia says, breaking through the stiff silence. "Does anyone know what's in that direction?" Botalia points to where the explosion and black out occurred.

Tenebrant opens an eye to see which direction she points. He closes it and sighs.

"I'm surprised it's not burned into your memory," Tenebrant responds, keeping his voice monotone. "Not too far in that direction is the Magistrate Association building."

Botalia peers northeast. An attack on the Association building. In biting curiosity, she throws open the door and leans over the rail of the balcony. She focuses her eyes and sees the fireworks of life force to fill the sky. Tenebrant, who also draws his life force to his eyes, leans forward at the spectacular display. His jaw drops.

"A revolution," Tenebrant whispers. "The Scholars bring their tank prototypes. The Professionals bring quickly thought up strategies. No one was quite ready for this. Not even the Magistrate Association."

"The Magistrate Association should always be ready for a fight, though," Nix says, not necessarily to anyone in particular. Confusion laces his tone. "They start wars in so many places, you'd think this would be nothing."

Botalia's blood rises with Nix's comment. Tenebrant smirks and looks to Botalia, amusement alight in his eyes. She reflects on Tenebrant's and Tanten's words from earlier. She never understood their lack of respect for the Magistrate Association.

"Rhys has to be there. And *he's* there. He has to be close..." Botalia thinks as she stares in the direction of the Association.

"We'll see what's become of it in the morning," Tenebrant says as he takes a soothing tone. Botalia turns to him, her eyes softening.

"Some things never change, I guess..." she thinks.

"Nix, Koepp. Time to close your eyes and forget we're in a warzone. Botalia," he looks up to see she's already peering at him. "You need to rest and rejuvenate your life force. If we're to head in that direction tomorrow, you better bet they're on high alert."

Botalia walks over to the bed where the boys are laying. Koepp scoots closer to the middle and Botalia takes her place on the edge. Turning to her side, Botalia places a hand on Koepp's arm. A slight grin leaves him before a it fades to a neutral expression. She starts to inch her hand toward Nix. He flinches.

"You don't have to use your powers on me. I don't need a lot of sleep anyway. What kind of assassin would I have been if I get tired easily?"

Botalia smiles, retracting her arm. Her eyes drift towards Tenebrant. He stares out the window with a solemn expression. A small wisp of life force escapes from his fingertips and circles his arms. Botalia blinks her eyes, trying to lose focus of her observation of his life force. She bites her lip.

"He senses death."

The horizon fills with light before the sun can be seen. Botalia sits up slowly, wishing not to disturb Koepp. Nix stares at the ceiling, obviously thinking the same of not wishing to wake his friend with any movements. Tenebrant stands out on the balcony. Life force flows from him to the ground, stemming to different nearby locations.

Botalia approaches him.

"The sky seems to have settled," she says. He doesn't acknowledge she's there, his entire focus on his scouting life force. "If you wanted to search the city, it would go much faster if we both took a part. Divide and c-"

"I don't need your help."

Tenebrant makes no movements visible to the average eye. To the trained eye, his aura swirls with greater ferocity, but his life force retracts very little, proving his recalcitrant nature. Botalia surrenders before attempting any further.

She pops open a bag of bread cakes Nix found the night before. Found. Stole. Nix said the food machine didn't put up a fight. With a whiff of the air, Koepp darts up, hands moving to his stomach.

"I'm so hungry," he states with eyes moving to the bag in Botalia's hand.

She giggles and tosses him the rest of the bag, taking a bite of the sweet food. Throughout the bread, sweet berries are interspersed. Blueberries, roseberries, bouganberries. Botalia forgot how good processed foods were. The sugar hits and her stomach rumbles. She grimaces.

As Koepp reaches to grab the bag from the air, Nix's hand bolts out and he rolls out of the bed, bread cakes in hand. He sticks out his tongue and hurriedly shoves a cake in his mouth.

"Hey!" Koepp shouts with a smile on his face.

"If you want it, you'll have to fight me. I hope you've been practicing," Nix says as he eats another cake, taunting his friend.

Koepp jumps out of bed and the two commence their chase about the room. Nix opens the door and runs into the hallway, Koepp not hesitating before following. Botalia jumps to follow, but Tenebrant interrupts her worries.

"There's no one around."

"No officers? No rebels?"

"It is no more than a hunch, but I believe the attack at the Magistrate Association scared even the rebels. No doubt the Magistrate's officials have secured a perimeter about the building."

"How will we ever get through?" Botalia asks, crossing her arms in deep thought.

Tenebrant shakes his head, falling back to reality as he repeats her words.

"Get through? We're here to fight Tanten. Atlas. Not meet up with your old friends at the Association."

"How many deaths were there?"

"What?" Tenebrant asks, not knowing she could sense it. Several articles he's read state that experienced life force users sense life force utilization in the necromantic skill tree. As if sensing the dead differs greatly from life force meant to find life. He was always skeptical. He remains so. He smirks, his back to her. She simply knows him too well.

"Eighteen. Most of them from a rebel group comprised of informants. The others either ran or were arrested. But... no, nevermind."

"What is it?"

"There was a large group that escaped from the scene. The amount of life force from the group... it probably surpasses..."

Botalia's presence appears at his side causing him to jump. Her senses are heightened, her movements silent. Her serious expression demonstrates her understanding.

"They weren't rebels?"

Tenebrant shakes his head.

"If a group of that caliber would have involved themselves in the fight, we would have sensed that life force from here."

"Magistrate officials?"

"It's possible. But the source of the life force... I couldn't sense the outline of a human form. Unless the user focused their life force in a strange way, I'd even bet the source wasn't human."

Botalia gazes at Tenebrant, a hollow knocking on her chest. She paces back and forth for a minute before finding her way to the balcony window. She stares in the direction on the Magistrate Association building.

"Let's go."

She turns and walks toward the door.

"Koepp! Nix! Time for another adventure!"

Tenebrant hears their shouts of excitement in the distance. He chuckles and shakes his head.

"This puzzle is far from complete," he says before erasing any life force signatures from the room and exiting.

Chapter Nineteen

The four leave the abandoned hotel, Tenebrant and Nix having scouted the nearby area before Koepp and Botalia followed. None revealed themselves for quite some distance. Tenebrant says those who refuse to mask their life force are those who wish the others to know of their presence. Magistrate officials and arrogant rebels. In the light of day, the rebels hide or cover their faces, protecting them from public ridicule should history fall on the wrong side of their group. But the end will see no victors. All will be judged poorly by history.

Tenebrant silences the group's footsteps as they continue forward. His life force attaches to the bottom of their feet, absorbing every sound and vibration. Attempting to go without detection, Botalia masks their auras. Nix zips from one position to the next to analyze their surroundings from many angles. Koepp stares at the road ahead, fearing his incompetence may be their downfall.

The intersection which leads to the Magistrate Association lay ahead. Botalia gulps the saliva buildup in her mouth. Her anxiety of addressing the very institution to outcast her bites at her mind, pounds at her chest. Life force leaves in thin wisps from her fingertips. Botalia retracts what life force she can.

Nix peeks around a building at the intersection and down the street. He shakes his head, his eyes forming no more than slits.

"It's gonna be tricky."

"A highly skilled assassin should know that the main headquarters for the Magistrate Association would be heavily under guard. If you could not sense that you should assume there to be a problem."

Nix rolls his eyes and peeks around the building. With the speed and the expression of being hit by a lightning strike, Nix pulls back from his spying position. His eyes threaten to give nothing away but Botalia senses the urgency of his calm. Tenebrant worries himself in life force patrol and misses Nix's expression but senses the need to panic.

A sapphire finch flies past the building, silent and determined. Before a call escapes its syrinx, Tenebrant aims a concentrated life force missile at its chest. The bird vanishes into a cloud of stray life force, unable to manifest or return to its sender.

"We need to back track and find another way," Tenebrant advises, pulling Nix away from the edge of the building. Nix glares at him before walking back toward the way they came.

Koepp turns to the first alleyway and points.

"Why not a shortcut?"

"The rebels could be using such passages as traps for unsuspecting officers. Day or night, city alleyways are used for dirty business. Trust me," Tenebrant says with a slight smirk.

"What about we try phase walking?"

"What?" Botalia asks, never having heard the term. Her eyes find Tenebrant, his eyebrows raised as he considers the notion.

"It's an assassination technique," Nix explains. "It's like masking your movements without masking your aura. They know you're there, they just don't know where. They're already paranoid, they know there are others here that they can't see. It'll give us the chance to sneak past while they drive themselves crazy trying to find what they can't see."

"A psychological tactic as well as strategic one..."

Botalia considers the idea but wonders how it will work against these higher ranked life force users. She places a palm against the building and closes her eyes. The denser forms of life force earlier guarding the doors to the Magistrate Association are no longer there. Two lesser forms draw near to the edge where they previously stood. Botalia blinks several times. She cannot decide whether it be her deteriorating mental state blurring the life force or some sort of life force jammer affecting her signal. Botalia pulls Koepp with her into the alleyway. Nix and Tenebrant, who sensed those who approach, await the forms, a competition growing between the two.

Botalia cups a hand about Koepp's nose and mouth, more so her own fear than the believe that he may yell or make any other unnecessary noises. A flash of life force occurs around the corner of the building. Botalia backs further away, dragging Koepp along with her. Nix and Tenebrant leave her field of vision.

With life force, she enhances her senses to understand their positioning and state of being. An odd sensation tingles at her back as she picks up on another. Her eyes widen as the hand wraps about her hair and pulls her down.

Tenebrant and Nix look to one another, challenge alight in their eyes. A sizzling sound can be heard and several small firecrackers zip from around the corner. Nix swats at them as they fly in front of his face and pop. Tenebrant encloses a fist around each firecracker, biting his lip as his eyes flicker with excitement at the pain. Smoke lifts from his palm upon opening it to view the damage. Tenebrant chuckles. Their attackers round the corner.

Both wear uniforms akin to magistrate officers. Colorful pins line their pockets, demonstrating their incredible achievements as magistrates. Tenebrant licks his lips as he notices the middle-aged man with the bald head has a blue flame pin. A sign he's successfully dealt with reanimated beings. A worthy adversary.

"You take the young one," Tenebrant whispers to Nix, his eyes focus in on his prey.

"Why do you think you get to choose my victim?" Nix pouts and crosses his arms.

The two officers look to one another, confused by the exchange. Neither realize exactly who their targets are.

"Listen, the dotard can manage the likes of you," Tenebrant says, no longer hiding his words in low volume. "The young one might be your only chance to show you're capable."

"I'm pretty certain I've killed more than you."

Nix's words paralyze Tenebrant. He shakes his head and gazes at the young assassin.

"I think you'd be surprised-"

"Forty-six. I've killed forty-six since I was eight."

The officials' jaws drop.

"Who are these kids?" the bald man says to the other. The young man shrugs and removes his gun from its holster.

"Not bad," Tenebrant responds, rolling his eyes at the assassin's immaturity. "To be honest, I never started counting. I never think I'll kill another until I do. Just like now."

Black smoke whirls about Tenebrant's hands. Tiny bolts of lightning flash as if he holds dark, cumulonimbus clouds in his hands. At this sight, the magistrate officials raise their guards.

"Stop what you're doing there, sir," the young man warns as he aims his gun. "We don't wish to injure anyone. We're looking for the criminals who stole from the Association building last night."

Tenebrant raises his eyebrows, curiosity itching at him. Nix, who fails to understand the weight of the officer's words itches to attack.

"Don't make any sudden movements," the bald man says, his life force moving to his hands.

"We're gonna be taking you both in to the station to ask some questions."

"What did they steal?" Tenebrant asks, wondering what kind of information they'll let slip.

"That is classified information, sir."

"So you don't know," Tenebrant says, eyebrows arched in an unamused expression. He pushes more life force to his hands, not wishing to waste any more time.

"Calm down and place your hands on the ground, sir," the young officer instructs with a tremble in his tone.

"Make me," Tenebrant tempts with a smirk.

"You said he was mine," Nix mumbles, his eyes forming slits.

"Then take him before I do."

Nix raises his left hand and moves his right hand about it, transmuting his life force to the likeness of a sharp object, an extension of his arm.

"They both know life force!" the bald man gasps.

Nix leaps at the young man, who turns his gun on the young boy. His movements prove too slow, hesitation in killing a child his downfall. Nix's hand, sharp as the blade of a katana, slices his wrist. The gun falls from his hand as the other hand reaches for the pouring blood.

The bald man acknowledges the imminent threat to his partner and turns to defend. He lunges, but out of his peripheral vision he realizes his mistake too late. Tenebrant shakes his head.

"And you leave your right side undefended. Such a shame. I thought you were worthy."

Before the bald man can channel his life force to his hands, a cutting pain slices through his gut. He looks down to see a smoky kris protruding from him. His body convulses as the curse moves through his blood and tears him apart from the inside out. His corpse falls to the pavement, twitching until the last ounce of life blows away with the breeze.

Nix hits the street and lunges at his opponent's back. His velocity proves far too great for the magistrate. The ex-assassin slices at the back of the heels then delivers a final blow to the neck.

"Not bad," Tenebrant smirks. He struts to the corpse and withdraws his kris before it dissolves into life force.

Meanwhile, Botalia and Koepp fight their own battle.

The stranger from the shadows pulls Botalia back. Botalia pushes Koepp away, hoping to send him from the danger. Three beings form from the shadows on the brick walls of the alleyway and wrap their contorted, almost transparent arms about him.

"No!" he screams as he wrestles with the force.

Botalia turns in a panic to reach for Koepp when a leg with knee-high, leather heeled boot slams into her chest knocking her back. The brick wall behind stops her from falling to the ground, her head pounding into the hard surface. A sharp pain reverberates throughout her skull. Botalia blinks away the black spots covering her vision as she tries to catch a glimpse of her attacker. Her heart races as she imagines something truly awful happening to Koepp.

A hand with long, manicured nails wraps about her neck. As if being formed from the wrist out, the enemy reveals herself. Half of her head is shaved, the other half with wispy, obsidian hair. Her attire appears made of the shadows themselves. A badge of a white diamond shines from her vest's collar.

"A magistrate," Botalia mumbles, examining her opponent.

"Children like you have no place in this city right now," the woman states in a strict tone. "This is a war zone."

"And whose side are you on?" Botalia presses, undecided as to whether she should reason with the attacker.

The woman smirks and licks her teeth. Her hand squeezes tighter about Botalia's neck. With the same movement, the shadows constricting Koepp do so with more force. Rage grows within Botalia as Koepp's fearful expression sinks into her memory.

"Unfortunately, I'll have to silence you both before you lead more magistrate officers in this direction. Those two should be rounding the corner any minute and I'll be far away from here by then," the woman says as she removes a thin knife from her vest and points it at Botalia's cheek. "You won't blow my cover to those hypocrites at the Magistrate Association. I'll get in and I'll take it. You were at the wrong place at the wrong time. You kids made a big mistake."

Koepp winces as the shadowy arms restrict his movements. His strength proves insufficient to protect himself from this conjurer's life force. Botalia takes a breath and looks the woman dead in the eye.

"I'm not a kid," Botalia whispers. Both of her hands jolt up to grab the wrists of the woman. The enemy's eyes widen. "And the mistake is yours."

Botalia's life force manifests into a large, shady golem that forms between the two. The presence forces the woman to lose grip of Botalia.

The woman steps back, eyes focused on the shadow beast. She bites her lip in her ultimate decision to free Koepp and reabsorb her life force to defend against Botalia's creature. Shielding herself in her own life force, the woman gathers the strength she possesses in the palm of her hand. She directs her palm at the beast and grunts as her life force emits in a blinding white light. A hole bores through the shadow beast at the point of contact but reforms after the attack finishes. Fully healed as if nothing had happened.

"Who are you?" the woman asks, pushing her hair from her face in her panic. "Are you a Professional? A Scholar?"

"As far as they're concerned, I shouldn't even exist," Botalia answers.

She telepathically instructs her shadow beast to pin the woman against the wall. Her thoughts turn violent as the creature within her rages with its desire to protect. Botalia bites her lip, not wishing for these thoughts to reach the beast. Not wishing to do more harm to the woman.

Her heart beats with a rapid fury. Images of the past resurface, reminding Botalia of what it's capable of. She shakes her head. The icy morning air fills her lungs at temperatures much lower than those that surround her.

"Koepp!" Nix's scream as he runs toward his friend pulls Botalia from her mind.

"Botalia."

A desperate voice calls to her. She turns to see Tenebrant, with wide eyes and soft expression. He finished his battle, blood lust and adrenaline pulling at his heart, his lungs working double to calm his breathing and racing thoughts. His eyes look at her not as if she is the girl who protected those years ago but as if she were the monster. The shadow beast disintegrates, and the woman flees the scene.

"Crazy lot of kids," the woman mutters as she rounds the corner.

Botalia shakes her head and returns to reality.

"There's something... Something she's after... that other people are after..."

Botalia mumbles, trying to piece the puzzle together.

"And they have it," Tenebrant states. "The magistrate officers let it slip. They stole it last night. No doubt it's that group with the large concentration of life force that we sensed."

"Let's get going," Botalia says in an urgent tone. She backs away from the wall and stumbles. Her head turns to face Tenebrant. She mouths, "Thank you."

Koepp nods as Nix asks if he's okay. His jaw trembles, but Koepp's eyes shine with his desire to live. Botalia clenches her fists and follows the path to the other side of the alleyway. Botalia senses the woman they encountered far away, as if she had given up hope in her original plans. Or perhaps she now understands that what she sought no longer lie within the Magistrate Association.

"We should start doing the phase walking technique, so they don't see us coming," Nix says as he peeks into street to observe the army. Fifteen officers and five life force sculpts stand in the courtyard outside the Association building. Botalia gulps and gazes at Koepp.

"The entire point of phase walking is that the enemy sees a frozen frame of you. After they first have a line of sight, then begin to phase walk. Unless using their life force as a shield, they should remain focused on the image of you that isn't you."

Nix rolls his eyes with Tenebrant's correction of his error.

"Whatever. I'll go first."

Nix steps into the street, hands in his pockets, and starts to whistle to attract the attention of the officers.

"Hey, you!" one yells, their voice amplified by life force.

Nix smirks and starts his phase walk. Tenebrant nods and the three follow Nix's lead.

Upon seeing the three, the officer's raise their guard, all turning to what they assume to be a joke, as four kids couldn't possibly be a threat. Botalia examines Tenebrant as he steps into his phase walk. As if leaving a shell of himself behind, he steps from his image, walking in beat to his heart, and moves straight to the building. With a blink, Botalia no longer sees him but only the frozen image.

"It requires vast amount of life force to see the one casting this technique. Though perhaps he's using his life force to cloak his actual position. He's much stronger than I thought he was..."

Botalia squeezes Koepp's hand and commits to the phase walk. If she doubts in her ability for even a moment, the officers will detect their position. With intense concentration and a deep exhale, Botalia freezes their image to the backdrop. She pauses and looks to Koepp, all life drained from his eyes.

"Don't panic, Koepp," Botalia thinks as she offers a gentle squeeze of his hand. "Even if they sense us, no harm will come to you."

Botalia leads them forward, the air with the consistency and friction of water. Botalia pushes on, stepping to the beat she hears in her eardrum. If she breaks the rhythm, she knows it will break the phase. With caution, they walk past the officers, who focus their attention on the frozen images. The officer's forms are blurred. Botalia is not convinced the position she views are the correct ones of the officers, the phase walk messing with her perception.

She blinks from the phase and sees Nix and Tenebrant hiding behind potted cypress bushes near the front door. Nix rolls his eyes at Tenebrant's smirk, Tenebrant obviously arriving before the ex-assassin despite his lead. Every officer and sculpt have wandered from the courtyard and search the alleyway they previously exited, looking for the children who got away. Botalia takes a deep breath and smiles at the team.

They enter the building, observing the chaos of the workers around them. The phones ring nonstop and the officials constantly ask and answer questions yelled to and by others. The group approach the front desk.

Botalia stands in front of the three. "Hello?" she calls in a regular tone, no one looking in her direction. She places her hands on her hips, exhausted by being ignored after all they'd been through. "Hello?" Botalia yells. A woman, who appears rather irritated, walks up to the desk.

"Sorry, but if you cannot tell, we're a little busy right now. If you wouldn't mind leaving and returning at another time." The woman forces a smile, though her sardonic tone reveals her true attitude. She looks curiously at the boys and continues. "How did you get past the-"

Botalia pulls out her Magistrate license. "I'm a magistrate. I came to help."

"We're busy at the moment. And this is no place for children," the lady responds. Murmurs begin in the background, along with occasional glances at Tenebrant as the workers recognize him. He looks to the ground, feeling he can't do anything rash in Botalia's presence. Though far from being in her strongest state, she's glowing with resolve.

"I want to help!" Botalia pleads. "I can-"

"Leave!" the lady screams. Botalia leans back, shocked by the response. "The Council is looking to the top magistrates for assistance. They don't need the help of two children, a criminal, and an overeager amateur."

Tenebrant chuckles. The woman glares at him and walks away with arms crossed.

"Can you just tell them Botalia Ulton was here," Botalia calls after her.

The woman keeps her back turned and waves her hand. Botalia sighs. An elderly worker turns to Botalia, an expression of shock on his face. He walks over to her and grabs her arm. She looks at him, confused.

"I thought you were gone," the elderly man states, a happiness in his voice. "My, look at how you've grown." He looks her up and down in amazement. "I used to work for your parents way back. Conducting research and the such."

Botalia grins, happy her parents and their work are still remembered in a good light by some. A relief hits her to know the man knew her parents, but then the shock sets in. He must know what she is. She hopes his reaction proves genuine in its happiness, that anger nor fear will take over.

As her desires come to life, the man says, "Tell you what, I'll show you where the Council are so you can offer them assistance when their meeting is over."

"Thank you, Mr... I'm sorry, I can't remember your name," Botalia says.

"Oh, I shouldn't expect a two-year-old to have remembered my name. I'm Westin Sapotski. And it's my pleasure. Anything to help an Ulton," Westin replies.

Koepp and Nix join Botalia's side, smiling to express their gratitude. Westin leads the way down the corridor, no one caring enough to stop them.

"They're in deep trouble. You may be the savior they need."

Botalia's heart sinks as the walk to meet the Council triggers painful memories all too familiar in her tormented mind. She attempts to control her heartbeat with breathing exercises, but her aura reveals her nerves to anyone focusing on it. Tenebrant senses her anxiety, and internally laughs as he thinks about the girl who's stronger than anyone in terms of life force forgetting her own strength and abilities.

They walk down the hall and Westin stops in front of the door. Botalia instantly recognizes the location and crosses her arms in a nervous fashion, whether trying to hide herself by appearing smaller or preventing her heart from escaping her chest. Preparing for the wait, Koepp and Nix sit against the wall. Westin bows his head and walks away.

"Thank you. I hope we'll meet again one day," Botalia calls after.

Westin continues down the hall, a smile growing on his face as a tear slides down his cheek. The memories of his former life creep into the back of his mind, along with the guilt he now feels for participating in such acts against nature. He offers a prayer that any divine being that exists above may forgive him. However, seeing Botalia Ulton, strong, courageous, and selfless, almost like a normal human, gives him the bit of comfort he sought for so long. Westin turns the corner, hoping they may meet again.

Botalia leans against the wall, staring at the floor, thinking about what to say to the Council members. She wonders how she'll react if any of them remember her. Before Tanten's appearance, she thought they had forgotten her, but the possibility they remember her still exists.

The hallway they stand in remains quiet. Every so often, the four hear indistinct voices from within the meeting room. Minutes have passed since their arrival, but to Botalia it has felt much longer.

The sound of footsteps approaches the hallway. The man turns the corner and the four look up to see the newcomer. The man stops in his tracks, ten feet from the meeting room door. His eyes drift from Nix to Koepp. They pause as they settle on Tenebrant, a scowl forming. But his eyes continue to Botalia and freeze. His eyes widen. Botalia makes eye contact, realizing he must remember her as much as she remembers him.

Chapter Twenty

People rush through the hallways, papers and panic a common theme among each of them. Azriel Vayl maintains her composure despite being attacked by numerous questions from all around her. The Vice President continues down the hall, calmly and briefly answering the questions as she passes. A young woman rushes to her side, clipboard in hand.

"Turin Vitas has arrived. What time should I tell them the meeting will begin?" the young woman asks.

"Five minutes. I suspect that's not unreasonable seeing how long we had to wait for them," Vayl replies. The young woman nods and rushes down the hall to deliver the message.

Vayl continues on her path, a shaky breath and feigned confidence in every step. She enters a room with a large oval table and nineteen chairs surrounding it. The walls are empty to prevent distractions. No windows. No decor. An empty room only made entertaining by the characters to fill it. And magistrates are characters. She walks to the back of the room, dragging her fingertips along the backs of each and sits at the head of the table.

After a few seconds, another person enters the room. He tilts his head in the direction of the woman and takes his seat. A few minutes pass and only five chairs remain unfilled. The young woman with the clipboard enters and approaches Azriel Vayl. The young secretary hands her a stack of papers and exits the room.

A large, gruff man enters. He sits in his chair and turns to Azriel Vayl, who sits in a timid position at the head of the table. She leans forward with hands grabbing the opposite elbows.

"Cefni's takin' care o' some business. He said ta start the meeting," the man voices.

"Very well. Thank you, Mr. Champney," the Vice President responds.

"Just call me Rhys, Ms. Vayl."

"Very well. Shall we roll call?" Vayl asks.

The Council members stare blankly in her direction, as if the question posed should be rhetorical. For three of the four chairs that are empty are not currently in use, and they all knew the absent person to be the one forewarned about.

"For formality's sake?" Azriel Vayl asks again. With no response and a few eye rolls, she sighs.

The Council elected Vayl to serve as the Vice President (despite there being no President) of the Magistrate Association after several members abandoned the Council due to the ever-growing issue of the Schism. But not only for that reason. The issue crawled up after the President's death. The previous Vice President resigned along with four Council Members. Vayl, with great support from many of the newer Council members, attempted to lead the Council, hoping to mend the division and progress the Magistrate Association. However, she knows many of the veteran Council members will never quite see or respect her as the Vice President, despite their attempts.

"I believe we should discuss how to quell this chaos," asserts Lenora Kasper, a Philosophical and Literary Scholar. She joined the Council approximately nine months back, around the time of death of the President. Her jet black, curly hair and impatient personality place her outside of the stereotype of her field, however, she can be very insightful in difficult situations.

"Yes, well-" Vayl begins before being interrupted.

"Hey, Atheas. Shouldn't you be out leading your men against the separatist swarms?" Guto Robinson interjects. Guto works as a Professional, studying druidic rites and life force in nature. He is one of the two new recruits to join the Council without being elected by the populace. He treats others disrespectfully, but the Council members cannot deny his expanse of knowledge.

"Cefni can take care. And don't interrupt Ms. Vayl, Guto. She's the one leading the meeting here," Atheas Maynard responds. Atheas specializes in many Professional divisions. He has been on Council for the past sixteen years and took Tanten's bounty hunting position when he resigned. He mainly teaches manipulating and manifesting life force to his disciples.

"So, let's begin," Vayl states. "We can discuss any number of tactics we should be employing in the present, but this will do more harm than good in the long run. We need an adequate strategy to stop these attacks, not only here but in other nations where the Schism runs rampant. We don't need a war. We don't want a war. What we need is a cure to this disease."

"If we're talking medicines, there are quite a few poisons that may solve the problems we're facing. Curses, rituals... Xocopa, any suggestions?" Guto directs this final question to Xocopa Shauck. He scoffs in response, other veteran Council members shocked at his comments, though not as much as they would be if they hadn't thought it to be of character.

"Perhaps what we need is some form of uh...international propaganda by famous political figures both sides trust in. Convince them to stop. One who is both Professional and Scholar," Entzia says with voice fading in and out in her own doubts.

"Who do you suggest?" Turin says with an eyebrow raised and mockery lacing his tone.

"Umm…" Entzia's eyes scan the room as her answer creates greater hesitation. Her voice doesn't break a whisper. "Atlas Lurio?"

The room erupts in an uproar. Entzia lowers in her chair, as if lowering into a turtle shell.

As the Council continues to bicker ten minutes later, Vayl leans her head on her hand, her face expressing her dissatisfaction about the state of the meeting. All seemingly exists outside of her control at this point.

"If we can't secure this city, how can we begin to secure every other!" yells Lenora. Some of the members nod in agreement, but others wear an expression of being even more put-off by the suggestion.

"What we need is to restrain each separatist group. One at a time, being the most viable method," suggests Kiaran Szucs, a marine Scholar. He's one of the younger members, but one of the best in his field, incredibly intelligent and rational in all situations.

"That's impossible. Their numbers will keep growing. Most likely faster than we can restrain them," Gwyn Sanoba retorts. Gwyn is well-practiced in life force manipulation, dowsing, and astronomy, making her both a Professional and a Scholar. She was elected at the same time as Atheas Maynard. Though one of the older members, no one underestimates her abilities, both mental and physical.

"What do you suggest then?" Kiaran questions.

"I recommend we-"

"Do we have a budget?" Guto interrupts, directing his question to Azriel Vayl.

"It's civil war. We need to do whatever necessary to stop it," Vayl answers.

"What if we hire assassins to take out the leaders? The groups should quickly surrender if they have no one to follow," Xocopa Shauck (a Necromantic Professional) suggests.

The room erupts once more over his suggestion, for most people look down upon the use of assassins. Amidst the argument, the door opens. The Council members freeze and look toward it to see who has arrived in the middle of their heated discussion. Vayl raises her head. Cefni Medina enters, pausing in the doorway to peek into the room.

"I hope I'm not interrupting anything," Cefni states.

"Not at all, we're jus' having some fun," Rhys jokes. "We're jus' talkin' about-" He stops.

Cefni enters and stands at the opposite end of the table of Vayl, a young woman following close behind him. Gwyn Sanoba, Atheas Maynard, Ibovel Sobiski (an Alchemic Professional and Chemistry Scholar), and Merwyn Giacobbe (Professional considered a master in life force manifestation) express their shock from their faces to their body language to their auras. Their eyes focus in as they lean forward. The other Council members grow confused. Rhys frowns.

"Cefni..."

"Who is this broad?" Guto asks, the shock and confusion of the others having no effect on him.

"I ask your respect," Cefni directs at Guto. "Rhys, please, hear me out."

"She can't be here." Rhys responds.

"Who are you?" Vayl asks, focusing her eyes on Botalia. Azriel examines Botalia's aura and notices its strange flow, unlike any she has ever seen before. Not to mention the curious concentration of life force in her chest.

Botalia swallows. Cefni places his hand on her shoulder. She glances up at him and he nods.

"My name is Botalia Ulton," she answers.

"And why are you here, Ms. Ulton?" Vayl continues. A grin spreads across her face as she recognizes the name. She didn't know the famous Ulton's had a descendant.

"I want to help," Botalia replies.

The Council members laugh, excluding the members who remember her and Vayl. Botalia looks to the ground. Her heart beats against her chest. Anger or embarrassment she cannot decipher, but she wishes to escape before doing something she may regret. Her head shakes slightly. She's in control. She has to be...

"Silence!" Rhys shouts to end the laughter. He knows well the prediction made by the President came true, for the President never predicted incorrectly. Rhys is aware of the power Botalia must possess, and he can tell, solely by looking at her aura, how powerful she must be, understanding her current state not to be her full strength.

He stands. Vayl turns to him, attempting to understand the seriousness of the older members, for only the veterans appear changed since her entrance.

Rhys continues, "Ms. Ulton, you know well you shouldn' be here."

"Rhys, she-" Cefni begins, but Botalia's gaze urges him to stop.

"Mr. Champney," Botalia starts, making eye contact with Rhys. "I can't deny that all of your assumptions of me may have some truth to them. But, please, listen. I want to help."

"What can a being like you do to help us?" Atheas jabs. Botalia turns to him, the two exchanging glares. However, Botalia decides to be grateful he withheld the term "monster," for an otherwise offensive reaction on her part may lead to them being forcefully removed from the building. The other Council members look at Atheas, confused by his question.

"I won' deny you'd be of great advantage," Rhys states. "But, we can't be responsible for a tickin' time bomb."

"But Mr. Champney-" Botalia starts but is interrupted.

"We already got trouble on our hands, we don't need another-"

"I agreed with you. Ten years ago. I was out of control and dangerous. I know that. But I disagree with you now. I've gotten stronger. I can control it. I swear. Please, let me prove myself," Botalia pleads. They lock eyes and he can sense her determination. He can't deny she's become more powerful, but whether she has more control or not is questionable.

"I believe, if the President predicted accurately, her strength to be far superior to any of our own. From examining her aura and life force, we can confirm this," Cefni states.

The Council members not familiar with her did not think to focus their eyes and analyze her aura. The reactions of the Council members vary from awe, to disbelief, to fear, granted they did not know she was still in the process of rejuvenating her storehouse.

"How do you wish to help us, Ms. Ulton?" Vayl questions. The fact the late President saw incredible potential in Botalia means Azriel cannot let this chance slip through her grasp.

"Obviously she should fight the separatist groups," interjects Guto before Botalia has the chance to respond.

"Her power may be better suited aiding in the protection and transportation of civilians," Rania Sturgess suggests.

"What about securing and guarding this building? That should be our first priority," Turin Vitas declares.

"The girl's intelligence is better suited for developing strategies, you know, if she truly learned under her parents," Orphacia Glatz chimes in.

Some of the Council members continue to argue, their talking hurriedly evolving into screaming.

Vayl coughs and Rhys understands his cue. "Silence!" he screams. "I believe Ms. Vayl asked Botalia. Go 'head, Ms. Ulton."

"While the civil war concerns me, there is another matter that I feel may be more life threatening and catastrophic, though I don't know why. Instinct, I guess," Botalia states.

"What concerns you more than the war?" Vayl asks, squinting at Botalia, realizing the girl knows more than she may have first assumed. With Botalia's silence, Vayl takes a deep breath. "You know something, but you still lack information, it appears. Well, Ms. Ulton. Ask us anything. And we'll answer as honestly as our laws permit."

Botalia, impressed by Vayl's insight, knows the question she chooses may remain unanswered, thinking about Vayl's wording. With care, she sculpts a question she feels may not pry too deep.

"What did they steal?" Botalia questions, her nerves shaking her entire body. Every eye in the room stares at her. A thick silence fills the space. Time freezes. Botalia remains patient, not adding to or retracting her question. Vayl giggles.

"May I ask for context?" Vayl urges.

"A couple of officers suggested someone broke into this building. And I cannot think they lied of the matter due to the increase in security and the strange events to occur last night. Those who entered did not do so without a reason. Not to mention they must have been strong to have accomplished their goal without being caught. I want to know what they stole," Botalia tries to salvage her question. "If I know what they stole, it may be easier to stop them."

"Who?" Azriel Vayl questions.

"I'd rather not say, for it's only a theory and I don't wish to inaccurately criminalize anyone. Please, what did they steal?" Botalia pleads.

Vayl's eyes connect with Botalia for a second before peering down at the stack of papers laying before her. She quickly shuffles through the stack and pulls out a picture. Vayl raises the image for all to see. The Council members unaware of the theft gasp in horror, as does Botalia.

It can't be...

The picture in Vayl's hand shows a white slab, inlaid with gold and sapphire.

"They stole the altar piece! We spent a tremendous amount of time and energy excavating the holy artifact just for it to fall into the hands of some ruffians!" Orphacia screams, expressing her shock at the reveal. Orphacia Glatz joined the Council at the same time as Guto. She is an Archaeological and Geological Scholar. Her team spent several months cautiously digging out and cleaning the altar piece after discovering the edge of it in one of their sites.

"Ms. Ulton, to steal an artifact so precious and dangerous means they are only after one thing: infinite power. If this group of thieves find the location of the altar and refit it with the missing piece, the world may be in peril."

Vayl realizes how dramatic the scenario sounds, but she understands how dangerous power can be when used by those with little self-control.

"We'll deal with the civil war. Your job includes stopping the group and returning the altar piece to us. Well, Ms. Ulton? Are you up for the challenge?" Vayl asks.

Botalia nods.

"Good. However, I feel it's in the Magistrate Association's best interest if we send supervision along with you. If I gather correctly, you are an exile after all. We wouldn't want you running away or betraying your word."

"I'll accept the supervision, however, I also have a team I'd like to take along with me," Botalia says.

Botalia walks to the door and beckons the others into the room. Koepp, Nix and Tenebrant enter and take their place behind Botalia. The Council members drop their jaws, primarily from noticing Tenebrant among her team. The Council breaks into an uproar. They turn to Vayl, yelling statements like: "They're only kids!" and "He's a murderer!" and "She's insane if she believes she can get away with this!" Vayl sighs as she listens to the numerous complaints. Her eyes shift to Rhys who again yells for silence.

"If you believe they can be of value to you, I will not reject your proposal," Vayl begins. "However, I would like for you, Ms. Ulton, to introduce your team to us, telling us how they may serve in your mission."

"Alright."

Botalia looks behind her left-shoulder and sees Tenebrant. She sighs. *I should have known this wasn't going to be easy...* She observes the Council members, all of them growing impatient.

"Tenebrant Mortu. A strong ally, capable of holding his own in combat. He's masterful with the use of life force and quickly deduces any scenario."

The Council mumbles, but Botalia ignores it.

"Nix Kufuta." The Council members grow louder, but rapidly quiet themselves. "Extremely agile and observant. He's a student of mine."

She turns to Koepp, nervous to state his name in front of the Council. Tanten was never well-liked by the Council members.

"Koepp Flynn." The Council members erupt into a hailstorm of disagreement. Rhys attempts to silence them, but they continue to scream at Vayl, pointing fingers at Koepp. Botalia decides to talk over them, raising the volume of her voice. "He's strong and highly motivated and perseverant. He was my first student and I believe he has the potential to do incredible things."

The Council stares at Botalia, having quieted down.

"I trust each of these people with my life. They are my team. We've already agreed to go on this mission together, and I refuse to abandon them."

"Your loyalty is admirable," Vayl smiles. "Cefni, I would send you to supervise, given your history with the girl. However, we need you here to advise your forces. Unless... Atheas, do you think you could handle Cefni's forces as well as your own?"

"I won't deny it will be difficult, but my forces already have their orders. Leading Cefni's forces will be my first priority if given the opportunity. That is, if Cefni accepts," Atheas responds.

"I wish for Cefni and Merwyn to accompany the team." Vayl looks to Botalia. "I have my own theory as to who the thieves are. And if my intuition is correct, offering up two of the finest and strongest magistrates to accompany you is the least I can do."

"I accept," Merwyn answers. Botalia smiles. She peers up at Cefni, his eyes closed.

Cefni cannot help but remember walking into the scene of the crime ten years ago. He was called to the scene when officers realized the massacre deserved a proper investigation by an official magistrate detective.

As he entered the building, Cefni froze in disbelief. Mutilated bodies covered the ground, the smell of blood overwhelming. The attacks appeared to be from a monster of sorts. He focused his eyes to see if the fight included life force. The residue of life force projectiles covered the walls and floors, the victims marked by their attacks. A strange concentration of aura led him to a survivor.

In the midst of the carnage lay a young girl, unscathed by the attack. The blood on her hands and clothing being not her own. He reached down his hand in an attempt to check the girl's condition. A burning sensation seethed his flesh at the border of her aura. He instinctively pulled his hand back. He examined his skin only to discover blisters forming, much like the reaction from a chemical burn. In that moment, he became fully conscious of the power this girl possessed, for all other possibilities disappeared. This girl was the sole attacker. This girl was the monster. This girl was Botalia Ulton.

The images circle Cefni's mind. He returns to reality and observes the room around him. He understands none of the Council members contain a power stronger than Botalia. *If the monster escapes again, there's no way for me to stop it.* Everyone looks to Cefni, waiting for his response. Cefni takes a deep breath.

"I will accompany Botalia if she so wishes it," Cefni answers. Botalia forces a grin, but she senses all is not right. Cefni appears distracted.

"Ms. Ulton?" Vayl questions. Botalia locks eyes with Cefni.

"I would feel honored to be accompanied by Cefni Medina," Botalia states. "And equally as honored with Merwyn Giacobbe." Botalia glimpses the excited expressions on Koepp's and Nix's face. Tenebrant scratches his forehead and grumbles slightly.

Tenebrant very much dislikes the idea of being supervised, especially by Council members. Simply being in their presence awakens his hostility and he shakes from the anxiety and excitement. Each person around the table possesses great strength, possibly paralleling his own. Their hatred of him tempts him even more. But if he jumps, he may not get the chance to fight Tanten one on one. No distractions. No rules. A fight to the death against his long-time adversary. Tenebrant knows it's in his grasp. He can't let a little whim ruin his opportunity.

"Well, they already have the altar piece. The last we'd need is for them to make it to the altar's location in Qoterra. Orphacia, prepare a booklet for our team so they can be informed of what they are chasing. Lenora, please locate the journals from the adventurers, those which you uncovered with the discovery of the altar piece. Guto, we'll need a short essay on the druidic tribes of the region as well as rituals and rites the team need to be aware of when crossing through druidic lands. Mairo, this team will need a vaccine for Pterosicaria as there are plenty of Sanguine Arthropoda, the Blood Moth, in Qoterra, also a supply of any medicines you deem necessary for the region. Atheas, get them a private plane with the local airport, back way entrance and minimize media trying to catch a glimpse. If they see Council members leaving the city, it will surely divulge our plan."

Vayl leans back and presses a finger to her lips, wondering what else she may be forgetting. Her eyes scan the group once more, focusing in on their auras. Surprisingly, one of the younger boys has an aura that appears quite tame. Botalia's, moving about her like some form of energetic field, spikes curiosity. And Tenebrant's, twisting and hostile, forces her to stay on edge.

"Ibovel, Rhys, bring me the latest reports of this Schism issue. Gwyn, test if you can predict where the next large attacks may take place so we can work to prevent them. We'll reconvene tomorrow, in hopes someone has thought of a plan to end this Schism. And tomorrow, this team will depart on their journey. Unfortunately, we don't have the time to properly train you. But I do not worry, for you all appear quite capable."

Tenebrant scoffs as he believes he senses a tad of sarcasm. He gives a slight shake of his head and looks to the ground with amusement in his eyes. Those around the room glare at his form, amusing him all the more.

Vayl rises with a clearing of her throat to get the others' attention. They rise in suit, collecting their belongings before exiting to the hallway. As Ibovel Sobiski and Gwyn Sanoba pass, they bow to the team in respect of them and their mission. Koepp and Nix turn to one another in their surprise. A smile escapes Botalia, not knowing how much their acceptance of her would mean.

Merwyn and Cefni bow in the direction of their acquaintances, and Merwyn leads the way out of the room. Once in the hall, the team shares their last farewells.

"If this ain't a team o' heroes. I don' know what is," Rhys states. "They often say those destined for greatness are attracted to one 'nother by fate. Whoever they are, they may be right."

Vayl stares at the team, admiration and delight in her eyes. Tenebrant notices her strange glow. He focuses his eyes and watches as her aura flurries around in a similar manner to a blizzard. "She's hiding something..." is the first thought to intuitively enter Tenebrant's mind.

A hand falls on Botalia's shoulder, causing her to jump. She turns to see Azriel Vayl.

"Ms. Ulton, please take care. The moment you retrieve the altar piece, get it back here as soon as possible. We can talk about the terms of your status upon your return. Anyways," Vayl extends her hand. "I'm honored to be a witness of your rise to legend."

Botalia's nerves resume at the sight of Vayl's extended hand. In her current state, Botalia may collapse if the instant causes too much pain, not to mention the scene it may cause. Botalia ignores her hand and instead bows.

"I feel honored to have stood in your presence," Botalia states.

Vayl puts her arm back to her side and frowns, staring at Botalia with a curious, and malicious, expression. Botalia returns to Koepp and Nix, who both hop up and down as they giggle to each other discussing the crazy adventures they imagine they'll have.

Meanwhile, Cefni and Rhys stand against the wall not too far down the hall. Rhys occasionally glances at Botalia.

"What do you plan on doin' if she gets out of hand?" Rhys asks. Cefni closes his eyes and sighs.

"In the worst case scenario, I'll either leave her behind or... I may have no choice but to kill her," Cefni responds, apprehension lacing his voice.

"Aye," Rhys says. He looks to the ground before returning his eyes to Cefni. "If you hesitate, you may lose more than jus' your life," Rhys says nodding towards the young boys. "Jus' remember, the monster's not her. It will kill if it decides ta come out ta play."

The last farewell is said, and the party of six set out on their mission. Merwyn leads with a confident stride, engaging himself in pleasant conversation with Koepp and Nix. Tenebrant follows behind them, his arms crossed. Botalia and Cefni walk alongside one another in the back. The two can't help but feel the unwanted memories creeping in.

Ten years ago, they walked down the same hall together, side by side. The environment felt much more grim and hostile then, for both of them. At the time, Botalia marched to her inescapable life of solitude and nonexistence.

After hearing the discussion of sentencing her to exile, Botalia lost all motivation to fight back. Her body numbed. Her mind blanked. Cefni knows he will never forget that day, her hopelessness and despair filtered out of her, leaving nothing but a kinetic body behind. They both remember getting into the vehicle and heading to the docks. The silence of the journey made the parting all the more lonely for Botalia. She felt she had nothing left. And her feeling mirrored what Cefni saw in her and himself. The two were meant to exist as hollow shells.

Cefni thought the purpose of his life was to fill the shell every time it emptied, only to find the shell was cracked. It could never contain anything, and, despite his efforts, Cefni was never able to mend the cracks. Even when the contents would stay for a period of time, a parasite found a way in through the cracks, devouring all within it. Cefni theorized if he could fill the shell he would find true happiness. But the truth is, happiness falls easily through the cracks of a broken shell.

Chapter Twenty-One

Despite the change in location, the team continues to train. Day and night, they work to improve their abilities and increase their life force. Many of the team begin to shake, sweat forming rivers down their faces. Their long and tasking training created a bond between every individual. They know and understand everyone's strengths and weaknesses. They may not be the strongest individuals, but as a team, they are unbeatable. United.

This is why they respect their boss, why their loyalty unto him is unshakable and no doubt ever increases. He treasured them all as individuals despite their obvious weaknesses because he knew together, as a team, each weakness could be countered by another's strength. He treated them all with an unwavering respect and care, not wanting to lose any of his precious gems for the fear it may upset the balance. He saw the potential in each of them and understood their desire to grow stronger would perpetuate for centuries if it needed to, even more so now they feel a part of a team.

Keniph walks out of the gym and sits next to Atlas.

"Is the wall really that interestin'? You been staring at it for four hours," Keniph jokes.

He knows Atlas has a lot on his mind, but constantly thinking about the situations and possible strategies will only increase his doubt of their standing. Atlas's solemn demeanor and poor posture prove he is starting to question everything.

Keniph continues, "We can't turn back now. The team has worked too hard for you to just abandon them."

Atlas sighs. The thought of abandoning those who proved their loyalty to him never crossed his mind. His connections are precious. He would rarely sacrifice his bonds, unless of course those broken bonds would prove more useful. Atlas closes his eyes.

"I've done things in the past few days I'd swore I'd never do. I blatantly betrayed each of my allies," Atlas states. He looks at Keniph who appears to be listening intently to his words. "I know we talked about it, how neither team could help us achieve our goals, but I feel ashamed now. What if our team begins to question my loyalty to them seeing how readily I threw it away for the others?"

"Atlas," Keniph begins, a glow in his eyes. "You've stayed true to every word you've told us thus far. The team respects you and will follow you to the end of the nations just to see you succeed."

"Keniph." Atlas looks at Keniph with an unrelenting expression. Keniph senses Atlas continues to shift his attention elsewhere. To Atlas, the conversation hasn't been about his concern with loyalty, but about his desire for his own form of justice to prevail and needing a team that will help him achieve his will. Atlas's thoughts appear to be his worst enemy, tearing him apart from the inside, not allowing him any tranquility. "We must destroy them. We must not let them reach the altar. Tanten, Bysciw, or Jevid (the Crusader's leader)... We can't let them win. For humanity's sake."

Keniph nods and stands. Atlas looks up at him, a softer expression on his face.

"Red," Keniph says with a look of resolve. "We won't let you down."

Keniph returns to the gym. Atlas chuckles as Keniph walks through the doors, realizing his fortune in finding a magnificent lead.

He stretches his legs out and puts his arms behind his head, returning to his thoughts once more. Though less vicious than before, Atlas's thoughts continue to instill fear in him.

The possible outcomes of this mission are infinite, and he knows he must be willing to accept all possibilities. Atlas knows well that you can't take one's life without being prepared to lose your own.

Since becoming a magistrate, he has held fast to this ideal. Though he only holds the purest of intentions, Atlas understands his goal cannot be achieved without the evilest of actions. Atlas undertook this mission to prevent power from falling into the hands of selfish and careless individuals. To create a good and just world, power must be in the hands of those who aren't hungry for it. Power must be wielded for the whole and not the individual. Yet, those not hungry for power often do not search for it due to their disinterest. Though wielding said power does not interest him, Atlas feels he must be the one to wield it. Only he can make good of unlimited power. He's willing to sacrifice anything and everything to attain power, thus depriving others of it. The world's burden will rest upon Atlas's shoulders. And Atlas will kill all who threaten the sanctuary he seeks to create.

Thinking such thoughts exhausts Atlas as his heart weighs down on him.

"Playing hero sure is tough," Atlas whispers. He stands and walks into the gym.

As he gazes around, Atlas can't help but smile at the cohesion of his team. Targe, whose real name is Artoria, continues to strengthen her life force wall. Her life force concentrates itself in a stable crystalline formation. Very few people are capable of their life force bonding in such a manner. That is why Atlas chose Artoria. Though only Atlas's disciple, Artoria has a natural talent for bonding her own life force. Its crystalline structure makes it impenetrable to projectiles consisting of concentrated life force and hardly shakes with the explosion of man-made projectiles.

The nineteen-year-old boy named Ilric spends his training time running his hands along different blades and guns. After examining each of them for an extended period, he walks away. With his back to the weaponry, Ilric concentrates on conjuring each weapon, attempting to create a facsimile of each of them. Not only can he replicate the blades and guns down to the smallest detail, but each weapon is inch by inch stronger than the original due to them being constructed of his life force. At the beginning of his training, Ilric was given a set of weapons to copy. Every day since, the weapons have been different. Over time, his senses quickly examined all aspects of the weaponry in short periods. Atlas knows Ilric's abilities don't solely work for weaponry, but other objects as well. If Ilric can perfect conjuring complex objects like guns, basic objects will be simple for him.

Some other members work on their physical build. Strengthening their muscles and training their bodies for endurance and agility. Fighting with fists, swords, and life force means all members must be versatile in their combat styles. The members spar with one another, not holding back in their techniques. The team's medic, or residential shaman as they refer to her, Leda, observes as the sparring occurs. She focuses her eyes, ready to pull out any person who sustains what she considers too much damage. Though often annoyed by her motherly nags, the team deeply respects Leda and her medicinal wisdom.

Atlas steps to the punching bag in the corner of the room. He removes his suit jacket and rolls up his sleeves. The anger and frustrations he's bottled over the past year, the resurfaced memories, find their release through his fists and legs. Atlas's hostility, though amused, is unsatisfied with the exercise.

Atlas' phone vibrates in his pocket, the shock of which causes him to punch the bag off of the line tethering it in place and launch it against the wall. The resounding boom causes all to turn to him. Some laugh when they see the punching bag detached from the line, the hole in the wall also amusing them. Atlas sighs. He throws his suit jacket over his shoulder and exits the gym, taking his phone from his pocket.

"Hello?" Atlas answers, his breathing heavy.

"Hello, well don't you sound exhausted? Is it really so tiring turtling away?" Azriel Vayl jokingly questions. Atlas lets out an unamused chuckle.

"Any news of Tanten's whereabouts?" Atlas asks. He looks around in a paranoid manner, guaranteeing his solitude.

"Nothing as of yet. Atheas Maynard sent his troops to the supposed locations of each base. He said each building was empty, though signs of life were found. I can't help but wonder why you didn't give us the location of the primary base." Vayl says, curiosity in her voice. Atlas squints, staring at nothing in particular but deep in thought.

"I'm not surprised Tanten didn't go to one of the secondary or tertiary bases, but where could he have gone?" Atlas wonders. He speaks into the phone, "Never mind where the main base was, I took care of it." Vayl giggles. Atlas continues, "So, how did the Council meeting go? Did you learn anything?"

"Well," Vayl begins, amusement in her tone. "That's exactly why I was so eager to call. The Council decided it best to deal with the Schism first."

"Perfect, just as-"

"But that's not quite all," Vayl interjects. Atlas's heart accelerates. He licks his lips, his nerves and the suspense torturing him. Vayl continues. "Do you know a girl named Botalia Ulton?"

Atlas's eyes widen and his jaw drops. He shakily laughs in disbelief. He worked close to Vayl to make certain Botalia's name was never found out by any of the higher ups. Atlas knew the possibility existed that some of the members may remember Botalia, being especially certain Cefni and Rhys would remember her. Atlas felt the distraction of the Schism would be enough to maintain the separation between her and them. Atlas deduces the only way Vayl could know of Botalia would be to have made contact with her. He shakes his head, unable to grasp the situation, denying what he heard Vayl say.

"I take it by your reaction you know her, or at least know of her."

Vayl frowns, realizing Atlas may be hiding other information from her if he failed to mention this. At first, Vayl regretted allowing Botalia and the team attempt the mission, understanding the possible dangers it may prove for Atlas. But Vayl knew if she refused, the Council would question her motives. It was a risk Vayl was not willing to take. *Anyways... What can a couple of children, a criminal, and an emotionally unstable girl truly be capable of?* Vayl reconsiders her thought, noting the discomfort Botalia's name causes Atlas. Atlas is an extremely strong and powerful life force user, as well as combatant and strategist. The few Council members who remembered Botalia had strange reactions to her presence as well. *Perhaps the girl is a threat...*

"Yes, I know of her," Atlas says. He tries to swallow his nerves but finds difficulty in doing so. "The question is how do you know of her?"

"She stopped by the Associa-"

"Was she alone?" Atlas presses.

"What's with the urgency, Atlas?"

"What did she want? Did anyone recognize her? Please tell me you turned her away. What could she possibly desire from the Association?"

"Calm down. I'm only capable of answering one question at a time," Vayl grows frustrated. She remains exhausted from the meeting, which ended only an hour ago, and the constant flooding of questions and updates dealing with the Schism. Vayl finds herself slowly being drained, the pressure pushing her to her limits. But, she knows the rewards for sticking by her alliances may be unparalleled to any she'll receive as Vice President of the Magistrate Association. However, if she gains the reward and maintains her position in the Association, all the better.

"First question: Are you ready?" Atlas asks, calming himself and attempting to slow his heart beat.

"Yes," Vayl responds.

"Was she alone?" Atlas asks in a very serious tone. Since hearing Botalia's name, Atlas continues to look around, worried someone may be listening to their conversation. He sees no one, yet his unsettled mind forces him to check time and time again.

"No," Vayl replies after several seconds of contemplation. "The girl was not alone. Accompanying her was a man and two children."

"Two?" Atlas's eyes widen as this word echoes in his head. "Little Flynn and the Kufuta boy are with her. And Tenebrant Mortu beside them. What kind of dysfunctional team is Botalia forming?" Atlas wonders. The thought of the four together almost amuses him, but he knows better than to underestimate a team despite the individuals that make it up, and he knows better than to underestimate Botalia's strength.

Atlas responds to Vayl, "Interesting. Next question: Did anyone recognize her?"

"The Council members who have served for many years froze when they caught a glimpse of her. Granted her presence alone is quite astounding, but a familiarity, a recalling of the past seemed to hit the Council members who did know of her. When Cefni entered the room with her, his expression appeared rather solemn and distracted, like he was caught in a bad memory."

Atlas nervously laughs once more, the information almost too much to digest. It's not worth denying anymore because the story must be true. All of the information fits with everything Atlas knows, and he understands more about the Botalia case than anyone. Atlas knew and sponsored several of the Ulton's experiments and expeditions, including turning their daughter into a lab rat. Atlas knew Botalia's DNA was not completely human as a result of the experimentation. He knew about the existence of the organ pirates Botalia brutally slaughtered. Atlas knew Cefni was the first official magistrate called to the case, having been the one to assign him. He knew Cefni had lost his daughter and wife to criminals exactly one month before. Atlas knew Cefni could not let Botalia die, Cefni had to save her or his heart may have truly shattered. Atlas knew everyone would call for her exile, though it did not surprise him when Tanten Flynn argued against it. Atlas knows the ins and outs of Botalia's life, yet for her to show up to the Magistrate Association, let alone with Cefni Medina, seems too much.

"Ms. Ulton wished to help us, the Association. However, she wished to assist us in a way we didn't expect," Vayl says. She pauses, whether for dramatic effect or to allow Atlas to prepare himself for the next shock. Vayl continues. "She knows Tanten Flynn stole it. And she wishes to help us get it back."

"Impossible," Atlas replies. He shakes his head. "No one even knew the altar piece existed outside of the excavators, Council, and the security who poorly protected it. How can a girl who's been exiled for ten years know of its existence?"

"Well, that's the interesting part. She didn't know about the altar piece, she simply knew Tanten's team stole something. She clearly understands your ploy to use the Schism as a red herring. But here's the stranger part. When I showed her a picture of the altar piece, her eyes widened as if she recalled a memory or had a vision. Though I'm not sure why, intuitively, I know she's seen it before. The questions unanswered are when, where, and why her." Vayl stops. Atlas chuckles.

"Don't lie. Many other questions remain unanswered. Though, if she's after Tanten my nerves can calm," Atlas replies, finally breathing in a collected fashion once more. "Anything else to report?"

"To appease the Council, I sent two members with the girl to supervise her," responds Vayl. Atlas sighs.

He understands the Council simply wants the altar piece to return to the Association building. He knows they may also be weary accepting Botalia's help. However, not even the Council members can parallel Botalia's strength if she chooses to rebel. With Tenebrant on her team, there is definitely bound to be friction with the Council members already. Atlas says nothing but waits to hear who Vayl chose to accompany Botalia. Vayl notes his silence and continues.

"I sent Merwyn Giacobbe and Cefni Medina."

Atlas shakes his head and violently throws his suit jacket on a chair. With his free hand he hides his face.

"Of all the Council members she had to choose from, she chose the strongest two," Atlas thinks, still in shock. "With Cefni at her side, there is no way Botalia will rebel. Tenebrant may be our only hope for causing a break in the team... But if the team as a whole runs into my team, I have no doubt they could easily apprehend, no, destroy us." Atlas softly chuckles, sifting through his thoughts. "Merwyn's experience in life force manifestation more than likely far exceeds my team's assigned manifesters, Artoria and Ilric, making their talents useless. Cefni has no need to fear any form of combat with him being an Elemental Professional, easily the strongest and most difficult category among Professionals. Botalia... she's strong and powerful, we all know that. Her abilities may as well be infinite with the immense amount of life force within her. And Tenebrant Mortu. My team works hard training in combat from day to day, but most their training began eight months back. Mortu has been fighting and killing for near a decade. His experience in combat and the pleasure he finds in killing means combat should not even be attempted with him near. But, their team does have a weakness. Those two kids... If anything were to happen to them, no doubt their team would fall apart. It's my last hope if the team is whole when we meet."

Vayl impatiently looks around, understanding Atlas takes all she's said into consideration and adjust his plans to fit this new information. But she herself finds she lacks the time to wait from him to strategize. Vayl continues. "That is all I have to report."

Her voice breaking the silence pulls Atlas from his thoughts. He squints and looks around. At length he says, "Thank you for the news. After stealing the piece, Tanten's team will probably hide for a few days, not wishing to risk being caught. This means they've either just left or will leave tomorrow. However, if we beat him to the altar's location, we can stop them before it's too late."

"Do you have a plan?" Vayl asks, sensing his doubt and fear of the mission and its success. Atlas chuckles.

"I have a few tricks up my sleeve yet," Atlas claims and looks around himself. "You know, some people refer to Professionals as magicians, and as our namesake suggests, we never reveal our secrets. Fortunately for me, I know many people's secrets while keeping my own hidden away. Of all the possible outcomes, the staff falling into possession of Bysciw or Tanten is the worst. They must be destroyed, and I'll unveil any secret I have to do so." The doors of the gym sound as his team starts to exit. "I need to go."

"Be careful," Vayl urges. "And stand tall."

Atlas chuckles. "I will.

"Oh, and Atlas?"

"Yes?"

"Mortu. He's the team's weakness. He snaps and the team breaks."

"Right..." Her words echo in his head. "Bye."

Atlas hangs up the phone and returns it to his pocket. He gazes at his exhausted team and begins to feel despair. Atlas envisions the suffering and pain they will endure in the foreseeable future and the guilt consumes him for leading them all to their death.

Atlas thinks, "We can't win, not against such odds. But I can't let them see my doubt, for then they may hesitate in battle. They pledged to follow me until death, and may it be honorable." Atlas locks eyes with Keniph, and Keniph walks over to him.

"You had quite a show in there earlier," Keniph smiles while pointing toward the gym. Atlas smugly grins. Keniph scratches his head. "So what did she have to say?"

Atlas realizes he refers to Azriel Vayl, yet feels issuing his orders may be the best first move. Atlas nods. "Gather the troops. We're moving out."

Keniph's eyes widen at the orders, but he senses the subdued urgency in Atlas's voice. He takes his soldier stance and openly listens to all commands.

"Tonight, we start our journey to Praecantatis Tepui. We must beat Tanten to the altar... We must."

Keniph salutes and rushes off to gather the team, shouting commands. The members run about, excitement and anxiety coursing through their veins. They occasionally gaze at Atlas who sits in a chair, eyes closed and head in his hands. His calm composure emanates throughout the room causing everyone to feel at peace. The room slowly empties, leaving Atlas to the silence and solitude. He chuckles. His eyes open in a flash as he remembers something.

Atlas removes his phone from his pocket. He analyzes it, squinting his eyes to focus on it. He surrounds it in life force and throws it away from himself.

Once fifteen feet from him, the phone encased in life force freezes in midair. It floats and Atlas continues to glare at it. He scoffs and shakes his head. In that moment, the phone detonates in a contained explosion. Every piece and part disintegrate. Atlas releases his life force and the debris falls to the ground.

"Underestimate no one," Atlas whispers to himself.

He rises from his chair and leaves the room, turning out the lights and closing the door behind him. He'll never return to that room. His journey, like the many others, lays beyond.

Exclusive Sneak Peek

THEIR LOYALTY TO LEGEND

Book 2 of The Chimera's Requiem

Tenebrant lurks at the back of the cathedral, watching as Atlas, Naht, and the others leave the area, heading toward the floodplains. Whether marching for the altar or simply advancing, Tenebrant could not be sure of their objective. Naht told him earlier that Atlas doesn't have a strong desire concerning the attainment of the staff and its power. Atlas is more obsessed with his twisted ideal of justice. The thought makes Tenebrant chuckle.

As Tenebrant scales the deteriorating marble columns of the cathedral, he takes care to conceal his aura. His ability to conceal of his aura and life force make him near impossible to spot. Not even Naht steals a glimpse, whether because he sensed it was Tenebrant or discovering the presence was outside of his own ability as well.

Tenebrant watches as Atlas's team heads north from this new vantage point, examining how they cope with the loss of two team members. Grief takes many forms in humans, yet the resilience, or in the least faking it, takes a drastic toll on the mind. Not even the soldier on the battlefield can maintain a stone composure after the retreat. That is... unless the mind morphs... no longer fully human.

He grins and glances down at his minions below. Developing a strategy to lure the members from their group proved rather tricky given the heightened climate of fear. Tenebrant could not fault them for showing courage until the end. Taking life grows easier every day for him. Granting them life from his own hands, reanimating the corpses, was complex, the outcome never up to his standards of satisfaction. His necromancy skills were rusty, fully manipulating the corpses was no simple task. Giving a corpse back its own spirit was a skill he had not achieved, yet.

In the distance, Tenebrant notices Merwyn leading the group in the direction of the cathedral. The necromancer quickly hides behind the dome, windows either shattered or stained from centuries of buffeting sandstorms. Hostility grows within him as Cefni enters his view, Botalia beside him. Using his life force as a buffer between his feet and the ground, Tenebrant jumps off the cathedral roof. He commands his undead allies to follow him, his thoughts unstable. Fighting... killing... the rush of excitement, seeing his strength, feeling Atlas's apprehensive aura... the combination of these experiences puts his mind in a flurry. He wants more. More excitement. But the ones nearest him are also the members of the team he betrayed... Does betrayal have a limit?

His minions limp after him, his pace too fast for them to keep up. Tenebrant scopes out the area, wondering where to hide himself or if he wants to adhere to that option at all. His mind tells him to let the group be, but his body refuses to listen. Standing approximately fifty meters from the cathedral, Tenebrant stares at the building, frozen to the spot. Around him lay marble slabs, some buried within the ground while others protrude. A cemetery.

His face turns to the sky as a soft laugh thanks whichever druidic gods must be on his side. Demented and as sadistic as him. His life force seeps into the soil and feels the remnants of creatures, or perhaps humans, who were laid to rest, their corpses long decomposed. Tenebrant closes his eyes as the dusty breeze caresses his skin. The wind carries voices to his ears, begging for his regenerative life force to wake them from their long rest.

Tenebrant grows alert to his presence before he sees him. An enraged and aggressive aura, laced with bloodlust and revenge. A foolish and immature mixture of emotions. Why would people wish to give in to something as lowly as revenge?

Without placing eyes upon his adversary, Tenebrant turns and strolls away. He smiles as the man pursues him. The necromancer and his undead allies create a maze in the marble ruins of mausoleums, obelisks, and weathered statues. Tenebrant loops left, right, then right again. The man quickens pace to close the distance so as to not lose sight of Tenebrant.

Tenebrant swiftly ducks behind the corner of a marble division wall and pauses. The corpses had taken a different path through the maze of ruins, waiting for their master's command. This man paid no mind to the minions, intent on his pursuit of Tenebrant.

The presence disappears. Tenebrant pushes a palm against the marble wall and searches for a heartbeat in this field of the dead. He detects nothing. Peeking his head around the wall, Tenebrant sees no one. He successfully evaded the enemy. With a shake of the head, he sighs.

"I thought you'd put up a better chase," he disappointingly mumbles.

The loud bang of a shot fires.

Tenebrant leaps into the air, fast as an eagle taking flight, and lands atop the wall he had been leaning against. Not a second later, the marble wall shatters into thousands of small shards, launching like shrapnel in all directions. Tenebrant had catapulted himself into the air as the bullet made contact, leaving him with no more than superficial scratches from the marble pellets. Where the wall once stood lay a burnt and smoky foundation.

Tenebrant studies the surrounding area, attempting to use the angle of incidence to determine the origin of the bullet. However, he realizes the ineffectiveness in doing so, for another bullet already targets him. He launches and somersaults to the side. Despite the dodge, the bullet, encapsulated in its own aura, tracks him. Tenebrant grins, amused by the challenge.

He runs around the ruins, not only evading the bullet but assembling his allies. Finding a marble slab, Tenebrant lifts it with his life force to act as a shield. The bullet strikes and the shield disintegrates. His vision blurs and the city rotates about him. A concussive shot. He lowers himself, placing his hands on the dry soil and closing his eyes to return to equilibrium.

"You're not giving up already, are you, coward?" Cefni Medina questions. Tenebrant chuckles, Cefni's hostility fueling his strength.

"You ask as if I would surrender to the pitiful likes of you, Cefni Medina."

Tenebrant opens his eyes and stares at the rough presence of the Council member before him. Cefni aims his revolver at Tenebrant's chest. Though powerful, Tenebrant knows the previous two shots were not set to murder him. The Magistrate Association deems Cefni one of the best life force users in the world, and Tenebrant does not deny that claim. Tenebrant knows the limits of his own strength and intelligence, which gives him an advantage in most battles. Granted, he's never met an adversary as worthy or respectable as Cefni Medina.

Cefni feels no fear in the face of Tenebrant. A stone wall. Both mentally and physically on the battlefield. Tenebrant's raw ability means little to his years of experience. Cefni patiently waits for the moment to reveal his true strength both to his opponent and himself. That is, if his true strength even warrants revealing itself.

"Arrogance is a pretty shade on no one."

"Nor revenge," Tenebrant flashes a devious grin. "But it seems a natural fit for you."

"Why would I seek revenge against you?"

"Not specifically me... I simply assumed you have a hard heart set against all murderers and criminals... Considering your past..."

Cefni cocks the revolver. "I'm not gonna warn you again. The Association would have no qualms if I ended you here."

"You don't have to be kind," Tenebrant laughs. His face grows solemn in a flash. "No one would."

Tenebrant and Cefni stare into each other's eyes, though Cefni carefully pays attention to the reanimated corpses in his peripheral vision. He steadily aims the revolver at Tenebrant. Cefni's heartbeat is as tranquil as an undisturbed pond, but his mind swirls as if in the outer ring of a hurricane. Tenebrant tilts his head to the side. He observes Cefni's aura, appearing like a star experiencing solar flares and coronal mass ejections.

"What are you fighting for?" Tenebrant inquires. His eyes do not deviate from their position, slowly breaking through Cefni's defenses. Finding the weakness his body and aura attempt to keep hidden, but his eyes and soul cannot hide. Cefni understands Tenebrant's state of hostility and psyched aura cannot be quelled until he kills others. Until he encounters an attempt to bring back life before the spirit finds its way from the body. Until he can prove to those long gone that he will never worry to lose those closest to him again. The pity that no one close remains...

"I fight for the protection of those things still lovely in the world and to squash those trying to damage it," Cefni answers. Tenebrant erupts in laughter. Cefni stands, stolid, his resolve cements itself in his expression. Tenebrant notices and falls silent.

Furrowing his brow at Cefni, Tenebrant remarks, "Liar."

No sounds occur in the environment around them. No rustling of the brush under their feet, no settling of the rubble from the marble ruins. As if the environment understands that only silence can fill the moment. The tension increases between the two enemies.

"You speak of a lovely world, a world we both know ceases to exist in our eyes. Others still see it, some will never see anything but. Many who lose that image deny its reality to begin with, as if a false projection was torn down to reveal the cruel world we live in. They reject the idea of a lovely world for now they see the truth. Or is it the truth? Can we say a lovely world never existed if so many claim to live in it? Can we say they are wrong, that they don't understand because they're blinded by a false pretense?"

"Is it so wrong to hope for a lovely world?"

"No. Not if one wishes to suffer. Hope is but a sad excuse for exerting a belief we know borderlines reality and imaginary. Scholars cling to the hope for a panacea to save the world from disease, yet understand it to be outside the realm of possibility. Many hope for worldly happiness and peace yet understand humans would cease to exist if the world were to come to that. Hope is a tortuous artifice used to destroy the soul. To prove the world is not a lovely place. Because those who rely on hope know the world is cruel. Hope is the first step in a cycle of suffering. You hope for a lovely world, but your hope is another's suffering. To protect your so called "lovely world," someone has to take the fall."

"Those attempting to destroy-"

"Isn't that subjective? Your lovely world will never be everyone's lovely world and therefore will only live as it exists today. Your lovely world is devoid of what you deem evil acts, your hope a smiling fourteen-year-old girl who embodied your ideals of eradicating those who do wrong."

"The world has no need for murderers."

"And yet someone must if the world is to be rid of them. No matter the way you approach the situation, she's a killer. You're a killer. I'm a killer."

"Don't compare yourself to us." Cefni's frustration is evident as his aura experiences more frequent disruptions than before.

"We're more alike than you know," Tenebrant quietly mutters. He closes his eyes, feeling their exchange of conflicting ideals to be dissolving his excitement and hostility. However, he refuses to find despair in his new emotions. With his bloodlust gone, his mind is clear to discern why Cefni is a true enemy.

Superficial disagreements. The two words perfectly encapsulate Tenebrant's reaction to every felony of his involvement. Eradicating narrow-minded, weak, arrogant, unintelligent, ignorant weeds became a job to Tenebrant. It reaffirmed in him his own strength, his abilities. No one could bully or overpower him. He wouldn't allow it. He had control. Always. Whether it be the psychological lure or the physical strikes, Tenebrant began to find little satisfaction in killing those who were no more than weeds to society. They weren't even comparable to the colossal weeds that never seem to die, for those are a greater pain than those he murdered. His hostility and excitement assisted in his killing sprees. If not for a rapid flood of emotion, he would not find satisfaction whatsoever. But, in the face of Tanten and Cefni, he finds a contorted obsession. As if winning a fight against either would solve his internal conflict. He wishes for that control, for that strength, to reclaim himself.

Tenebrant cracks his neck and sighs. He glances at his allies then back at Cefni, who appears unwavering in his stance.

"How about we settle this?" Tenebrant questions. He slides his right hand along his left arm, revealing a glowing language tattooed on it. A necromantic rite inscribed with his own life force, allowing for him to easily command and summon undead minions.

Cefni does not shoot, but rather lowers his revolver, understanding the practice of a fair fight. He prepares his life force, concentrating a large portion into his hands and feet, a small portion moving to his eyes to carefully watch Tenebrant's execution of life force. He's investigated too many cases where necromancers used their life force to conceal curses, therefore rendering the opponent weak, confused, or paralyzed. Cefni glances at the undead warriors, understanding them to be weak but an effective tool for drawing attention and fire away from his primary opponent.

Both men take a defensive stance. They lock eyes, hesitating to initiate the battle.

"Don't hold back," Cefni orders, "If you do, I'll tell the world you died a coward's death."

"As you should," Tenebrant responds with a smile. He cracks his fingers and points his index finger at Cefni. "Prepare to join my army."

www.ingramcontent.com/pod-product-compliance
Lightning Source LLC
Chambersburg PA
CBHW020305200626
46814CB00006BA/2096